LAID OUT
TO
REST

LAID OUT TO REST

A CHARCUTERIE SHOP MYSTERY

J.C. EATON

LEVEL
BEST BOOKS

Author Photo Credit: Larry Finkelstein

Cover Art Image Credit: Dar Albert of Wicked Smart Designs

First edition

ISBN: 978-1-68512-152-5

Cover art by Level Best Designs

This book was professionally typeset on Reedsy.
Find out more at reedsy.com

In memory of Nancy Davis, amazing English teacher and friend. And to the real Speedbump, her extraordinary cat who kept all of us in stitches. We, along with the village of Penn Yan, New York, miss you every day.

Praise for Books by the Author

Booklist Starred Review for *Booked 4 Murder*:

"A thoroughly entertaining series debut, with enjoyable, yet realistic characters and enough plot twists-and dead ends- to appeal form beginning to end."

Suspense Magazine for *Molded 4 Murder*:

"Filled with clues that make you go 'Huh?' and a list of potential subjects that range from the charming to the witty to the intense. Readers root for Phee as she goes up against a killer who may not stop until Phee is taken out well before her time. Enjoy this laugh-out-loud funny mystery that will make you scream for the authors to get busy on the next one."

Chapter One

Chandler, Arizona

"That's it? A done deal?" Another few syllables and my mother's voice would have breached the sound barrier. I was sure it was accompanied by a frantic fluffing of her recently bronze-highlighted tips. It was a little past eight in the evening and I was fast at work packing kitchen utensils. Thankfully, a neighbor had recently moved into the complex where I rented an upscale condo for the past five years and offered me her cardboard moving boxes.

"If you're referring to the fact that I submitted my letter of resignation to the CEO of Chan-Tech Industries, then yes, it's a done deal. Unless of course, you called to talk about something else. Usually, people provide some background before they start a conversation."

"You know very well what I'm talking about, Katie. You've got a business degree and you worked your tail off to get to where you are in that company and now what? You want to give it all up to make cucarachas in some godforsaken place?"

"Charcuterie boards. Not cucarachas." *Heaven help me. I can only imagine what she's telling everyone.* "And since when is Cave Creek a godforsaken place? I've done my research and I know what I want. I also know what I don't want. I'm only thirty-two and already I'm burned out with the high-tech business world. The pressure to make a sale. The unrelenting push to get a deal through. It never ends. I want to use my energy in a more creative way. I need a venue that blends art and taste."

"Since when is putting deli meat and cheese on a plate an artistic expression?"

"Since the French introduced it in the fifteenth century. And it's an art form. An edible art form. For your information, the entire idea of salting and preserving meats came from Ancient Rome."

"This isn't Ancient Rome. We have refrigerators now. And freezers. We don't have to salt and save anything. Honestly, this is the worst idea you've ever come up with. How on earth do you plan to make a living?"

"By catering high-end parties and events in the social hub of the valley—Scottsdale, Paradise Valley, and Fountain Hills. And I'll have a home base with a small grab-and-go shop in Cave Creek. I already signed the lease and secured a business loan. Besides, I got the deal of the century on a cute rental house not far from the shop. The owner passed away and the nephew who inherited it lives in Tacoma. Maddie found it for me. Lucky I have a friend in real estate, huh?"

"Please tell me the place comes with electricity and hot and cold running water."

"Aargh. Stop being so melodramatic. And before you ask how I intend to pay for all of this, I've managed my money wisely. Enough to take over the little sandwich shop and get my business started. The two full-time employees were thrilled that I agreed to keep them on."

"It's the breakup with Evan, isn't it? I've heard of things like that."

"Like what?"

"An early midlife crisis brought about by a stress-related incident."

"Stop reading all that psychobabble. Besides, Dad isn't all too bent out of shape. All he said, when I saw you guys last week was that he wanted me to be happy."

"What did you expect him to say? Of course, he wants you to be happy. I just hope your brother doesn't decide to leave dentistry."

"I doubt it. Too many college loans to pay off. Besides, I think he rather enjoys being the second prosthodontist in the family."

"You could have been the third, you know. The fourth if you count your

2

late grandfather."

"Ew! I like putting food in people's mouths, not staring into them. Ever since I worked summers for that golf resort and shadowed their chefs, I've been enamored by the idea of working in that field. Unfortunately, I was persuaded by big tech and the prestige that went with it. So much for illusion. Listen, I've got lots of packing to do, not to mention the odds and ends I've got to catch up on. I'll give you a call the end of the week."

"Call me sooner if you change your mind about this. But not tomorrow. I've got three client meetings for house staging. Then again, you can always leave a message. And big tech illusion translates into money. Like I said, you may have second thoughts."

"Doubtful. And remember, it's charcuterie, not cucarachas."

In a sense, I couldn't blame my mother for worrying about my livelihood. Both she and my father weren't exactly what someone would call risk takers. Before my mother became a home stager, she worked as a teaching assistant while my brother and I were growing up. Steady job. Steady hours. Same with my dad who took over his dad's dental practice around the same time. Nevertheless, her call unsettled me more than I cared to admit.

That conversation was on a Sunday, five days ago, and since then I had to juggle my current job and begin to transition the little sandwich shop I bought into a grab-and-go place that would morph into a charcuterie business. I figured it would be a slow transition as I gradually introduced preprepared mini cheese, fruit, and meat plates. I'd managed to get the advertising set up and touched base with the current vendors. The downside was that I was sleep-deprived. Completely and totally sleep-deprived. I figured once I got settled in my new place, I'd make up for all those lost z's. Lamentably, I was wrong. Dead wrong. But at the time it sounded good.

Now, facing my last week at Chan-Tech, I felt hopeful. Two Guys and a Truck were scheduled to move my belongings to Cave Creek tomorrow, and I'd commute to Chandler for that last week while juggling my time with the sandwich shop. The catering end of my venture would have to wait a bit. Superwoman, I wasn't.

Lilly-Ann Wentworth, a late fifty-something retired elementary school teaching assistant, and Matt Lindon, a part-time student at Paradise Valley Community College, ran the 7:00 a.m. to 2:30 p.m. shop during the week and on Saturdays. Of course, the prior owner also worked there, and I'd have to step into his shoes. Experience or not. At least with the doors closed on Sundays, I could concentrate on charcuterie boards when the catering end took off.

Like my current rental, the little house in Cave Creek came completely furnished. The only thing I replaced was the instrument of torture in the master bedroom. I purchased a new queen-size mattress that didn't boast a sagging middle and a lumpy exterior. As far as everything else went, I could live with the prior occupant's design choices, eclectic at best. The elderly lady who last slept here filled the place with Moroccan ottomans and Russian samovars. As for the overall décor, it was a jarring combination of early American farmhouse and Southwestern style. Still, it was functional, even if not a personal preference, and that's all I needed.

Its owner, the nephew in Tacoma, offered to have it painted but not for a few months. At least he did have it professionally cleaned so it wasn't as if I would be stepping into a *Flip or Flop* nightmare, complete with termites, plumbing issues, and years of decay.

The only uptick to my new venture was the encouragement I got from my longtime friend, Maddie. She and I attended the same elementary school before her family moved from Chandler to Paradise Valley where she now works as a real estate agent. If it wasn't for her perseverance, I would have wound up renting something way too pricy.

"This is the only house within your budget," she said a month ago when we looked at properties. "It's in a somewhat historic part of town and it does check off a number of boxes."

"*Historic* is a euphemism for *old*," I remembered telling her.

"Think about it, will you? It's almost walking distance to the sandwich shop and it's a quick drive to Scottsdale, Paradise Valley, and Fountain Hills. So what if the prior owner liked ochre and puce? It'll be painted in a few months. Just dim the lights."

That, or walk around blindfolded.

CHAPTER ONE

Maddie arranged her schedule so she could help me unpack and settle in once the movers unloaded my cartons of books, clothing, and miscellaneous household goods in the morning. The worst part of the entire ordeal was having to do without technology. At least I had the iPhone and if I could have had it permanently attached to my hand, I would have. The thought of going two full days before the cable company hooked up my computer and TV was unbearable, and I swore I developed a twitch under my left eye.

Surrounded by boxes, I no longer had my digital alarm clock by the bed or my computer a few feet away. And other than an M.C. Beaton novel left on the nightstand, there was nothing to entertain me, except of course for that nagging thought about calling my mother before vacating my apartment in less than twenty-four hours. We had texted during the week, and I had to reassure her with each message, that everything was going smoothly and that I didn't need her to help with the packing. I promised to call and it couldn't wait.

Fumbling with my neck rest and pillow, I tapped the number from my list of contacts. "Hope it's not too late, Mom," I said. "This is the first chance I got to catch my breath."

"You should have told me sooner. I would have come over to help you."

"I know. And thanks, but I had it under control. Maddie's going to help me unpack and the movers will be at the new place by eight. Tuft and Needle already delivered my mattress."

"Then there's no going back?"

"Um, no."

"That's what I told your father. Listen, should you change your mind, you can always move in with us until you find another position in your own field."

Unless I find a Harikari knife first.

"I'm not about to change my mind and everything will be fine. Cave Creek is less than an hour from here. It's not as if I signed up to join Lewis and Clark. Once I get unpacked and get the sandwich shop going, I want you and Dad to come over for dinner. Okay?"

"Will it be one of those cuca-charerie plates?"

I laughed. "Only if you insist. And by the way, I'm changing the name of the shop from Cave Creek Sandwiches to The Char-Board. Kind of like a take-off on 'chalkboard' where sandwich shop menus are written."

"It sounds like cardboard. People will think you're selling boxes. What about "A Cut Above?""

"That sounds like a hairdresser. The Char-Board it is. Once customers see the place, they'll get the reference. Besides, I've designed a neat logo and I had a graphic designer incorporate it into our ads and our business cards. I even had magnetic signs made for my KIA Sorento. Nothing like advertising on the move."

"It sounds like you know what you're doing, Katie, even if I'm struggling to accept it."

"Thanks. That was the most encouraging thing you've said this entire month."

"Send me some of those business cards and I'll pass them around to my clients. How's that for encouraging?"

"It's great. I'll text you with updates and we can chat once things settle. Give Dad a hug from me."

"I'll do better. I'll insist he put those business cards in the lobby of his office. Right next to the ones about teeth whitening."

With little to do except stare at the ceiling, I picked up the cozy mystery and read until I could no longer keep my eyelids from closing. If Agatha Raisin could start all over, Katie Lynn Aubrey certainly could.

Even if she wasn't a fictional character.

Chapter Two

Ever since I was little, if I had to get up early for anything out of the ordinary, I never slept well and last night was no exception. From lying flat on my back to rolling from left to right, my bout in bed was more of an exercise routine than the ones I got at Chan-Tech's gym. When the alarm went off at six, I wondered if I could begin a new trend—burn calories in your sleep.

I took my last shower in the condo, toweling off with two hand towels because I had packed the larger bath ones along with my electric toothbrush, compelling me to use one of the freebee toothbrushes from my father's office. *Fine. Packing for a move isn't one of my strengths.*

A quick damp dry of my wavy red chin-length hair coupled with an application of tinted sunblock, and I was all set. I stuffed yesterday's clothes into a plastic grocery bag and threw on the t-shirt and worn capris that I set out the night before. Then, I hightailed it to the elevator and returned from the coffee shop in the lobby with a blueberry muffin and large coffee. It would have to suffice for the time being.

Next, I scurried around the place, gathered the last-minute odds and ends that were still in sight, and crammed them into the oversize backpack that I last used during my freshman year in college. No sooner did I zip it up when the movers arrived. Two muscular men with broad shoulders, beards, and a variety of tattoos on their arms.

They immediately got to work loading my cartons, electronics, and small kitchen appliances onto dollies. I stood open-mouthed, coffee cup in hand praying they wouldn't drop anything. The entire process took less than an hour and a half. At least at this end.

"We'll see you over in Cave Creek," one of the men said. "Are you following us, or will someone be at your new place to let us in?"

"My girlfriend Maddie will let you in. I've got to give this place a quick once over before I lock up and leave the key."

"Sounds like a plan. Catch you in a bit."

One of the perks of having a real estate agent for a friend is the connection she had with cleaning services. At her insistence, I hired Wanda's Wonders to make sure the condo would be spotless enough so I could get my entire security deposit back. True, I didn't have any pets, but I wasn't exactly what someone would call fastidious when it came to house cleaning. I made up my mind to do better at the next place.

It took me longer to drive from Chandler to Cave Creek than it did for me to make sure I didn't leave anything behind. From drawers to cabinets and closets, I scrutinized everything. Satisfied, I left the key on the kitchen table and locked the bottom non-deadbolt lock in the door. All the cleaning service would have to do is contact the manager. Goodbye Chandler and hello Char-Board!

Yep, I had no doubt I'd made the right decision about Cave Creek. It was a cross between an artist's haven and an Arizona frontier town. Complete with quirky shops like the Rusty Javelina featuring metal art, and Miners to Finders, with an array of rocks, minerals, and gems, it also showcased new-age getaways that promoted healing oils, body massages, and meditation. Most of all, Cave Creek was known for its unique coffee shops and an abundance of watering holes like the Thirsty Lizard. Some of the shops, like mine, were connected to others in a rustic strip-mall sort of way while others were stand-alone with large parking lots and a plethora of cacti, mesquite trees, and agaves. With the Continental Mountains on one side of the main drag and the Black Mountains on the other, it was a veritable picture postcard. It was also well within driving distance to the Greater Phoenix area.

"I thought you'd never get here," Maddie shouted from the porch of the rental house. She gave her shoulder-length blond hair a flip and smiled.

Perfect teeth thanks to years of braces and retainers. And a perfect figure, too, a result of early morning workouts, a penchant for fruits and vegetables, and great genes. "The movers are almost done. Hope you remembered some money to give them a tip. All I have is my debit card."

"Not a problem. Does everything look all right in there?"

"Sure. Try not to fixate on the wall colors. It'll take some getting used to."

"Don't worry. I'll be too busy fixating on getting my business started."

For the next hour or so, Maddie helped me unpack the essentials—kitchen and bathroom stuff. "You can always work out of boxes for clothing," she said. "And you've got all day tomorrow."

"Not all day. I'm meeting my employees at noon to go over a few things, so I want to get as much done now as possible. And that includes making a stop later at the nearest supermarket for provisions. The only things I had left in my apartment were three pods of dark roast coffee, a few cans of soup, a box of crackers, dishwashing liquid, and Minute rice."

"Yeesh. Don't have me over for dinner any time soon. How about I run to the nearest fast-food place and bring us back some sustenance? I don't know about you but I'm ready to chew my arm off."

Just then one of the movers came out of the house and shouted, "You should have told us you had a dog. That thing scared the daylights out of us. When we opened your bedroom door, he or she was on the bed, and didn't look too happy we had intruded on its privacy."

I froze and widened my eyes. "I don't have a dog. Are you sure it's a dog and not a coyote? Those things are all over the area. Maybe one of them got into the house."

"Unless there's a new breed that has a striking resemblance to a beagle, I'd say no."

"Must be some neighbor's dog got into your house while the men were unloading the truck and—" Maddie said. Before she finished her sentence, I brushed past her and ran straight for the master bedroom. Sure enough, a slightly chunky beagle was curled up on the bed. It lifted its head and then licked a front paw.

"You need to go back to your own house," I announced. "Come on, off of

9

my new mattress. Good thing the plastic is still on it."

The dog looked at me and edged forward.

"Come on, get down from there."

I made a motion with my hand and watched as the beagle left the cozy spot on the bed.

"Okay, one mystery solved," I said. "You're a male. And from the look of things, a neutered one. Your owner is probably looking for you."

Maddie, who was a few feet behind me, approached the dog and proceeded to pat his head. "Sweet guy. You can't simply toss him out of here. Anything could happen. It's summer and for all we know, he could die of dehydration."

I shrugged. "He hasn't died yet. What are you suggesting?"

"Well, he doesn't have a collar so that's no help. There's a veterinary office on the main street. We should check for a microchip. I've got one of Sir Walter's leashes in my car. I'll loop it around this guy, and it'll be fine. Besides, this is a small town. Chances are, that office may know who the owner is."

"Guess we don't have much choice, huh? Maybe I can find a bowl in the kitchen and get him some water. There were a few pots and pans left in the cabinets as part of the rental."

I narrowly missed bumping into one of the movers as I walked out of the bedroom.

"Not your dog, huh? Must have wandered in to get out of the heat. At least it's early June so it's not that bad."

"I, um, er..."

The man was already down the hall and headed for the other bedroom before words could form in my mouth. The last thing I needed was to deal with a dog. I had enough on my plate with a new business. Not to mention the unpacking and shopping for groceries.

Thankfully the movers were as efficient with this end of the process as they were with the first. I thanked them and gave them decent tips, having already paid the fee prior with a credit card. As their truck pulled out of the gravel driveway, I returned to the house where Maddie was seated at the kitchen table, the dog at her side. She turned toward me and widened her eyes. "What are you going to do if there's no microchip?"

"What do you mean, 'What am I going to do?' Can't you take him home with you? Sir Walter might like a friend."

"Sir Walter is a spoiled mini-schnauzer who barely tolerates me. You should keep the beagle. This place isn't as secure as your condo complex in Chandler. A dog provides protection."

"Protection? Look at him. He's curled up on the braided rug by the sink."

"You can't turn him over to the county shelter. He'll be put to sleep."

"We're jumping ahead of ourselves. Chances are he's a neighbor's dog and we'll return him to his owner once we go to the vet."

Maddie stood. "On our way. With one stop—fast food hamburgers for the three of us."

Since Maddie's car was a larger SUV, she drove us to the nearest McDonald's where we downed Big Macs and fries and the dog inhaled two plain burgers. Then it was off to the veterinary practice on the main drag.

"Don't look so despondent," Maddie said when the three of us pulled into my driveway. "Just because the dog doesn't have a microchip and no one in that veterinary practice recognized him, doesn't mean he isn't someone's pet. And, so what if your next-door neighbors didn't know where he belonged. Hey, at least you introduced yourself to the neighborhood. We'll post info on Facebook and social media, and I'll take a photo with my phone and make up some posters for you to put around."

I opened the hatchback of the SUV and lugged the bag of Royal Canin dog food that I purchased at the vet's office into the house. The beagle trotted behind Maddie and me as if he had just won the Mega Million jackpot.

"I can't believe this is happening," I said. "A beagle. Of all things. The last pet I owned was a turtle and that didn't go well at all."

"You were in the fourth grade and turtles don't live that long. It's about time you had a companion."

"I had Evan and we both know how that worked out."

"This isn't the same. Beagles are known for their loyalty."

"It's a dog for crying out loud. Not a significant other."

"No, it's better. You get to call the shots."

"Yeah, well, tell that to Sir Walter."

LAID OUT TO REST

We both laughed as I unlocked the door to my new place. Again, cartons everywhere.

"I suppose I should start in the kitchen and find a plate or something for his food," I said. "How long can you stick around?"

Maddie looked at her phone. "About an hour or Sir Walter may punish me for being late."

"Terrific. And you're convincing me to keep this dog?"

"Foster. Babysit. Call it what you want."

"Hmm, I need to call him something. Judging from his mannerisms, he's not exactly a fast mover."

"That's because you've only seen him indoors. It may be different if he spies a rabbit or something."

I looked at the beagle, now snoring on the braided rug. "Speedbump. I think that says it all. At least temporarily. Maybe his real name is Buddy or Charlie or—"

Maddie grinned like the Cheshire Cat. "Speedbump it is. Hey, at least you won't be sleeping alone in here tonight."

At the time, I thought she meant the dog, but I was mistaken. Seriously mistaken.

Chapter Three

"It's serendipitous," Maddie said as she headed out the front door. "The backyard is fenced and there's a doggie door in the utility room. Must be the prior owner had a dog at one time. When I spoke to her nephew, he told me his aunt passed away peacefully in her sleep. No mention of pets whatsoever."

"Serendipitous my you-know-what. Speedbump is simply visiting."

"I'll get the social media going and work on those posters for you. Promise. Talk to you tomorrow."

"Thanks, Maddie." I gave her a hug and watched as she drove off.

Serendipitous, huh? Preposterous would be a better word.

Speedbump's snores oscillated from soft buzzing to rigorous snorts. I immediately sifted through my cartons to find my Bose radio and plugged it in. Any kind of background music would have been better.

"Sorry you have to use an old spaghetti pot for your water dish," I said. "If no one claims you by tomorrow I'll have to spring for a water dish, a food bowl, and a leash. Don't worry, I have faith in social media. If your owner is out there, they'll be anxious to get you home."

The dog continued to snore, and I went about my business unpacking and drinking water like a camel. Fortunately, the refrigerator was a fairly new one with a decent water filter and ice maker. Absolute necessities in the Arizona heat. The microwave was fairly new, too, but not built in. At least I had enough counter space to plug in my Keurig and my toaster oven.

I was pretty wiped out by six, not to mention ravenous.

"It's a toss-up," I said to the dog. "Chicken noodle soup or vegetarian vegetable."

He looked up from his spot on the rug and ambled into the kitchen. "Chicken noodle it is. I can always pour some of it on your kibble. Not that it matters. You devoured a full bowl of it when we got back from the vet."

Speedbump watched my every move as if he understood and needed to ensure I'd keep my word about the kibble. When we were both done eating, I motioned for him to follow me. "Come on, might as well check out the doggie door and backyard while it's still light out."

Either the dog was used to the process, or he was a quick learner. Watching him, it seemed as if he'd done it a thousand times.

"I'm not going to get attached to you," I said, giving him a pat on the head. "You're someone else's dog and that's that."

By eight-fifteen, I was ready to throw myself on the bed and sleep like nobody's business. Only one problem—I never made up the bed. Lifting a queen-size mattress wasn't the easiest feat in the world, especially while trying to pull the plastic covering off but after a few tries, complete with expletives, I was able to get down to business and add the mattress cover and sheets.

Thankfully the pillows were in reach since I shoved them into an empty laundry basket earlier that day. As I bent down to get them, Speedbump was already on top of the bed making himself comfortable.

"No!" I shouted. "You're not about to sleep on my bed. For all I know you might have fleas. Or worse." True, the dog didn't appear to be itching and his fur looked fine, but it was the "ick factor" that gave me the willies.

"I absolutely cannot believe I'm about to do this," I muttered, "but you're going into the shower before you set one paw on my bed."

I swore the dog rolled his eyes, but he acquiesced and let me bathe him with the remaining Johnson & Johnson Baby Shampoo that I packed.

"It's a good thing I saved all my ratty towels for the move. No sense using a good one. These are perfectly clean, even if they do have a few holes and are frayed at the ends."

If nothing else, Speedbump was as mellow as could be. Maybe it wouldn't be so bad having a dog around. Then again, I reminded myself, he had to be someone's lost dog.

Too exhausted to do anything else, I let him out in the yard for a few minutes before pulling down the lightweight cover from the bed and getting in. My back melted into the mattress, and I drifted asleep. The last sound I heard was Speedbump snoring, his body pressed against my leg. Unlike earlier in the evening, the sound was soft and rhythmic.

With a new moon and the shades drawn, the only light came from the digital clock on the nightstand. Fuzzy bluish light with a two-inch radius at most. I don't know how long I slept before the dog's low growl forced me to open my eyes.

The light from the digital clock seemed to have expanded, creating a cloudlike haze in the room. I pressed my elbows to the mattress and sat up. Speedbump continued to growl as the haze intensified for a minute before vanishing completely, leaving only the short radius of light around the clock.

"Must have been someone's car headlights," I mumbled. "Maybe their engine woke you. Come on, boy, go back to sleep."

The dog lifted his head and perused the room before circling in the bed a few times and finally taking my advice. I was out cold for the remainder of the night but got the shock of my life when I stepped out of bed the next day and felt something under one of my feet. Looking down, I saw a pair of worn pinkish slippers and they weren't mine.

"Did you roam around the place while I slept and found these?" I asked the dog. "Tell me yes because this is way too much Stephen King and Dean Koontz for me."

Speedbump sniffed the clumped fleece edge on one of the shoes and recoiled.

"They've probably been mothballed in a closet somewhere. No worries. Straight in the trash they go. I don't have time to speculate. You need to go outside, and I need to plunk a K-cup into that Keurig. After that, I'll feed you and unpack my clothes and a few more boxes."

I can't believe I'm explaining my every move to that dog.

A few seconds later, my phone vibrated. It was a text from my brother asking if I needed any help. I texted back, "Only if you want to foster a dog. Long story but I'm all set thanks to Maddie. Call you later. Xx's."

My breakfast consisted of dry Premium saltines and a second K-cup of dark roast. Emphasis on dark since I hadn't gone shopping yet for milk or creamer. Speedbump fared better and gobbled his kibble. I worked like the Dickens organizing my clothes closet and bureau before jumping into the shower so I wouldn't look like I slept on a bus station bench all night before meeting with my new employees.

I'd only met Lilly-Ann and Matt once before and that was cursory at best. Both of them were eager to retain their jobs and from the looks of things, they appeared to be well-organized and energetic. Maddie had orchestrated the business purchase as well and told me it was one of the fastest-moving transactions she had ever done. The prior owner, who started the shop over fifteen years ago, was anxious to move to Florida in order to be around his grandkids. Deal done. I was anxious to leave Chan-Tech.

Now, pulling up to the storefront on Cave Creek Road, just past the town hall and Skyline Drive, I eyed the closed sign dangling from the door. In a few minutes, Lilly-Ann and Matt would arrive. No matter what, I couldn't let them see the fear that suddenly took hold of me. It was as if an iron fist had grabbed my gut and refused to let go. I told myself it was the lousy breakfast I had but I knew better.

Whatever was I thinking when I made this decision? Even with my business background, it was daunting. Daunting? It was downright terrifying, but I'd never say that out loud.

I unlocked the door, turned on the lights, and took a good long look at the place. Cave Creek Sandwiches, soon to be The Char-Board, was a cozy coffee shop, flanked by two other stores. It still had its original round tables and ice cream parlor chairs that I intended to update or replace. Same for the blue and white checkered tablecloths and matching curtains circa 1950. There were three square-shaped metal tables outside, each with four chairs. Not enough to boast outdoor seating but still, better than nothing.

The menu was simple—a variety of breakfast and cold cut sandwiches on different breads, as well as ham, tuna, and egg salad sandwiches. Juice and soft drinks, along with coffee, tea, hot chocolate, and apple cider were also the norm. Nothing fancy, just your average lunch place. Specialty breakfast breads that were delivered from a bakery in Scottsdale were also available—corn, zucchini, cranberry, and apricot with walnut. Toasted or plain.

I planned to add mini-charcuterie plates that would include cheeses, meats, nuts, pickles, olives, and whatever else I fancied. It would be a good way to introduce customers to the idea of charcuterie boards. Maddie had joked that the sandwich shop was really a front for my real enterprise—the catering business. Well, I had to get it off the ground somewhere.

While the seating area was on the small size, the working kitchen in back was perfect for my greater enterprise. With a long prep table and ample counter space, I could easily work my magic with the charcuterie boards. As far as delivery went, my KIA Sorento had plenty of room, especially since there were two extra rows of seats in back that could go underneath to form a flatbed of sorts.

A sharp rap on the door and my daydreaming ceased. "Come on in," I shouted to the sandy-haired kid in jeans and a red Cardinals t-shirt.

"Lilly-Ann's on her way," he said. "She texted me a few minutes ago. Um, it's nice to see you again. We really didn't have a whole lot of time to talk. Look, I'll just spit it out—we really want to keep our jobs. Lilly-Ann especially. She gets a pension from being a TA but it's not much. And I've got all sorts of college expenses. Especially since I plan to go to ASU once I get my associate's degree."

I motioned for him to sit and joined him. "I need honest, reliable employees who don't mind learning new skills. And since both of you are conversant with this operation, it will help me as we transition to a charcuterie board catering service."

Matt crinkled his nose. "A charcoal what?"

At least he didn't say cucarachas.

"Think fancy cheese platters for parties, meetings, celebrations. That sort of thing. I'll explain more when Lilly-Ann gets here."

"She's here now. That's her, getting out of the silver Toyota."

I turned and stared at the woman with a ponytail and sweatshirt who waved and smiled as she opened the door and stepped in a few seconds later. "Lots of parking out front on Sundays. Hi! I'm Lilly-Ann. Oh gee, of course, you know who I am. Duh. I'm just nervous."

She held out her hand and I shook it. "Good to see you again, too. Last time was kind of a whirlwind. Before I forget, both of you are on the clock today so your time will be compensated. It's not fair to make you give up a Sunday."

Matt turned to Lilly-Ann and back to me. "Wow. We weren't expecting that. Cool. Thanks."

"Yes, thanks," Lilly-Ann said. "We appreciate it."

"Not something Mr. Kuss would do," Matt chuckled. "He's the only person I've met who could get six cents out of nickel." Then he flinched. "Oops, I really need to keep my thoughts to myself. Sorry."

I winked. "Only if they're about me. Unless of course, they're accolades. Then you can spread them around like butter on toast."

Chapter Four

For the next hour, I had Lilly-Ann and Matt go over the daily routine. Prior to my ownership, Mr. Kuss handled all food orders, payroll, and maintenance. Once a month a cleaning service came in to do a deep cleaning, but Lilly-Ann and Matt did the daily clean-up before they left each day. And that included dishes and mopping.

As I listened, I could feel all of my free time being whittled away. At least I had the good sense to arrange for an accounting service to handle the tax matters.

"I'll be juggling two jobs this week," I said. "After that, the sandwich shop will have my full attention." I went on to explain about my vision for a charcuterie board enterprise and to my surprise, Lilly-Ann knew exactly what I meant.

"I love those!" she exclaimed. "Especially when the cold cuts are formed into flower blossoms."

Matt rolled his eyes. "Bologna is bologna. I don't care what it looks like as long as it tastes good. Oh heck. I did it again. Didn't I? Put my foot in my mouth. Listen, if I have to learn how to make cold cuts look like flowers, I will. No problem."

"You can relax. As long as you and Lilly-Ann work the sandwich shop, I'll design the charcuterie boards. I'll be working with two sizes—two by four, and three by six."

"If you don't mind teaching me," Lilly-Ann said, "I really want to learn. One can never add too much to their repertoire."

"Terrific. Starting tomorrow, I'll be here at six to help you get started. At eight I'll need to drive to Chandler for my final week at Chan-Tech. Leave me any notes on the counter because I'll be back around seven to review everything. You can also call me or text me if there's an issue."

"I can put in our regular orders if you want," Lilly-Ann offered. "I've done that quite a few times for the prior owner. We order monthly so you should be all set. If we run short, I can always contact our distributors. Much too expensive to run to the grocery if we run out."

"I'll have you walk me through it sometime this week if you don't mind coming back in at night."

"Not a problem. By the way, how was your move? We heard you're renting the old Cooperman place. Well, at least that's what everyone called it. The Cooperman's built it in the seventies then sold it to a food critic. Poor old lady died there. Peacefully in her bed from what I've been told."

Ew! Thank goodness I have my own new mattress.

"Uh, fine. More or less. Do you happen to know if she had a dog?"

Lilly-Ann shook her head. "The Cooperman's raised Golden Retrievers. Some of their offspring are probably still in the valley, but I don't know about the woman who died there."

"One of our customers knew her," Matt said. "It was months ago. The woman mentioned getting a lousy review for her restaurant in Fountain Hills. Apparently, a lot hinged on that review. Also went on and on about cat hair on her clothing from being in the house. Guess she went over there to have it out with the woman."

I shrugged. "So no dog, huh?"

Lilly-Ann looked perplexed. "Why do you ask?"

I told her and Matt about finding Speedbump in the house, and they laughed.

"Desert dogs get dropped off here all the time," Matt said. "I volunteer when I can for a local animal shelter. Chances are he got dumped."

Oh no. That dog's going to wind up living with me after all.

My meeting with the new employees was reassuring, alleviating much of the tension I felt earlier that day. From there, I went south on Cave Creek Road to Tatum Boulevard where the nearest Frys Supermarket was located.

With a stack of coupons itching to be used, I stocked up on food, sundries, and paper goods. I also bought two different kinds of dog biscuits, two dog bowls, a leash, and a collar. I rationalized that it might take a while for Speedbump's owners to be found but in the back of my mind, Matt's words surfaced—"Desert dogs get dropped here all the time."

By late afternoon I was ready to crash. Unloading the groceries didn't help either and the fact that I had to endure another hour or so without technology was unbearable. The iPhone could only do so much.

"I don't know why you're wagging your tail, dog," I said, "Your life is in more of a flux than mine." I gave him a dog biscuit and rubbed his chin before making myself a ham and cheese sandwich.

I don't know how Maddie did it, or who she bribed, but she got the cable company to agree to install my TV and internet between seven and eight pm that night. I was flabbergasted when she sent me a text. I'd made arrangements for the install, but it was a few days off. "Call U later or U call me," the text read. "Have fun unpacking."

"If all goes well, we won't be living in the Dark Ages tonight," I announced to the dog. "In fact, we can watch TV in bed since I'm getting a mini-box connection to go with the Contour package."

Speedbump inhaled his second biscuit, then darted out the doggie door while I tackled more boxes. If nothing else, the 'poor-old-lady-who-died-peacefully-in-her-sleep' didn't mess around when it came to a decent HVAC system. The cool air was a relief from the oven that would linger in the valley until October.

True to the text, the cable company truck pulled into my driveway at a little past seven, and the installation was completed before eight.

"Textbook job," the technician said as he handed me the iPad to sign off on it. "By the way, your dog is really laidback. Our Jack Russell can't stay still for a second."

"He's not—" And then I paused. "Very active at night."

"How old is he?"

I tried to remember what the vet said. "Around three. He's a rescue."

The technician rubbed Speedbump behind the ears. "He's a keeper for

21

sure."

"Did you hear that?" I asked the dog once I closed the door behind the guy. "A keeper. Don't let that go to your head."

Too exhausted to do any more unpacking, I microwaved some popcorn and flipped on the TV. The Sunday night lineup wasn't all that exciting, but it was better than staring at the ceiling. I gave Speedbump more kibble and another biscuit before calling Maddie.

"No takers yet on Facebook or Twitter," Maddie said before I even said hello. "I didn't want to post your phone number or email on the internet. I'll stop by tomorrow after work and we can go around your neighborhood with the flyers."

"Thanks. And double thanks for getting my cable and computer hooked up. Another night like the last one and I'd be ready for the looney bin. I don't know how people managed before technology."

"They read, and had a zillion kids. How'd the meeting go with your employees?"

"I think it will work out fine. Lilly-Ann seems pretty sensible and so does Matt. Still, I'm not about to leave them on their own. This first week will be tough but after that, things should settle in for me."

If nothing else, I will never, NEVER ever say that things will settle in because they never do. Something always pops up, and in my case, it happened well into the night.

Speedbump and I got into bed at a little after eleven. I was totally and completely drained but at least I was able to channel surf my way through late-night TV, The Weather Channel, and a few news sources before checking on Agatha Raisin's progress in the mystery I was reading.

Bleary-eyed, I pulled the chain on my beside lamp at eleven fifty-one and slipped into oblivion for exactly three hours and four minutes according to the digital clock. That's when Speedbump growled. Loud enough to wake me up.

"Go back to sleep," I said, refusing to open my eyes. "You probably heard that car again. Must be someone in this neighborhood works late hours. Or frequents bars."

His growl got louder and this time I did open my eyes. That's when I noticed the time. Two fifty-five. But it wasn't the first thing I noticed. That would have to be the haze and it didn't come from the digital clock.

It appeared the same way it did the night before in a cloudlike formation that hung next to the bed. Only this time it seemed to have more form, more definition, but of what I couldn't be sure. Then I heard a voice that cut through every fiber in my body.

"You threw out my favorite house shoes. I don't go around tossing your clothes in the garbage, although I have to admit, some of those bland outfits of yours would be better off in the landfill. I've never seen so many unappetizing neutral colors in one place."

I bolted upright. Absolutely indignant. "You rooted through my closet?"

"You mean *my* closet. And to answer your question, I was bored. By the way, you could use some help with style sense."

"Those are business suits. I'm a professional—I mean, I *was* a professional—" And then, poof! Just like that, the haze vanished, and Speedbump circled around at the foot of bed before going back to sleep.

I leaned over the bed and spit three times. It was a silly reaction but something my grandmother taught me to do whenever I had a nightmare.

"Whoa. Talk about an insulting nightmare," I muttered. "I'm worn out and stretched too thin. That has to be what's going on. I rarely get nightmares. Not even when Evan and I broke up."

The dog snored intermittently, and I realized I was talking to myself. What was that line from *A Christmas Carol?* Something about an undigested bit of beef or a blot of mustard? I blamed the fast food and popcorn for my nightly encounter with, with…what? It was a woman's voice that had somehow seeped into my subconscious only to manifest itself in a dreamlike state. Freud and my college psych professor would have been proud.

I pulled the cover up to my neck and went back to sleep. The alarm went off at a quarter to five and all appeared to be "right with the world." Speedbump dashed out his doggie door while I poured kibble into his bowl. Following a quick cup of coffee, this time with cream and a giant muffin from the supermarket, I took a fast shower and toweled off.

"Unappetizing neutral colors, my you-know-what," I laughed. "Maybe it's my subconscious telling me to spring for a new wardrobe. Anyway, this is the last week I'll be in business suits. Starting this weekend, I can be as creative as I want."

I pulled out a top from my dresser and walked over to the closet to grab the nearest suit and hightail out the door. That's when the breath was literally sucked out of me. Instead of the neat row of suits that I hung according to color and season, colorful boas looped around them as if it was a Mardi Gras display.

I froze. No way could Speedbump have done this. Not with a closed closet door and a five-foot-high clothing bar. My breath seemed to come out in waves as I stared at the reds, corals, and magentas that ensconced my business attire.

There was only one answer. Maddie had to have pranked me. I reached for my phone and tapped her number.

Her voice was groggy and slow. "Huh? Who? What's going on?"

"My clothes," I shrieked. "The boas! It's not funny."

"Katie? I don't understand."

When I told her what I had discovered, the line grew incredibly still. Finally, she spoke. "I've been home all night. Last thing I'd do would be to traipse all the way back to Cave Creek to play a trick on you. Look—get the locks changed on your house and put security bars on the windowsills. Maybe there's an unhinged neighbor floating around."

Terrific. Just what I need. An unhinged neighbor with a penchant for boas.

I told her I'd see her later when she came over with the posters and I apologized for waking her up. The thought of an unhinged neighbor was unsettling, but the alternative gave me goosebumps that didn't go away until I got to the sandwich shop a few minutes before six. That's when Maddie called with yet another theory.

Chapter Five

"We overlooked something," she said as I juggled my phone with one hand and closed the car door with the other.

"What? What did we overlook? We already unleashed the possibility of an unbalanced nutcase in the neighborhood."

"Sleepwalking. Maybe you did it in your sleep."

"Huh? I've never walked in my sleep. Not ever. Once I'm out, I'm out."

"That was the same deal with my aunt Doris until she got up in the middle of the night and made curried chicken salad. It was in the fridge the next morning. Next to some leftover chicken."

"How do you know she was the one who made the salad?"

"She lives alone."

"Aargh. Stop telling me these things. I'll see you tonight after work."

The second I got to the sandwich shop, I unlocked the door and raced to start up the coffee machine. At Lilly-Ann's enthusiastic "Good Morning!" I nearly jumped out of my skin. "Hey!" I said. "I didn't hear you walk in."

"Sorry. Didn't mean to scare you. Matt should be here any second. Do you want me to go through the morning ritual with you? And then if you want anything done differently, you can just tell us."

"You can tell me," Matt called out, breezing through the door. "I'm not set in my ways like Lilly-Ann."

Lilly-Ann shot him a look. "Being organized doesn't mean being set in my ways. I have a system and it works. Even if you did beat me to step one, making the coffee."

"Okay," I said. "I've got less than two hours so start showing me. That'll give me a better idea of where I'm needed most."

"We start with the salads," Lilly-Ann explained. "Usually, we've got plenty of hardboiled eggs to fill a decent size bowl but if not, we get some on the stove. For the most part, the ingredients are the same for all of the salads, so we portion out bowls of tuna, chopped ham, and of course, the eggs."

Matt walked to a small side sink and washed his hands before donning an apron and proceeding to the larger sink. "I'm the official veggie chopper. I check what's left over in the containers and determine if it's palate-worthy or garbage ready. Then it's off to work. We add all of the ingredients except for the mayo. That's done individually since mayo tends to get kind of watery the more it sits around in a salad."

"Not many places do that," I said.

Lilly-Ann dried her hands having soaped up while Matt and I talked. "It pays off. Same deal with adding lemon to the tuna."

I watched the two of them as they finalized the salads and made sure there were enough cold cuts for the sandwiches.

"'Brioche, Toast, and Most'" should be here any second," Matt announced. "We get a big order on Mondays and freeze the sandwich and specialty breads, so we have enough until Thursday when they come back for the second round. We've had the same bakery delivery guy for over a year and he's pretty reliable. Only got here late once and that was because there was an accident on the 101. Desert Delectable Foods brings us a huge delivery once a month. Meats and cheeses mainly. Mr. Kuss did the shopping for vegetables and miscellaneous stuff."

"Um, yeah. He left me a long laundry list."

"Most of our orders are take-out but some of our customers like to chitchat over coffee and breakfast sandwiches. It's an easy setup. The milk, creamers, sugar, and sugar substitutes are all on the counter by the coffee machine. Along with cinnamon and nutmeg for fancy-schmancy connoisseurs. We use plastic utensils, Styrofoam cups, and plastic reusable plates with liners."

"What about a dishwasher?"

Matt laughed. "At your service. It's only the large salad bowls and the coffee machine once a week. The health department didn't seem to have a problem with that. In fact, we've got an A+ rating."

How soon can you make it over to my place?

Fifty minutes later, our first customers drifted in and out in spurts. One or two people followed by six or seven, then nothing for a few minutes before the intermittent barrages continued.

Matt was right about the chit-chatters. Judging from what I observed, some of the folks were downright territorial about their tables with comments like "You know that's my seat, Linda," and "I always sit next to the window." I supposed that was what gave the shop its hometown feel.

Sometime in the midst of all of this, Lilly-Ann introduced me to the delivery guy, and we talked briefly. Billing and invoices came from the bakery shop so his job was simply to deliver the goods on time and in one piece. Fine with me.

The time at the sandwich shop was gone in a nanosecond and I reminded Lilly-Ann and Matt to leave me any notes on the counter and that I'd see the two of them the following morning.

"Any luck with the dog?" Matt asked as I was about to leave.

I shook my head. "Not yet. I told the vet I'd bring him in on Wednesday for a rabies shot if his owner didn't claim him."

Matt and Lilly-Ann exchanged glances from behind the counter. "Ka-ching, Ka-ching, is all I can say," Matt laughed. Then Lilly-Ann elbowed him just as the door closed behind me.

Traffic was higher than usual but I made it on time to work, thankful I only had four more days of the early morning rush. All day long, co-workers asked me if I wouldn't consider staying on and one even bribed me with a candy bar. "They'll probably hire some stuck-up stick-in-the-mud who won't be any fun at all," she said.

"Nah, chances are they'll hire some hunky dude who'll make Tom Cruise look like a toad."

She shook her head. "Only in my dreams."

By late afternoon, I was exhausted. I still had those posters to tack up around town and Maddie promised to be at my place around six. I figured we could nuke something I picked up from the store yesterday or we could go all Cave Creek touristy and eat at The Lazy Lizard or Big Earls on the main drag. It didn't matter. My head was a mess of cobwebs and I seriously wondered how I'd keep it together until the weekend.

The past two nightly visits or sleep-deprivation apparitions didn't help. I'd always been a logical person so finding brightly colored boas that I didn't own draped over my business suits was one puzzle I was anxious to solve.

It wasn't as if the movers stuffed them there, because I was the one who unpacked my own clothing. The more I thought about it on the ride home, the twitchier I got. What if someone really did sneak in. But how? The windows were closed tight since I had the AC running and the doors were deadbolted shut. Besides, wouldn't Speedbump have barked? Or howled? Or something?

I forced myself to push that incident to the back of my mind and instead focus on the business plan I had roughly sketched out for my charcuterie business. It gave me great comfort to concentrate on something tangible like a marketing plan and accounting software. Once those were in place, there'd be no stopping me when it came to design elements for those platters.

My mind drifted from combining dried figs with tangy olives to setting up an Excel spreadsheet and by the time I pulled into my driveway, the thought of those boas was all but gone.

Speedbump trotted to the utility room door when I came in from the garage. His tail was in fast motion, and he gave me an enthusiastic bump.

"Guess I gave you the right moniker for a while," I said, giving him an ear rub. "I suppose you ate all the kibble I left. Come on, I'll get you a refill and put some ice cubes in your water dish. This heat is something else, huh?"

With that done, I grabbed an unsweetened Pure Leaf iced tea from the fridge and took a giant gulp before I walked into the bedroom to swap my office attire for capris and a t-shirt. "Maddie's going to be here in about a half-hour," I called out. "If you're good, you can join us as we drive around the neighborhood."

All I heard were chomping sounds as I hung up my suit. The boas were still in the closet, but I had folded them and stuffed them on the shelf above the clothing rod. Their next stop would be the local charity shop. With phone in hand, I sank down on my bed and called my landlord, the nephew of "the-elderly-lady-who-died-peacefully-in-her-sleep."

"Mr. Fitzpatrick?" I asked.

"At the ready."

"Hi! I'm Katie Aubrey, your new renter in Cave Creek."

"Uh-oh. Don't tell me something went wrong already. An appliance? I wanted to contract with a maintenance company, but I figured with only one house I could manage."

"No, no, nothing like that. But I want to change the locks and I need your permission. You see, last night—"

"Oh no. Don't tell me someone tried to break in. Or did break in."

The alarm in his voice rivaled my mother's when the cable went out or her internet went down.

"This may sound weird. I unpacked my business suits and hung them in the master bedroom closet last night. This morning when I opened the closet, I found colorful boas looped around them. Mr. Fitzpatrick, I don't own colorful boas. I don't even own bland ones."

"Boas? Like in feather boas from the nineteen twenties? That kind of boa?"

Trust me. If they'd been constrictors, I would have been in Iceland by now.

"Uh-huh. At first, I thought one of my girlfriends might have played a trick on me but that wasn't the case, leading me to believe maybe some nutcase was floating around the neighborhood and found a way inside. Although, there was no sign of a break-in. Still, changing the locks would make me feel more secure."

"Of course. Of course. Call a locksmith and send me a copy of the bill. I'll reimburse you or take it off next month's rent."

"Are you sure? You don't have to do this. I can pay."

"It's not a problem. Boas, huh? You know, they may have belonged to my late aunt and quite possibly fell down from the shelf above the clothing bar. I didn't spend a lot of time in the house when she passed. With the exception of some artwork, jewelry, and family items, everything else is still there. Well, not everything. I donated her clothing to a woman's shelter in

Phoenix. It was either that or a theater company. Oh, I also stashed that relic of a computer of hers in the shed in the backyard. It was a miracle I could fit it in. Had to wedge it next to some hideous gargoyles and a rusty old bicycle with balloon tires. If I ever sell the place, an estate liquidation company can deal with it."

"You didn't want to keep her computer?"

"Only if I planned to open a museum. She was still using WORD 97. Frankly, I didn't have the time to deal with it. At least donating her wardrobe was easy, even though Edith's style wasn't exactly what one would call establishment. No, if I could describe it in one word it would be flamboyant. It went along well with her lifestyle I suppose. Aunt Edith, world traveler, food critic, and fussbudget. Not to mention cat lover."

"What about dogs? Was she a dog lover, too?" *Maybe Speedbump was hers.*

"Nope. Adored cats. I'm surprised she didn't own forty-nine of them. Anyway, those boas had to have been hers. Classic Edith Ellory style."

"Edith Ellory? *The* Edith Ellory who had the audacity to criticize one of Gordon Ramsay's signature dishes? *That* Edith Ellory?"

"The very one, I'm afraid. The Ramsay incident, as my family still refers to it, made every headline in culinary magazines for the entire fall season that year. So yes, *that* Edith Ellory."

"Wow. Not to sound critical of this house, but I would have expected someone with her wealth and prestige to live in Fountain Hills or maybe even Paradise Valley."

"Funny, isn't it? For someone whose style and mannerisms could intimidate a four-star general, you'd think she'd live in the same fashion. But no, she was closer to 'off the grid' than high society. Anyway, get those locks changed and you'll have a better night's sleep."

Lamentably, he was wrong. But how was he to know I wasn't dealing with a neighborhood fruitcake who liked to embellish people's wardrobes?

Chapter Six

"I'm dying of thirst," Maddie said the second I opened the door. "You'd think I'd remember to keep a bottle of water in the car with me this time of year." She bent down to pet Speedbump who nuzzled against her leg. "Got your posters ready to go and even brought sticky tape with me. I figure we'll be okay putting them on utility poles. Heck, everyone else announces garage sales and all sorts of stuff."

I handed her a bottle of iced tea and motioned for the kitchen table. "Take a five-minute break and then we can get going. FYI, I called Daniel Fitzpatrick to tell him about the boa incident. He was really understanding and offered to pay for new locks. But get this, he said his aunt was really eccentric and a flashy dresser. Thought maybe those were her boas that slipped down from the closet."

Maddie took a quick swallow of her tea. "Isn't that what I said?"

"Yeah, among other things. Like sleepwalking and a neighborhood lunatic."

"Hey, it's important to cover all of the bases."

"Aargh. Um, I kind of told Speedbump he could join us if you don't mind. He's absolutely clean because I actually gave him a bath. Poor guy's been stuck in the house all day."

Maddie continued to pet the dog. "He doesn't seem to mind. Besides, he can go out in the backyard anytime. But sure, he can tag along. I take it you didn't get any messages from the posts I put on social media."

I shook my head. "It's still early. Someone will claim him."

Unlike the new housing developments in the area, my house was in an established neighborhood that allowed for space and privacy between buildings. It was built before homeowner associations became the norm, so the owners didn't have to contend with all sorts of covenants, rules, and restrictions. Or the monthly meetings where residents could catch up on the local scuttlebutt. Still, it didn't mean the area was free from the usual rumors and gossip as Maddie and I quickly found out. We did a general drive-around and posted our "Found Dog" signs wherever we could. When we finished that task, we leashed Speedbump and knocked on the doors of the houses that we missed when the dog first arrived on scene.

"I'm surprised Edith's house is still standing," the man next door said. He appeared to be in his late fifties and in need of a shave. "That woman had a way of getting under everyone's skin. No wonder she never got married."

"Can you be a bit more specific?" I asked.

"Where do you want me to begin? See the house across the street? The lady who lives there had her grandson stay with her for a few months as well as her live-in boyfriend. Edith approached the woman one day demanding to know 'just how many men she had in there.' Does that answer your question?"

I flinched. "Yeesh."

Maddie and I also learned that Edith left notes for people regarding their recycling if she happened to notice inappropriate items in their bins during pick-up day. According to another neighbor, she put an AA flyer on that person's door with a note mentioning an abundance of empty wine bottles.

"She was persnickety all right. I suppose that's why she chose her line of work," I said to Maddie. "You know, being a food critic and all."

"It also sounded like none of the neighbors were all too broken up about her passing."

"Broken up? From what you and I heard I'm surprised they didn't celebrate."

We returned to the house an hour and a half later. Tired, thirsty, and no closer to finding Speedbump's owners. No one recognized the dog, and I grew closer to the realization that I'd be spending the next decade or so with him sleeping on my feet.

We left Speedbump with a full bowl of kibble and took off for the sandwich shop so I could see what notes my staff of two left for me. Thankfully, only one and it read, "We're still in business!" It was signed with initials and a smiley face.

From there, Maddie and I went to El Encanto, a classy Mexican restaurant and a Cave Creek favorite. No wonder. Who can resist mission-style arches and a fabulous water feature? Maddie was insistent on genuine Mexican food having tired of all the chain restaurants in her corner of the valley.

"I've got enough leftovers to last for two days," I said when we returned to my place. "By the way, I can't believe you keep a food cooler in your car."

"What did you expect? We grew up in the valley. I'm surprised you don't have one."

I shrugged. "I don't usually eat out at fine dining places with generous portions. Or prices for that matter."

"You've been stuck in that high-tech building for way too long. It'll be different now that you're going to be your own boss. Listen, as much as I'd like to hang out with you, I've got two showings tomorrow, and judging from the fact your eyes are drooping, you'll want to hit the sack, too."

I thanked Maddie, gave her a hug, and promised to connect with her during the week. "If I'm still vertical by the end of the week, let's get together. Toggling two jobs is worse than I pictured and today was only day one. Good thing Lilly-Ann and Matt know what they're doing. As far as Chan-Tech is concerned, I can do that on overdrive."

"Yeah," Maddie laughed. "What's the worst they can do? Fire you?"

I made sure to check the deadbolt twice when Maddie left the house. Chances are she and my landlord were right about the boas but what if someone still thought Edith was alive and well and they wanted to, to…I shuddered, trying not to say it out loud.

"Come on, Speedbump. It's late and I need to make up for last night's horrible attempt at sleep. Tomorrow I'll call a locksmith."

The dog followed me into the bedroom and jumped on the bed.

Yep. Another decade of this for sure.

"I need a good night's sleep," I said to the dog. "In fact, I'm too tired to do any channel surfing and too unfocused to read. Lights out, it is. We'll be up with the roosters again."

My body sank into the mattress, same as it did the night before, and I blotted out the hum of the air conditioner and the whirl of the overhead fan. It was absolute oblivion. Until it wasn't.

A rustling sound woke me at a little past three according to my alarm clock. It was only Speedbump re-positioning himself in the bed. I turned over and started to drift off when I heard his low growl again.

The bluish haze had returned to the room only it wasn't as nebulous as it was the prior two nights. In fact, it appeared to form the silhouette of a woman. A silhouette that hovered over the bed.

Convinced I was in a dream state, I pulled the cover over my head and faced the opposite direction. That's when Speedbump's growl intensified and the raspy woman's voice I heard the night before cut through the stillness in the room.

"You're not going back into La-La Land, are you? I need you to do something for me."

"Huh? What?"

I rubbed my eyes and watched as the silhouette's form became sharper. It was a woman all right with a headful of curls and a floral top.

"I'm just dreaming," I mumbled. "Go away."

"Not until you help me."

At that instant, Speedbump barked, and I sat bolt upright. If I had been asleep, I wasn't anymore. The woman's form moved closer to the bed, and she sat down at its foot. Speedbump immediately jumped off and stood at attention.

"At least you didn't put my boas in the garbage like you did with my slippers," she said.

"Is that what this is about? Your boas?"

"Don't be ridiculous. I need you to find out who killed me."

Okay. I'm dreaming for sure. It just feels like I'm awake, but I'm dreaming.

I squinted and took a closer look at the apparition or silhouette or whatever she was. The details got clearer. Older woman. Well put together. *For a specter.* Stylish ensemble but perhaps a bit bold for my liking. Especially those dangling earrings. What the heck was I saying? The apparition of a dead woman was having a conversation with me at the foot of my bed as if we were enjoying a latte in a coffee shop somewhere.

"Who are you?"

"Oh, cut it out. You know very well who I am. I'm Edith Ellory. You're living in my house, sleeping in my bedroom, and picking up where I left off as far as feeding that stray dog is concerned. He showed up right before my unfortunate demise. Frankly, I've always been more of a cat person but my last cat, Lulu Fondoola, passed away a few months before I did."

"I'm sorry to hear—Oh good grief. None of this is real. I'm dreaming."

Just then, the overhead fan picked up speed and my bedside lamp flickered on and off.

"Want to see what else I can do?" Edith asked. "I'm still learning."

"All right. All right. I get it. You've got some unfinished business and can't move on. Classic textbook ghost."

"So now you're an expert on departed spirits?"

"That's not what I said."

Meanwhile, Speedbump moved to the small throw rug by my dresser and curled up. I figured he didn't think Edith's appearance was much of a threat.

"Like I mentioned earlier, you need to find out who was responsible for putting me in an early grave."

"You're buried around here?" I tried to wrap my head around the bizarre conversation.

"That was a figure of speech. I was cremated for your information. Easier for the rat-scallion who did me in to cover the evidence."

"Um, listen, as much as I'd like to help you, I'm starting a new business in the area and that's going to require hours of work. Hours! Do you have any idea how many new businesses fail in their first year? Especially in the food industry."

"Oh honey, I'm more than familiar with the food industry. Whining never helps."

"Can't you wait it out a bit until your murderer winds up where you are and then you can deal with it? You know, confront them in the netherworld or wherever you are."

"It doesn't work like that. It's not as if I'm at Sandals, sipping on a Mai-Tai waiting to chat with one of the guests. Besides, I don't know who killed me."

"Um, uh, I don't want to insult you, but are you sure you were killed? Everyone said you died peacefully in your sleep as a result of old age."

"Old age? Old age? I died at the age of seventy-seven. Since when is that old age? I could understand it, maybe, if I passed away in my late nineties, but seventy-seven? I was in the epitome of life. So, yes or no? Are you going to help me, or do I have to resort to nagging?"

Nagging, huh? Take a number and join my mother.

"You think it over," she said. "We'll talk more tomorrow. The food business you said? What kind of food business?"

"A charcuterie catering service and sandwich shop. I bought the Cave Creek Sandwich Shop, and it will be my home base."

"We may be able to work out a deal. I'm quite accomplished at creating charcuterie boards."

"So far all I've seen you do is get a fan to blow and a light to flicker."

"I suppose you'd tell Monet all he could do was wash paint brushes."

"Now that's not fair. In fact—" I never got to finish because in that instant, the specter vanished, Speedbump returned to the foot of the bed and the fan slowed down. To be on the safe side once again, I spit three times before going back to sleep.

Chapter Seven

"It's stress," I told the dog the next morning. The sun hadn't even come up and I stumbled around the kitchen getting his food in a bowl and my coffee in a cup. "Once I settle in to one job in one place, all of this nighttime nonsense will vanish. Edith's ghost? Can you imagine? And murdered no less. My imagination is working overtime."

Speedbump sat at attention, more interested in his food bowl than what I had to say. "Maybe today will be your lucky day and someone will claim you. If not, it's off to the vet tomorrow morning for a rabies shot. It's not worth taking chances around here. Too many coyotes and foxes."

The dog gobbled his kibble and slurped the iced water that I had placed next to his food bowl. "We were lucky they open at seven. We'll be really rushed this time tomorrow. I'll have to do a quick in and out at the sandwich shop, then swing back and get you before taking off for Chan-Tech. Ugh. Only a few more days of that. No wonder I'm stressed and seeing apparitions in my sleep."

I toasted an English muffin and followed it with a second cup of coffee before jumping into the shower. Speedbump followed me into the bedroom but instead of getting back on the bed, he settled by the dresser again.

"I can't believe I'm this fanatic about making my bed," I announced once I had toweled dry and put on my undergarments. "I would have done well in the armed forces. They have to make their beds every day at dawn, too."

I threw back the lightweight comforter and was about to straighten the sheets when something caught my eye—a two-toned gold chandelier drop earring. I don't know how long I stood there, but it couldn't have been for more than a few seconds.

"Those dangling earrings of hers." The words choked out of me as I reached for it. "Coincidence, my patootie." It was a lovely piece of jewelry in a style that I would never wear. Somehow, I never got used to the feel of earrings bobbing around my lobes and much preferred the studded ones.

"It's real all right. Solid as can be," I said to Speedbump. "And I'm calling that locksmith company this instant. I don't care if I wake them up."

The dog looked at me and then went back to his resting position. "Okay, so maybe I'm overreacting. There has to be a rational explanation. Meanwhile, I'll get on Valley Locksmiths' schedule."

I wound up leaving a voicemail on their system since it wasn't a dire emergency. And what was I supposed to tell them? That I found an earring in my bed? Or had nightly encounters with an annoying apparition? The only explanation I could think of was that Speedbump must have found it somewhere in the house and deposited it in my bed while I slept.

All sorts of little odds and ends wind up in corners of houses when people move in and out. Still, the earring bore an unusual resemblance to the ones Edith wore during her nightly visit.

Hustling, I grabbed a lovely pinstripe suit from the closet, snatched a cute pair of Mary Janes, and was out the door in record time. Lilly-Ann and Matt were already fast at work when I got to the shop.

"You look like you've been chased by the devil," Matt said when he saw me.

"What do you mean? Is my hair a mess?" I immediately patted down the bouncy waves.

"No, not that. I don't know. Just that look on your face. Like you've been running from something. My girlfriend gets that same look when we watch a horror movie."

"I'm fine. Just a bit harried. How's it going?"

"Everything's fine back here!" Lilly-Ann called out. "Salads are made, coffee's on, and we'll be ready to open as usual. Any luck finding your dog's owner?"

"Not yet. In fact, I brought along a few flyers we can leave on the counter. Also, I've got an appointment tomorrow morning to get him a rabies shot.

That means I'll only be in here for a few minutes."

"You don't have to drive yourself nuts," she said. "Matt and I can manage. Take care of the dog, go to Chandler and then stop by after your work there. This place can run on autopilot for a few more days. By the way, I took care of the bank deposits like you directed and all of the information is in the drawer under the register. Not much cash these days thanks to debit and credit cards. Seriously, give yourself a break. Wrangling two jobs in two different parts of the valley has got to be a nightmare."

"I'll be fine, but I'll let you know if I decide to take you up on that offer and skip stopping in tomorrow."

Like yesterday, I shadowed Lilly-Ann and Matt, served a few customers, and started to become somewhat familiar with the ebb and flow of the place. The opening hour went fast—customers in and out and staff on the go. Pulse racing for sure, but satisfying. This was the first venture, and it was truly my own. That's why I didn't want to louse things up by asking Lilly-Ann or Matt if either of them had realistic nighttime dreams where they had an ongoing dialogue with a phantasm. Yep, last thing I needed was to have my employees think their boss was unbalanced.

Edith insisted she'd been murdered. But maybe Edith was a fabrication my own mind created as a result of stress. But murder? The consensus was that she had died peacefully in her sleep. No evidence of foul play whatsoever. After all, that sort of thing would have to be disclosed to buyers and/or renters.

Then again, Edith wasn't exactly the most likable neighbor, giving rise to lots of motives for murder. Not to mention those restaurant owners whose businesses got slapped in the face by her reviews.

I'm reading way too many murder mysteries. Maybe I should switch to romance for a while.

"If I don't see you guys tomorrow," I said to Lilly-Ann and Matt, "then it will be bright and early Thursday morning." I retrieved my bag from the desk in the kitchen and started for the door when I remembered something Matt said.

"Hey Matt, before I head out, you wouldn't happen to know the name of that restaurant in Fountain Hills that got a scalding review from Edith, do you?"

"Everyone does. It's The Chanterelle on Parkview Avenue. They're still in business so I guess she didn't do too much damage. I don't suppose we'll have to worry about food critic reviews, will we?"

"If the charcuterie end of the business takes off, I would hope so. A stellar review translates to a high-profile business and that means more profits."

Matt grinned. "Fine with me. I could use a raise."

Lilly-Ann rolled her eyes. "Ignore him. We're getting paid a decent wage."

"Well," I said, "Who knows. If this business does thrive, I would certainly be amenable."

Day two of the rush to Chan-Tech mirrored day one. A frantic day complicated by a series of meetings designed to help my successors adjust to their growing workloads until a new hire could be made. Lunch was a bland ham and cheese sandwich from the snack bar in our building and my third cup of coffee for the day.

Worse yet, my fifteen-minute afternoon break wasn't a break at all. I used that time to respond to a four-word text my mother sent. "It's not too late." Really? And here I thought I was the delusional one with those nighttime visions. At least I was in the real world during the daylight hours.

Famished by the time I got into my car but too exhausted to get out, I stopped at the first McDonalds I spied and ate a Big Mac in the parking lot, washing it down with Coke this time. Same amount of caffeine but carbonated.

Like yesterday, Speedbump was eager to greet me. "Sorry guy," I said. "No calls came in for you today and no messages either. If I wasn't so dead tired, I'd take you for a walk around the neighborhood but that may have to wait until the weekend." Then it hit me. Three days had gone by, and the dog was no closer to reuniting with his owner than I was to keeping my job at Chan-Tech.

Three days? If my conversation with Edith had any validity, then it was longer than three days. What did she say? Something about Speedbump showing up before she passed away in her sleep. That wasn't days ago. It was weeks. If I really was communicating with the dead and not suffering from hallucinations, then Speedbump must have been scavenging around for the early part of the summer.

"You poor guy," I cooed, rubbing his head and ears. "Maybe it won't be so bad having a roommate after all." I texted Maddie the update and she texted back a heart and a smiley face.

Even though Chan-Tech kept their temperature slightly above freezing in the summer, the moisture dripping from my neck to my back forced me to take a cool shower before checking out the sandwich shop.

True, it was obsessive and compulsive, but I had to see for myself that the place was still standing, and everything was in order.

"Come on, Speedbump," I said. "It's after hours and I doubt you'll be a problem at the shop. We're only going to be a few minutes. Just don't expect to be as comfortable in my car as you were in Maddie's."

Everything was neat and in order when I unlocked the door and stepped inside. Speedbump lifted his head and sniffed before walking around. Again, a short note on the counter indicating that all was well.

"I'm taking you up on your offer," I added to the note. "I'll be in tomorrow evening. Call me if there are any problems. Thanks!" Like Lilly-Ann, I drew a smiley face before tucking the note under the same coffee cup she did.

Just then, my phone buzzed, and it was Valley Locksmiths. They had a cancellation and could be at my house in a half-hour.

"Got to move it, dog," I said. "If there's any validity to Maddie's theory about the wacko in the neighborhood, then this should put the kibosh on it for sure."

As Speedbump and I got into my car, I tried to envision how someone could get into a house without making noise. Even if they had a key. It simply didn't make sense, but neither did the other possibilities.

Chapter Eight

"You should be all set," Mitchell McClure said as he handed me an invoice. Tall, clean-shaven, and muscular, it looked as if the fifty-something locksmith spent his free time at the gym. "The front and back doors, as well as the door to the utility room are all keyed the same and the deadbolt's one of the best. If you continue to have problems, I'd look into getting security doors, too."

At least I didn't have to worry about sliding patio doors since the house featured large view windows in back and a regular outside door. I handed Mitchell my credit card and waited while he processed it on his iPad. "Um, would you happen to know if there have been issues in this neighborhood with break-ins? I mean, I know you're not the only locksmith company but you're the closest one around so I figured yours would be the one people called."

Mitchell returned my card and the iPad for a signature. "No break-ins but two folks on this block had their locks changed due to trespassers. That's all the information I have. You may want to check with the town marshal's office or check the AZ Spot Crime Map, but like I said, you should be fine. Keep the doors locked. Especially the one that goes from the garage into the house. If someone jockeys with the garage door opener, they'll still be locked out. But, I wouldn't rule out security doors."

I thanked him and immediately put one of my new keys on my keychain and the spare key in my desk drawer. Downing that Big Mac seemed centuries ago, and I was famished. Famished, but too tired to do more than plunk a Stouffers veggie lasagna in the microwave and give Speedbump a handful of kibble and a biscuit.

If anything decent was on TV, I wouldn't have known. I passed out on the couch once I finished eating and from there, I staggered into bed during an infomercial about water softeners. At a little after ten, as I shut off the lamp on my nightstand, I announced, "I know you said we'd chat tonight, but I'm too gosh-darned tired, Edith. Besides, you're not real."

At least I managed five or so hours of sleep before Speedbump nuzzled me and jumped from the bed. No growling this time. The usual blue haze was greenish and gradually morphed into Edith Ellory's form as I rubbed my eyes. An ostentatious tiara rested on her curls, and she was draped in a dark green fringed evening dress that looked like it came straight out of the 1940s. This time she had the audacity to sit at the foot of the bed.

"Go away," I said. "Your timing stinks."

"It is what it is," was her reply. "Now are you going to help me or not?"

"Not if this continues at three in the morning. For crying out loud, this is Cave Creek, not Gull Cottage and you're not the spirit of a cantankerous old sea captain. Well, not a sea captain at any rate. If you want my help, we have to agree on a more convenient time."

Sure, I can play along with this nightly delusion. Once I get into a decent schedule, all of this will disappear.

A sudden burst of cold air took me by surprise and I pulled the cover tighter to my chest. Edith seemed amused. "Do you expect me to take out my planner? Let's see, shall I schedule you for Mondays after my beauty parlor appointment or maybe Thursdays before my pedicures?"

"There's no reason for you to be sarcastic. I'm the one whose sleep keeps getting interrupted. Look, how about we make a deal? Evenings between nine and eleven. Here and only here. I don't need you showing up during the day in all sorts of places. I have enough to deal with."

"So it's agreed? You'll find out who murdered me."

"You realize I'm not a detective. Heck, I'm not even an amateur sleuth."

Good grief. I'm rationalizing with a dream fragment.

"You should be by now, with all of the cozy mysteries in those cartons by the big bureau in the living room. I would have thought you'd be unpacked

43

by now."

"They're not all cozies. Some are police procedurals and thrillers. And a few historicals and traditionals here and there." *Oh, for heaven's sake, now I'm arguing with a figment of my imagination.*

"By the way, highly doubtful it was a trespasser."

"Huh? Who?"

"Why the person who did me in, that's who. I overheard you talking with the locksmith. Always prudent to have the locks changed when moving into someone's prior residence but I don't think you have cause to worry. Unless of course you make up a charcuterie board and leave a pit in one of those olives or worse yet, a fig. Then it's lawsuit time or worse."

I decided to take the easy way out and get it over with. "Um, if you're really going to drag me into this so-called homicide investigation, then you'll need to tell me who had it in for you. Looking around, I doubt you were sent to the proverbial cabin-in-the-sky for money because, from what I found out, the only person who got your inheritance was your nephew in Tacoma, and he was nowhere near here during the time of your departure."

"Even if he was here, Danny would never commit such a heinous deed. He's a regular Boy Scout. And if you're thinking insurance monies, think again. I left enough for my nephew to take care of my obligations as well as a tidy little sum for his troubles. Not to mention the house."

"Anyone else cash in?"

"The Desert Hills Cat Rescue in Carefree. It's run by a group of former nuns. You can cross them off the list."

"Uh-huh. Back to where we started. If you were really murdered, then you need to figure out who you ticked off. And by the way, you weren't exactly Miss Congeniality as far as your neighbors were concerned."

"Bunch of old gossips and bats. And that curmudgeon who lives next door. Someone should introduce him to a razor and shaving cream."

"What about the eating establishments that got bad reviews from you? Any lingering hostilities?"

"Honey, it's a competitive business, not a feel-good walk in the park. If they can't take the criticism, they shouldn't be in the culinary world. Now, if you don't mind, your questions and constant badgering are getting on my nerves."

"What about a vendetta? Revenge?"

"Hers or mine?"

"Who?"

"Imogen Brodeur, that's who. The snotty owner of The Chanterelle. That woman never walked past a mirror she didn't like. I'm surprised her restaurant didn't have one on every wall."

With that, her form began to evaporate like a cloud.

"Wait! Are you missing an earring?"

But it was too late. Edith vanished and Speedbump returned to his spot on the bed.

The following morning while Speedbump and I waited in the lobby of the vet's office for his appointment, I texted Maddie. "Dinner Sunday at The Chanterelle?" I had to get rid of this stress-induced nighttime apparition and what better way than to play along with the script. Even if it was all a figment of my own imagination. After all, a little innocent sleuthing into a possible, but not likely murder, wouldn't hurt anyone. And Matt did mention the owner was furious at the biting review Edith gave her.

Maddie texted back, "Did U win at Mega Millions?" I wasted no time with a reply. "Okay. Lunch then. Cheaper menu items." A few seconds later, I read her response. "What's going on? Call me later."

I waited until midday to phone her in between bites of a chicken salad sandwich on rye.

"Speedbump's had all of his vaccines, a heartworm test, and then some. I've got the paperwork, so I'll get him licensed with the county."

"I knew you'd come around. Tell me, what's the deal with The Chanterelle? A glass of water will set me back. When I said I liked restaurants with generous portions, I meant portions, not prices."

I wasn't quite ready to give Maddie the real reason. *The woman who died peacefully in my house showed up in my bedroom and said she was murdered. Quite possibly by the owner of The Chanterelle. I'm investigating on behalf of the victim's ghost.*

"Curiosity, that's all. Edith Ellory, the former owner of this house, gave them a blistering review a while back. Besides, we never treat ourselves to a high-end meal."

"That's a reason all right, but it comes with a high-end cost. Oh well. If you're so adamant, I'll take you up on lunch. After all, how expensive can a salad be?"

I didn't have the heart to tell her I perused their website and small salads began at $14.95.

"Terrific. Come on over here around eleven so we can visit first. By then, the place should have some semblance of order. I've only got a few more cartons to unpack and as for decorative art, I think I'll let the current ceramics, wall hangings, and metal art stay."

"Really? You didn't seem to take a liking to them when I first showed you the house."

"Um, they kind of grow on you."

And if I swap them out for my own stuff, Edith will inevitably pitch a fit. She's unbearable enough as it is.

"If you say so. Not many people fancy Mexican Day of the Dead pottery in combination with Russian nesting dolls. Well, to each his or her own, I suppose. Got to run. I've got a showing in Tempe in an hour."

"Good luck. Talk to you later this week."

Like the day before, I arrived home from Chan-Tech sticky, hot, and exhausted. "Good thing you've got fur to insulate you," I said to Speedbump as I tossed my top into the laundry bin, "otherwise your skin would be covered in a layer of Arizona summer moisture. And not the refreshing kind."

Following a quick rinse-off in the shower, I opted for another microwave dinner, only this time eggplant parmesan, compliments of Michelangelo. I rationalized that since it was eggplant, it had to be somewhat healthy. Still, I couldn't wait for the week to end so I could prepare salads and cold soups.

"Tonight's the big test," I said. "If Edith doesn't show up after nine, then I'll know she's a hallucination brought on by lack of sleep and stress. Meanwhile,

I've got to check on the sandwich shop so off we go."

Speedbump raced to the car and pawed at the door. "Don't think this is going to be a nightly habit. Only a couple more days of it and things will be back to normal."

As it turned out, normal was the last word I'd use to describe the frenzy that took hold of my life since the first blue haze entered the bedroom.

It began with a different sort of note from Lilly-Ann and Matt when the dog and I entered the sandwich shop. It was in the usual place under the coffee cup on the counter and it read, "A new customer came in asking about the owner. Said she heard you rented Edith Ellory's place and wanted to give you this message. Here goes: 'Good luck living in Edith's old place. You may want to burn some sage sticks to remove the bad energy. The woman had unresolved issues.'" Lilly Ann and Matt's note went on to say, "We wouldn't worry about it if we were you. Lots of kooks and nutcases out there. Anyway, everything else is fine. See you tomorrow!"

Instead of a smiley face, Lilly-Ann and Matt, left one that looked like Munch's *The Scream*. I shoved it in my pocket, perused the kitchen, and left a few minutes later.

Unresolved issues, huh? Is that what they're calling murder these days?

Chapter Nine

"Who was the woman? What did she look like? Did she tell you where she lived? How did she know Edith?"

I upchucked those words as if my stomach had reacted to a tainted meal. No "Good Morning or How's it going?" Nope, I flew into the soon-to-be Char-Board without pausing to take a breath. Lilly-Ann and Matt looked at me wide-eyed with open mouths. I continued as if nothing was wrong. "Was she some sort of clairvoyant? Your note scared the daylights out of me last night."

Lilly-Ann walked a few feet past the counter to where Matt stood. She gave him a kick on the ankle and bristled. "I told you not to write that down. See what we've done?" Then she moved toward me. "I'm sorry, Katie. Matt's sorry, too. We didn't mean to upset you."

Matt shrugged. "I thought you'd get a good laugh out of it. Artsy-fartsy communities like ours are a magnet for weirdos. We're just one step behind Sedona and Jerome. Heck, last year some guy came in claiming he'd had a conversation with Elvis."

"It's that recreational marijuana," Lilly-Ann said. "Loosens people up to the point where they say anything."

"I don't think that woman had been smoking weed," Matt said. "Nope. She was in her own alternate universe if you ask me. At least she liked the egg salad she ordered."

The crazed fanaticism in my voice evaporated and I was able to continue a conversation like a normal person. "Starting Saturday, I'll be here full time. Let me know if she stops in again."

Matt nodded. "Don't worry. She won't be hard to miss. Pencil thin, long gaunt face, red lipstick, and one of those sequin tops that matched her leggings. No spring chicken, either. Probably in her fifties."

"What?" Lilly-Ann all but shrieked. "Is that how you describe me? 'No spring chicken?' And I'm in my fifties, too."

Matt's face turned beet red. "Yeah, but you don't act as old as you are. I don't think of you as being a certain age."

I laughed. "I think you better quit while you're ahead."

"It *is* odd," Lilly-Ann said, "that the woman mentioned bad vibes in your house. Or something to that effect. You haven't noticed anything bizarre, have you?"

You mean like my nightly visits from the former occupant who insists she was murdered?

"No, no. Nothing like that. Everything's fine."

Good grief. Everything was *not* fine. Not in the least. And while Lilly-Ann chatted, my mind returned to the prior night when Edith paid her usual visit. At least she kept her word. She arrived at 9:01 and plunked herself down on the couch inches away from me and just as a new episode of *Magnum* came on.

Her voice was louder than before and just as raspy. "I liked the old *Magnum* better. It's not the same without John Hillerman."

That night she wore an ivory silk chiffon Grecian dress. The kind I'd seen in those old *Topper* movies my grandmother liked to watch. Straight out of the late thirties.

"Edith! You can at least announce yourself. You know. The haze and all."

"I thought we were on more personal terms. No need for an entrance."

"Fine. Fine. Do you have a starting point for me? Like an inner circle of possible suspects? And before we go any further, exactly how *do* you know you were murdered? If there was any sign of foul play, it would have been in all of the papers and on the nightly news *ad nauseum*. Readership and viewership are drawn to words like *bludgeoned, suffocated, strangled, choked,* not to mention the usual descriptors like *blunt force trauma* and *stab wounds*."

"Well, aren't you a little breath of sunshine? For your information, honey,

49

I have reason to believe I was poisoned. After all, that would account for the lack of, shall we say, other, more overt evidence."

"Poisoned, huh? The body shows visible signs of poisoning, you know. Like blue lips."

"I believe that's from drowning."

"And your house. *My* house. There were no signs of a break-in according to my real estate agent. No police report. Simply, deceased body found on the premises. How do you explain that?"

"Ah-hah! The million-dollar question. The last thing I recall was enjoying a lovely cup of Earl Grey tea before retiring. Then, dead air space for lack of a better way to put it. I knew someone was responsible for my undoing and it certainly wasn't me. For your information, I went to bed as robust and vibrant as ever. Before waking up dead."

"You're saying you felt perfectly well in the days leading up to your death? Not unusually tired or headachy?"

"Are you daft? I just told you I was in perfect spirits—mind and body."

Not that perfect.

"Okay. Okay. Perfect health and then a serious case of rigor mort. Look, I don't want to come across argumentative, but if I'm really going to get answers, I'll need more help from you. Why don't you start by telling me everything you remember, from the time your lifeless body was discovered."

"That's just it. I don't know. That part of my ephemeral experience has been wiped clean. Putting it mildly, I don't know who the hell found me or when. You'll need to do the digging on that, I'm afraid."

Fantastic. Now I get to play research assistant in addition to amateur sleuth.

"I suppose I can check with the town marshal's office as well as the local mortuaries for starters."

"Yes, yes. Do something! I can't hang around like this forever. I find it very grating on my nerves."

"You find it grating? I'm all but chewing my nails."

"Then stop dilly-dallying around. Launch that ship already, honey. And by the way, I'd stay away from those microwave dinners if I were you. Don't you have any idea what the sodium levels are like? Tsk-Tsk. And to think, you're in the culinary business."

"I'm not cooking charcuterie boards, I'm—"

And again, in that very annoying way of hers, Edith faded from view. All that was left was an ivory haze that lingered a few seconds more.

"You don't look as if everything is all right," Lilly-Ann said, startling me from my reverie.

"Huh? What? Sorry, my mind drifted off for a second. Nothing a second cup of coffee won't fix."

With that, I helped myself to a full cup and reviewed the prior day's business with Lilly-Ann and Matt. A half-hour later, Matt put the Open sign in the window, and I took on the dual role of proprietress and waitress.

"That woman who left the message isn't here, is she?" I asked Lilly-Ann.

"No, if she was, we'd point her out immediately. Don't let it get under your skin."

I moseyed about the place, introducing myself and chit-chatting with customers. I broached the subject of charcuterie plates, and it piqued their interest. Hallelujah. Then I remembered something - I never told Lilly-Ann or Matt that I adopted Speedbump.

"That's super," Matt said. "Beagles are the best."

Lilly-Ann had a similar reaction and went on and on about how satisfying it was to rescue homeless pets.

"If that woman comes in later, try to find out who she is and if she knew Edith," I announced as I headed out the door. "I'll be back tonight to check on things." Then I paused, "I hope you don't think I'm being too, well, you know. I just have a very strong closure element and want to make sure everything's okay."

Matt chucked. "You and my mother. I mean about the need to get things done. Not the age thing because you're not anywhere near middle-age."

"Watch it, Matt." Lilly-Ann gave him one of those teacher scowls and I laughed as I closed the sandwich shop door behind me.

On the drive to Chandler, I realized Edith was right. Even if she was a manifestation of my imagination brought on by a sudden change in careers and a relationship gone sour. Not to mention the stress. It's always about stress. Maybe the woman-who-died-peacefully-in-her-sleep didn't die that peacefully after all. And what harm could it do for me to look into the matter?

I had already taken the first step by convincing Maddie to have lunch with me at The Chanterelle on Sunday. That establishment got a scalding review from Edith, and it might have been a motive for murder. And Edith *did* mention poisoning. Easy enough to concoct a deadly delectable and somehow get it into Edith's hands, or in this case, her mouth.

Still, I didn't have a plan. Not like the zillion amateur sleuths in my carton of cozies. All of them had an inkling of where to begin. From murder maps, victim profiles, and timelines, they knew what they were doing. What am I saying? They were fictional characters. Fictional!

I really am losing it, aren't I?

I took a breath as I pulled into Chan-Tech's enormous parking lot in hopes of securing a space that wasn't in the "north forty." By the time I reached the elevator and pushed the button for my floor, I had come to a decision. I would devise a clear and succinct plan for finding out who put Edith to rest, beginning with the timeline. Or maybe the crime report like Mitchell McClure suggested. What was it? Oh yeah, AZ Spot Crime. At least I'd have a jumping-off point if nothing else.

I'd seen some of the crime reports in the local paper but never went to the state website to delve further. In those 55+ communities, a number of posts read "deceased body found in house" and I feared that would be the case with Edith. Then again, if the post contained even a minor detail, it might prove useful.

Engrossed with my so-called starting point, I jumped when the elevator door opened and two men in khakis and golf tees stepped out. "Hold the elevator," a woman shouted from the lobby, "I can't afford to be late again."

There was no time to start up a conversation, only a mumbled, "Good Morning." She got out two floors below mine and charged straight ahead as the elevator door closed. I had to admit, even with the caveat of having Edith Ellory enter my life, it was going to be far better than dealing with this corporate routine for the next decade or so.

When five o'clock rolled around, I couldn't wait to head back to Cave Creek and Speedbump. Only one more day of this rat race. As I turned off my computer and stood, my cell phone vibrated with a call from my mother.

"Are you absolutely, positively sure you want to do this, Katie?"

"And hello to you, too, Mom. Yes, I'm sure."

"You have no idea how much restraint it took me to not pester you this week. Of course, it didn't help that your father kept reminding me you need to live your own life."

"Give him an extra big hug from me. Seriously, I'm fine and really excited about my new venture. The house is just about unpacked and since it came furnished with some décor, I don't have to worry about wall hangings and that sort of thing for a while."

"You don't mind living with someone else's tastes?"

"The condo I rented in Chandler was so cookie-cutter and bland, that it's kind of refreshing in an odd sort of way."

"If you say so."

"I know I told you I wanted to have you and Dad over when I got settled, but that may take longer than I anticipated. I've got so much on my plate, no pun intended, with the charcuterie business and sandwich shop." *And a fussy, assertive ghost who simply won't take no for an answer.*

"Take all the time you need. We're not going anywhere. Call me this week. Love you."

"Me, too."

The second I tapped to end the call, I was positive I heard another voice. One that had become all too familiar as of late. It was only a few words but irritating as all get-up-and-go— *My murder should be number one on your list.*

Chapter Ten

Lilly-Ann and Matt's note was absolutely benign when I read it later that evening. Speedbump had gone along for the ride and seemed to enjoy poking around the sandwich shop sniffing every corner.

"No more counting the days, buddy. Now it's hours. After tomorrow," I told him, "this will be our full-time job. Well, this and the new catering service I'm launching. I'm meeting with someone from an advertising agency this week to get a promotion going. And the new sign for the shop is supposed to be installed later this week. The Char-Board. If I wasn't so mentally and physically exhausted, I'd be doing cartwheels."

Speedbump cocked his head and then resumed sniffing around. "This week will be what the industry calls 'a soft opening,' especially since the sandwich shop isn't about to undergo too many changes. Then, I'll host a special charcuterie day where I showcase some of my platters and promote the new sideline. Oh, and don't let me forget the social media ads and local newspaper ones. I've got to make sure they're ready to go."

The dog turned away from the baseboard of the counter and looked up.

"I'll take that as a sign you're ready to go."

Flicking the lights off, I ushered him out the door and locked up. My car was parked right out in front since most businesses at that end of town had been closed for hours and there was an abundance of parking spaces.

What appeared to be a flyer was stuck underneath the windshield wiper blade and I pulled it out. "I hate these darn ads. So annoying. I'll remember not to do anything like it with our promo."

I gave it a quick glance and realized it was an announcement from the

Town of Cave Creek that read, "Celebrate our hometown fire rescue and coroner office workers this coming Saturday at the town hall, beginning at 9:00 a.m. Free coffee and donuts." My immediate thought was that the sandwich shop wouldn't get as many customers as usual. Then I felt guilty for not appreciating the job they did. Below the headline was a photo of twenty or so men and women standing in two lines in front of the town hall. I shoved the paper in the console once I got in the car and motioned for the dog.

Speedbump jumped into the backseat like a pro, and I hightailed it home in record time. "You'll have to quit bugging me about the darn sodium, Edith," I announced when I set foot in the house for the second time that night. "If you want me to figure out who poisoned you, you'll need to cut me some slack."

With that, I put a chicken pot pie in the microwave and unscrewed the lid of my Pure Leaf unsweetened iced tea. Forty minutes later, I was on the Spot Crime website and from there to three other crime mapping sites. As I feared, they all had the same text—"Deceased body found in house." But they also had pertinent information I needed—the date of the incident.

Having a viable date allowed me to peruse newspaper archives regarding the unpleasant discovery. There were short clips about "Noted food critic Edith Ellory dying of natural causes in her home," but one that added a new and useful detail. It was her cleaning lady who alerted the local authorities. No name given, but I figured I could coax it out of Edith. It was the least she could do.

Two hours later I called her out. "I know that's you, Edith. There's a reddish glow in the room and it's not from the TV." I was seated at my desk and turned around to the couch where she had made herself comfortable, sprawled out with one leg crossed over the other. Tonight, she wore a red and fuchsia lounging suit. All that was missing was one of those long cigarette holders with the black pointed end.

"How do you do that?" I asked.

"Do what?"

"Arrive in different outfits each night."

"Darned if I know. Saves on the dry cleaning, though."

"I think you left an earring here," I said.

"Drat. Hang on to it. I don't know how to get it back. Anyway, I'm sporting a new pair. Art deco diamond gold drops. White gold. Do you like them?"

"Uh, not my style, but nice."

I cannot believe I'm discussing earrings with a ghost.

"Well? Do you have good news for me?"

I shrugged. "I have a starting point."

"A starting point? You need to get to the end zone. That's what they call it, isn't it? The end zone. I'm not much of a sports aficionado."

"Me either. Listen, I need to know who your cleaning lady is. *Was.* She was the person who found your body. It was in the local papers."

"Cora Milbrand found my body? I'm surprised the entire street still has its hearing. She must have shrieked like a banshee."

"I wouldn't know. The paper didn't say. Anyway, I thought I'd get in touch with her and see what she can tell me."

"Cora's one of those non-stop yackers. If she runs out of things to talk about, she'll tell you what's in her freezer. She's also as abrasive as a scouring sponge."

Wonderful. Another delightful personality to deal with.

"All I need is her recollection of that day. Does she live around here?"

"She lives in Carefree, off of the North Bloody Basin Road. Bring along an earplug if you know what's good for you."

"Listen, Edith, I've got a full schedule this weekend, but I'll see what I can do. Maybe we can—"

And like that, she was gone.

"That's not fair!" I shouted. "You can't keep popping in and out of here."

I couldn't see her form, but I heard her loud and clear. "I'm sticking to your inflexible time schedule, honey, and for your information, *I* may have things to do as well."

"What?" I asked Speedbump who was curled up on the rug. "What could she possibly be doing?" Then I took a breath and pulled up the White Pages on my phone. "Cora's here all right," I told him. "Edith didn't lie about that.

Maybe I can give the woman a call and ask if she'd be willing to meet with me Sunday morning before my lunch with Maddie."

I couldn't believe I was about to give up valuable time when I should have been getting my business underway, but I figured I'd have plenty of workable hours starting next week. And frankly, I wanted to get the whole Edith mess over with so that I could get my new life in order.

She told me to quit procrastinating. Or dilly-dallying around as she put it. "Well, Edith, for your information, I'm pursuing two leads. Two! How's that for getting a move on?"

Good grief. Now I'm yelling into the air.

It was too late to disturb someone at night with a phone call. Especially someone I didn't know. I jotted down her number and told the dog I'd be phoning Cora in the morning. Then, I did what I should have done when Edith first told me she was murdered. I dug up an old notebook that somehow made it to my book stash, discovered it had plenty of unused pages, and wrote three words in large print—Motive, Means, and Opportunity.

Next, I jotted the usual reasons under the word *motive:* anger, jealousy, revenge, money, love, vendetta, and hatred. Yep, I'd read enough mysteries to recite the list by heart. Given Edith's abrasive personality, I could understand why the woman might have been disliked, but I didn't think that was a strong enough reason for someone to do her in. Even if the neighbors agreed she was a royal pain in the butt.

Then there was the money angle. I'd have to agree with Edith that it was unlikely the cat-loving nuns did her in and I seriously doubted it was her nephew. However, if Edith was in possession of something extremely rare and valuable, it might have been a motive. I made a mental note to ask her.

As for the other motives, I simply didn't have enough information to pursue vendettas or revenge, but maybe Cora would be able to fill in the blanks.

As for means and opportunity, it was anyone's guess. I figured if Edith really was poisoned, it wouldn't be too awfully hard to pull off. People can get their hands on all sorts of toxic concoctions without having to look any further than their own kitchens or gardens.

Recently, I read a novel where dried dieffenbachia leaves were mixed into someone's chewing tobacco. Then again, Edith wasn't the chewing tobacco type. Of course, that left scads of other choices—antifreeze, which is very sweet and can be put in tea, coffee, pudding, and sauce, as well as arsenic, an Agatha Christie favorite, not to mention the chemical in Visine that some woman in South Carolina used to kill her husband. And what about cardiac arrest from potassium chloride? That was recently in the news.

The possibilities were staggering. Anyone could have slipped something into Edith's food or beverage. That left opportunity, and in order to flush out that part of the murder equation, I'd have to start with what Cora saw when she came to work that day.

"I'll fill in the rest of this stuff when I have a better idea of what I'm doing," I said to Speedbump. "At least if Edith shows her ghastly face around here tomorrow, I can wave the notebook in the air and tell her to quit nagging me."

Just then, I heard a whooshing sound, and Speedbump's ears perked up. It came from the flap in his doggie dog and I realized it was the wind.

Yikes. Don't tell me monsoon season is here already.

I walked to the doggie door with the intent of pulling the plastic covering over it when I noticed a crumpled piece of paper that had blown in.

"Darn advertising flyers," I muttered as I snatched it and headed to the kitchen trash container. As I lifted the container's lid and stood poised to throw in the wadded-up paper, I glanced at the ad. It was for Lo-Salt, a combination of sodium and potassium chloride.

"Funny coincidence, huh?" I said to Speedbump. "Either that or maybe that was the pressing business Edith had to take care of. Then again, she could have simply mentioned it."

I threw the paper in the trash and called it a night.

Chapter Eleven

My last day at Chan-Tech was more of a send-off than an actual workday. I kept getting interrupted all day by co-workers who wished me well and promised to visit The Char-Board sometime soon. In addition, they had put together a surprise luncheon in the conference room complete with balloons and quirky gifts.

"If you ever get tired of the food industry," someone said, "Hurry back. The tech and business world needs you." I smiled and told them I'd keep it in mind, but I was anxious for a new venue.

At a little past three, I took a pause from finalizing some accounts and called Cora Milbrand.

"I'm not taking on any new clients," she said before I could even choke out a greeting.

"Um, that's not why I'm calling. This is Katie Aubrey and I'm the new tenant in Edith Ellory's house. I know you worked for her and in fact, had the unfortunate experience of finding her after she passed."

"Are you with the police? I told them everything I knew. I got to the house. She didn't answer the door. I walked around to look in the windows and that's when I saw her in bed. Dead as a doorknob."

"You didn't go inside?"

"The woman was dead. Hanging over the side of the bed as lifeless as they get. How could I have gone inside? And, no, I didn't have a key. Edith didn't trust many people even though I'd been cleaning that house for close to a decade. What is it you want?"

"Actually, some closure about her death. To be honest, it *is* a bit creepy sleeping in a place where the former resident died."

"Then why did you rent it in the first place?"

"Because I — Look, is there any chance we can meet? It's kind of complicated. Maybe Sunday morning for coffee somewhere?"

"I'm busy Sunday. What about this evening? I've got to clean a house not far from Edith's place this afternoon. I'll be working from four to seven. I suppose I could spare a few minutes before I drive home. Coffee Shop on Cave Creek Highway is open until nine but you're buying. Look for The Roastery."

"No problem. Seven-thirty, then?"

"How will I know it's you?"

Because I'll be so exhausted by then, I'll look like something the cat would drag in.

"I'm in my thirties with short wavy hair."

"Forget it. Look for me. I'm in my sixties, I've got salt and pepper hair and I'll be wearing a plaid button-down top."

"Thanks, I appreciate it."

Cora was off the line without saying another word. *Chatty, my foot!*

I hustled out of Chan-Tech by five and got home with enough time to make a ham and cheese sandwich and feed Speedbump before taking off for The Roastery. True, I could have ordered food there, but I didn't want to turn my conversation with Cora into a production. Especially if she decided to order a big meal. I figured coffee and a snack would suffice.

"I'll have to stop in the sandwich shop without you, tonight," I told the dog, "But I shouldn't be too long."

The Roastery, a Santa Fe-style structure with a wrap-around deck and patio, sat on a knoll surrounded by huge boulders and a plethora of desert landscape. A picture-perfect example of the southwest, complete with metal art on the sides of the beige and brown building.

It was easy to spot Cora. She was seated at a table on the front patio and motioned me over as soon as I got out of the car. She was right about the plaid top. I hadn't seen one of those since we visited my mother's aunts when I was little.

"Thought it would be better if we chatted outside," Cora said. "The sun's starting to go down, so we won't sweat to death. Besides, I don't like people overhearing my conversations and we have more privacy here."

"Um, good idea. I'll go inside and place our order. Do you know what you want?"

"Medium coffee, cream, and three sugars, bacon, cheese, and tomato panini. Oh, and one of their chocolate brownies."

I nodded and went inside. *Great. A brownie, too.*

"I may wind up keeping a tab for you, Edith," I mumbled under my breath as I opened the door.

"So, what is it you want to know?" Cora asked when I got back to our table. She had selected a two-person table on the end of the patio facing the mountains.

I took a breath and looked directly at her. "I purchased the former Cave Creek Sandwich Shop in town and plan to expand it to include a charcuterie catering service and charcuterie boards in the restaurant."

"What does that have to do with Edith? And what the heck is a charcuterie?"

It took me a few minutes to explain about cheese platters and by the time I finished, our coffees and Cora's food had arrived.

"Edith's house came on the market as a rental, and it was near the shop and affordable. That's why I signed a lease."

Cora took a sip of her coffee and then cut into her panini. "Listen, people die in their houses all the time. No big deal. It wasn't as if she was stabbed to death, or worse yet, hit over the head with a hammer. No bloody mess that I could see from the window."

"I take it you didn't go inside once the police arrived?"

"They wouldn't let me."

"If no one had a key, how did they get in?"

"One of those lock-picking things. Took them all of five seconds."

"Then what?"

"They sent some wet-behind-the-ears policewoman over to me to ask questions. I told her I was the cleaning lady and when Edith didn't answer the door, I looked inside. End of story. Next thing I knew, a coroner's van pulled up. I didn't stick around to watch the show. I know what gurneys look like. And I didn't need to see a black tarp draped over Edith's body."

"Do you know if she had been ill? Any medical issues?"

"I thought that woman would live to be a hundred and ten. She had the moxie for it. The only issue she had was that bum knee of hers. It would act up once in a while, but she didn't want to go in for surgery and get a replacement. She had those cortisone shots a few times a year. That's why I was surprised she slept in her bed."

"What do you mean?"

"Edith's knee was bothering her, and she told me she had an appointment later that week for another shot. Meantime, she slept in that Lift chair of hers in the living room. It was too hard for her to bend the knee to get into bed and she couldn't use the other knee because the rotten knee would have to support the good one, which would defeat the purpose."

"Apparently it didn't hurt her that much and she was able to get into bed."

"Unless someone put her there. I told you I didn't see anything violent but that doesn't mean she wasn't murdered."

"Did you tell that to the police?"

"They didn't ask. Frankly, I've learned it's best to keep my mouth shut. I figured they'd run a toxicology report to see if she had been poisoned but nope. Shipped to the mortuary from what I know and then cremated before you could say 'Mickey Mouse.'"

"Cora, do you think anyone had a motive to kill her?"

Cora cut off another piece of her panini and put it in her mouth. I waited a few seconds while she finished eating it. "Edith ticked off lots of people. Mainly with those food reviews of hers. Bad reviews mean bad business so yeah, I suppose lots of people had motives."

"What about her neighbors?"

"She probably riled them, too. Why is this such a concern for you? It's not as if her unholy spirit came back to haunt the place."

The minute she said that my hand shook and the coffee cup I held teetered as I put it down. Fortunately, Cora was too engrossed chomping into the brownie.

"It's just a feeling I have. I can't explain it but something's not kosher. Granted, seventy-seven isn't exactly middle age, but still, the woman was in perfectly good health."

"How did you know she was seventy-seven?"

"It was in the papers."

Cora nodded. "Right. Nothing's private anymore." She took a napkin and wiped the sides of her mouth. "If you think foul play was involved, I suggest you drop it. Nothing you can do about it now. I don't know where her ashes wound up, but even if the mortuary sent them to you wrapped up with a pretty pink bow, they'd be as useful as the dirt in a vacuum cleaner."

"Most likely her nephew in Tacoma took care of it. He's the one who rented me the house. She left it to him in her will."

"Danny something, right? Edith mentioned him once in a while. Fondly, I might add, which was unusual for her. Listen, much as I enjoyed the panini and brownie, it's getting late, and I need to get home."

"I won't keep you, but I've got one more question. Were you aware of Edith's schedule before showing up to clean her house that morning? Like maybe where she was the night or day before?"

"That's two questions, and the answer is no. But I will tell you this much - Edith was practically joined at the hip with that computer of hers. No doubt any schedule she kept was somewhere on that thing, along with those restaurant reviews she wrote. I once asked her why she didn't use a laptop or an iPad and she practically jumped down my throat. Something about not wasting her time learning how to use new gadgets when her desktop computer was all she needed."

"At least she didn't go all old school with paper, pencil, and a notebook."

"She was old school enough. When you get to be her age, it's impossible to read your own handwriting. I don't suppose the computer is still on her desk. Those are the first things family members claim when they show up like buzzards to clean out the place. They're afraid their dearly departed might have something on them."

"I, um, er..."

"I know I said I'm not taking on any new clients, but I know Edith's house like the back of my hand, so if you do want any cleaning done, call me. I charge thirty dollars an hour and I bring my own supplies. Commercial stuff, not that organic nonsense they charge an arm and a leg for. If you want that, you have to supply your own."

I was about to thank her and decline the offer when I thought better of it. Cora had been working for Edith for over a decade and people with that kind of knowledge often have a wealth of information they don't realize they've got.

"Actually, I may take you up on your offer. I've got your number and I'll be in touch. Thanks, by the way, for joining me tonight."

"It saved me from making dinner."

Cora stood and pushed her chair into the table. I said thanks again and watched as she stepped down from the patio and walked to her car. Then I muttered under my breath, "You were right, Edith. Abrasive as a Brillo pad. But she may know something. I just need to find out what."

Chapter Twelve

By the time I pulled the covers down and crept into bed, I was mentally and physically drained. Speedbump must have sensed it, too, because he snuggled against my leg and didn't make a move until morning.

"That's odd," I said when I changed his water and poured his food the next morning. "I fully expected Edith to make an appearance and badger me about Cora. Hmm, maybe there's a Mahjong game or something going on in the netherworld. Or maybe this whole craziness is gone."

Fat chance.

At that instant, the ice cube maker in the fridge went berserk and shot out at least two dozen cubes. Speedbump raced over to see what the ruckus was about but when he realized it was only ice, he retreated to his usual spot on the rug while I gathered up the cubes and tossed them in the sink.

"Ugh, technology. It's only good when it works." A few of the ice cubes slid under the fridge and I reached underneath to retrieve them. That's when I found a small ACE Hardware key.

"Don't say I don't do anything for you." Edith's voice was unusually chipper, but it was the faint aroma of honeysuckle that caught my attention. I hadn't noticed it before. Maybe a new embellishment from the ghostly world.

Wonderful. She's back.

"Were you eavesdropping on my conversation with Cora yesterday?" I asked as I looked around the room. "Where are you? Did your wardrobe mistress go on strike?"

"Watch the sassiness, honey." With that, the ice cube maker spat out a dozen or so more cubes and the fragrance of the honeysuckle disappeared.

I called out her name a few more times but she had retreated back to the great beyond. I stared at the small key, now in the palm of my hand, and chucked. "If I'm not mistaken, Speedbump, there's only one lock that this baby was meant for—the shed out back. Using it wasn't included in my rental agreement, but it doesn't matter. I don't have that much stuff. Besides, I don't want to put stuff in, I need to get Edith's computer out."

The time on the oven clock read 5:01 a.m. and I didn't have a second to spare if I was going to wash up and get to the sandwich shop for my first full day. A Saturday no less. "We're going to get that dinosaur out of there tonight," I went on. "That is, if I still have any energy left after today."

The good thing about living near one's place of work is that it saves on commuting time. I was washed, dressed, and had my first cup of coffee by 5:35 before I jumped in the car to get to work. Fifteen minutes later, I was inside the sandwich shop greeting Lilly-Ann and Matt.

After the first hour, one thing became clear. The prior owner, Merton Kuss, did a good job of hiring. Lilly-Ann and Matt made a solid team, each one working efficiently on their own, and in synch with the other one when it came to the distribution of duties.

I ambled along, taking breakfast orders, chatting with customers, and pitching in with food prep as needed. Which wasn't all that much. The breakfast hours were the busiest, but we were able to catch a breath before eleven when the lunchtime regulars arrived. Eat-in and take-out.

"I want to start introducing little charcuterie platters by the end of next week," I told them. "And our new sign should be installed by Thursday. The new menus will also be here by Wednesday, the latest, according to the printer."

"Sounds good," Lilly-Ann said.

I rested my arm on the counter and looked around. Only two customers remained, and they were finishing up. "There's so much I want to do, but I've got to take it one step at a time. We've got outdoor seating, but we can maximize it with smaller four-person tables and maybe even add a canopy to give the place a European look. Of course, I'll need to check with the town's zoning. Like I said, one step at a time. My first priority is to get the charcuterie catering part of the business up and running."

"What exactly does that entail?" Matt asked as he wiped down the counter. "Catering businesses are, well…huge."

I nodded. "Yeah, if you're thinking weddings, graduations, and Bar or Bat-Mitzvahs. Not to say, I wouldn't be thrilled to take on something like that, but what I have in mind is smaller. Much, much smaller. Like I explained when we first met, I would be creating specialized platters of cured meats, cheeses, fruits, nuts, and various sweets for parties and small gatherings."

Matt crinkled his nose. "But wouldn't you need a van or something for deliveries?"

"Hopefully, some of our orders will be local and people can pick them up or I can use my car. For orders in the adjacent towns, I'll use a delivery service. I already made arrangements with two different companies so I wouldn't be caught out in the cold, so to speak. Customers would need to pay the delivery charge and I'll try to keep it low. Right now, it's a matter of advertising and getting the word out. That's why I want to introduce the mini-boards."

Lilly-Ann smiled. "I can't wait to learn."

"Think of it like a mosaic. Individual pieces that combine to create an eye-catching and delectable image. Plus, it's all finger food. Well, hopefully, people will use tongs and utensils."

Matt rolled his eyes. "Unless you're catering for a football game. Then it'll be all bets off. And FYI, some of those guys lick their fingers."

"Ew."

"If I understand correctly," Lilly-Ann said, "The platters are all pre-made."

"Um, not exactly. I mean, they can be, and it certainly saves time, but for a quality experience, it's best if the charcuterie boards are prepared on-site. In that case, I can transport the ingredients in my own car, in coolers. Then, when I get to the venue, I simply arrange the items on the boards so that they're fresh and pleasing."

"I'll let some of my friends at the school know," she said. "They're always looking for refreshments at faculty meetings. Not to mention those mind-numbing parent meetings at night. A charcuterie board might liven things up."

"Better than potluck," Matt added. "At least that's what my mother always says. She refuses to eat anything that was prepared in someone's kitchen other than hers. If you must know, her favorite quote is, 'I always wash my hands, but I have no idea what other people do in their kitchens.'"

I all but flinched. "I hate to say it, but your mother makes a good point. By the way, you and Lilly-Ann should grab some of the business cards I set out on the counter and feel free to pass them around. I ordered tons of them."

Lilly-Ann picked up one of the cards. "Cute logo with the nuts and leaves on the round charcuterie board. Very eye-catching."

I smiled. "I wish I could take the credit for it, but it was the graphic designer. I'm lucky if I can draw a stick figure."

Just then, four people walked in, followed by three more.

"Looks like our unofficial break time is over," Lilly-Ann laughed. And while the lunch business wasn't as demanding as breakfast, it was still non-stop until two. I made a mental note to spring for some decent arch support sandals in lieu of my cutesy wedges.

At a few minutes past three, when everything was washed, wiped down, and ready for Monday, we headed out the door. I was anxious to get home and give my feet a break but not as anxious as I was to retrieve Edith's computer from the shed and get a good look at her files. Aargh! Too bad Edith had something to say about everything with the exception of the timeline leading up to her death. I suppose I should have been grateful about the key under the fridge, but in all fairness, it would have been a whole lot easier if Edith simply told me what she'd been up to.

"I'm home!" I shouted to Speedbump when I opened the door. He got up from the rug, wiggling his way to the door, tail wagging non-stop. I had to admit, he was a handsome fellow with tan and black splotches that ran from his neck down his back and an all-brown face with the exception of a thin white line that separated his brow. "Did you miss me? You don't look any worse for wear. Unlike me. I reek of cold cuts and cold sweat, but at least I ate at the sandwich shop so you and I can have plenty of time to play

Sherlock Holmes on Edith's computer."

Speedbump followed me to the bedroom where I slipped out of my sandwich shop attire and into a loose ratty t-shirt and shorts. "Come on, boy, we're off to the shed. This shouldn't take us more than a few minutes to grab that computer and plunk it on the table."

Ha! What world was I in? The second I removed the lock from the shed door and pulled it open, I knew I was in trouble. "I've seen episodes of *Hoarders* where they had less stuff," I grumbled. The dog took one look at the place before trotting off to roll on the ground. True, Daniel mentioned the shed being crammed but crammed didn't come close. It was mind-boggling.

The gargoyles were everywhere. On the ground, peeking out between old cartons, and in one instance, hanging from large nails on the side of the shed. That was the least of my worries. There were dead bugs everywhere and more cobwebs than in Mrs. Havisham's drawing room.

Okay, so maybe this is going to take a bit longer...

My first fear was scorpions. Cockroaches were bad enough and they thrive on old cardboard, but at least they weren't poisonous, just yucky. I couldn't very well stick my hand in there, rooting around for a computer. I had to move gingerly. Something that simply wasn't in my nature.

When Daniel mentioned putting the computer into the shed, I thought he just opened the door and stuffed it inside, but I was wrong. Space was at a premium, so he had to move things around in order to find a good resting place for it. Then I had another thought. A worse one. The computer might be in one spot, but the keyboard and screen may have been stashed in other crevices or corners. And forget the mouse. I would be more likely to find a flesh-and-blood one in the shed than hers. No matter. I could always unplug my computer mouse and use it.

In order to sift through the contents, I had to first remove a few old standing lamps and a boxy fan that probably hadn't been used since Eisenhower was in office. I got the fan out without any trouble but when I grasped the pole to one of the lamps, a yellow, red, and black snake slithered over one of my feet and I let out a primordial scream. Then, I screamed again. Maybe it was a reflex.

Speedbump ran to where I stood and remained motionless. He wasn't the only one. I held my breath and glanced at the ground. No sign of the thing.

"Did you find a body in there?" It was the "curmudgeon from next door," and he didn't waste a second peering over into my yard. "Wouldn't surprise me if that's what Edith did in her spare time when she wasn't poisoning cats or something of the sort."

"No!" I shouted back. "Only a snake."

"I saw you were still standing so I didn't think it was a medical emergency."

"Thanks. I'm fine. Sorry to disappoint you but no dead bodies here. Only junk and lots of it."

"Well, if you do find a body, try not to scream. I want to read my book in peace."

What did they do? Gather up all the obnoxious people and stick them on this block? Then again, Cora lives in Carefree.

"No problem." *And I want to get rid of Edith so I can have some peace.*

70

Chapter Thirteen

Broken lampshades, garden tools, cracked ceramic gnomes, broomsticks without the brushes, weathered spindly chairs, and enough cartons to make a moving company jealous, Edith's shed had it all. All, except the computer I was desperate to find. I began to think Daniel didn't just "shove it in there" as he indicated but took the time to put it in a carton.

Wonderful. Another carton.

"I can't do this without a break," I said to the dog. Only Speedbump wasn't anywhere near the shed. He was smarter than that. He moved to a spot on the back patio where some overhanging mesquite trees offered a bit of shade.

I made a quick jaunt into the house and grabbed an iced tea before returning to my special little spot in hell to continue the search for Edith's computer. This time the dog didn't bother to join me. He curled up on the rug and closed his eyes, oblivious to the agony I faced.

It was the giant wall lamp or the old trellis. Moving either of those would free up enough space for me to remove some smaller items and peer into the nearest carton. I tried to turn the process into a game, like Tetris, but it didn't fly. Work was work, and in the heat of the afternoon, it was even more unpleasant.

"You owe me, Edith," I mumbled at least half a dozen times. "And so help me, if another snake slithers its slimy self out of there, all bets are off."

A warm gust of wind took me by surprise, and I was positive Edith heard my every word. Four gnomes and three cartons later, I found her white

Dell computer, more yellowish than white, in a carton along with a small monitor and some cables. I also found a wobbly wheelbarrow that saved me the trouble of lugging the computer into the house.

As tempted as I was to find the nearest plug and delve into Edith's past, I couldn't very well ignore the trash and treasures that I took from the shed. They were scattered around in the yard as if a mini-burst put them there instead of me.

Ugh. I leaned the computer against one of the kitchen walls and returned to the great outdoors where I tortured myself in an attempt to fit everything back in the shed. This was worse than the BELIEVE blocks.

The BELIEVE blocks were seven hand-decorated holiday blocks, each with a separate letter, that I purchased a few years back for my windowsill in Chandler. They were wooden and came in different sizes in a reusable box for storage. The only problem was that the manufacturer didn't provide a key as to how to get them all back in the box so that they'd fit.

I spent more time arranging and rearranging those darn blocks than decorating my condo for the holidays. Finally, I gave up and stuck them in the box any old way. So what if the box didn't close? I guess Edith must have felt the same way about the precious items in her shed.

By the time I wiped the sweaty dirt from my hands onto my shorts and relocked the shed, I was really for a shower and not a computer search. At least I had gotten that far. I had a life, too, and I wasn't about to live it with perspiration droplets in my eyes and a musty scent that seemed to have attached itself to my clothes.

No wonder it was a little past nine when I finally lifted the old Dell onto the kitchen table and plugged everything in. With no need for the internet, since the program was already installed, I was in business. WORD 97 came up with no problem and I paused for a minute to thank the gods.

I opened the files under "My documents" and sure enough, Edith had a plethora of them dating back to 1998. With few exceptions, like files labeled "to do list," and "tax information," most began with the prefix RV, a date, and two or three capital letters.

"It's a random crapshoot," I announced, even though the dog was snoring

72

a few feet away from me. "I'm not touching anything that's two decades old, or longer." *At least not right away, and that's only if nothing else pans out.*

Taking a breath, I clicked on a file labeled RV March 3, 2021, TC. One mystery solved—RV stood for review and the last two letters were Edith's abbreviation for the name of the restaurant. Judging from the length of the review, I figured it was going to be a long night. What I didn't figure was that the review for The Chanterelle in Fountain Hills read more like a diatribe than a reflection of one's dining experience.

It began with, "The meal should have been given a merciful death and washed down the drain." Then, if that wasn't enough to deter customers, Edith provided an abundance of particulars including, "I wasn't sure if I had tasted a quail egg or a lump of week-old cheese," and "Totally devoid of flavor. Not sure if it was prime rib or the arm off of someone's leather couch."

I shuddered and selected another review to peruse. It was worse. Much worse. Had I been the chef, I would've begged the government to put me in the witness protection program somewhere in South Dakota.

By ten-fifteen, I had read twelve reviews and only one of them was positive. *If* a lukewarm review could have been considered positive. No wonder Edith was convinced she had been murdered. True, there were some redeeming comments, but they were few and far between. With the swipe of a pen, or in this case, the click of a computer keyboard, Edith Ellory most likely destroyed the livelihood of many an establishment. Talk about a motive for murder. Yeesh!

At least I had a viable plan, beginning with The Chanterelle, whose review was enough to get anyone's blood boiling. From there, I would isolate the other recent reviews and pay those restaurants a visit, even if the price tag might set me back. Then I realized something—*Of course, the price tag would set me back.* All of the restaurants that food critics write up are expensive. It's not as if they review fast food places like Taco Bell or Burger King. And I doubt they review chain restaurants. Aargh. Unless I was willing to shell out big bucks, there was no way I could dine in them and still pay rent for Edith's house and a mortgage for the sandwich shop. I was stuck.

"I can't afford to track down leads at all of these fancy places Edith wrote up. I can't—"

A sudden clack and Speedbump raced for the fridge. It was another ice cube that landed on the floor, and I rolled my eyes. "Don't tell me. You're back."

Edith's voice was unmistakable. "I'm getting pretty good at this. I wonder what I'll try next."

"Don't!"

"Use that noggin of yours, honey. You don't have to patronize those places. Figure out another way to get them to talk."

"I, um, er..." And like that, Edith had perfected her vanishing act.

Speedbump gnawed at the ice cube while I stood and stretched. "It's getting late and I'm exhausted. I'll boot this up tomorrow and write down the names of the recent reviews. *"Figure out another way to get them to talk." Easy for you to say, Edith.*

My late dinner consisted of a bag of tortilla chips and a bowl of chocolate ice cream. I gave it a gold star for its unique combination of salty and sweet before heading off to bed.

"Don't bother me, tonight," I announced. "I got your message."

As I drifted off to sleep, I thought about the sandwich shop, now The Char-Board, and how I couldn't wait to start creating delectable platters for parties, proms, and anything in-between. *Once I got it off the ground.* Establishing a new business was one thing, promoting it was the other.

Speedbump nuzzled next to me and I petted his head. "All I need is that first connection," I mumbled, "that first—" And then I sat straight up, forcing the dog to readjust his position. "Oh my gosh! I think I've got it. Not only that, but I can kill two birds with one stone. Well, not *kill*, but...oh my gosh, I should have thought of this sooner. Duh!"

I was surprised it took me so long to see something that was staring me in the face. I didn't need to make a reservation and dine at those restaurants Edith trashed, all I needed to do was to convince them I could create charcuterie boards for stunning appetizers at the bar or for catering parties.

So what if they said no? I could use the opportunity to eke out information about Edith's blasted review and gauge whether or not the owner was so incensed that he or she murdered her. And if the other half of the equation came to fruition, then I'd be all the better off for it. It was ingenious. Absolutely ingenious.

"I figured it out, Speedbump. I'm going to use my charcuterie catering business as my ticket to uncover a murderer."

Another loud clank on the floor, only this time it wasn't the ice cube maker. It was the upright paper towel holder that fell from the kitchen counter to the floor.

"Sorry about that." Edith sounded more annoyed than remorseful. "I'm still honing in on my newfound skills."

"Hone them in elsewhere," I called out. "I'm going to sleep."

Chapter Fourteen

I forced myself to get up early the next day so that I'd have time to read the recent reviews Edith had written and make a note of them before Maddie got here. It was strange, but with each passing day, Edith's spirit became more and more convincing. Maybe there was such a thing as the afterlife, and I unwittingly tapped into it. *In for a penny, in for a pound.* I told Maddie to come by at eleven so we'd have time to visit, and she could see what the place looked like without all my cartons strewn about. That was before I had a giant Dell computer sitting on my kitchen table.

Last thing I needed was to fabricate a reason for its presence, so I had to hustle and make sure I left ample time to stash it in a closet before her arrival. With a cup of coffee in one hand and the mouse in the other, I systematically extracted Edith's recent reviews and read them.

Each one was more toxic than the one before. "Remind me never to open a high-end restaurant," I said to Speedbump. "I'd have hives if it ever got a review like these."

Thankfully, Edith had only pummeled three establishments to the ground, not counting The Chanterelle, before she vacated her earthly abode and her Windows 98, Word 97 program. In order to make things easier for me when I paid those places a visit, I decided to jot down their names and a one or two-sentence description of hers in order to know who I was dealing with. After all, if Edith went to all that trouble, a mere "lousy meal" wouldn't suffice.

The first restaurant was The Flaming Pit in Scottsdale. It was a noted steakhouse that featured everything from the usual filet mignons and porterhouse steaks to carpaccio of roast beef and center-cut prime ribeye. I wrote down the following: "Did the chef not understand the dining experience was for people, not cows? The thinly sliced roast beef on the carpaccio could not be found, let alone tasted, under the weight of the basil and greenery."

Next was Savor in the Heights, located in Fountain Hills. Although meat dishes were on the menu, it featured a variety of seafood including Oregon trout, Pacific salmon, and a Louisiana bouillabaisse. Edith's comment stung like a lamprey. "If I wanted dishwater, I could have helped myself without leaving home to taste the bouillabaisse."

Finally, there was Randolph's Escapade in Paradise Valley. It touted international cuisine with world-renowned chefs who probably bought the first tickets home once they read Edith's review. In brief, "Chicken Romana should be seasoned with chunky tomatoes, not left drowning in it. It's called lobster soong, not ginger soong. Look up the word *moderation* in the dictionary." If that wasn't enough, she added, "Escargots Bourguignon should be delicately seasoned in garlic parsley butter, not overcooked with the texture of an eraser on a number two pencil."

Had Edith chosen a career in education, it would have caused the dropout rates to soar. On behalf of students everywhere, I was thankful she was a food critic, not an educator. By the time I finished scouring her reviews, it was five minutes to ten. I shut down the computer and found a spot for it in the spare bedroom closet next to a pile of shoes and my tennis racket.

Then, I raced to the shower and was dressed and ready to welcome Maddie with ten minutes to spare. I'd chosen a summery floral dress with a matching shrug and wedges. The thought of putting on another business suit was about as appealing as returning to Chan-Tech.

I heard Maddie's car in the driveway before she even knocked on the door. "Welcome to my humble abode," I called out as Speedbump trotted over there. His tail wagged like a fan. "Come on in before you melt in the heat."

From May to October, the heat in the valley can oscillate between the nineties and the triple digits, but heat is heat, no matter what, and the oven starts revving up shortly after nine.

"I can't believe you talked me into eating at The Chanterelle," Maddie said as she scratched the dog's head. "When I told some of the agents in my office, they said they were still waiting to make a million-dollar sale before going there."

I laughed. "Grab a seat at the table. I'll get us some iced teas. Unless you want coffee. I can make iced coffee, too."

"Tea's fine. Tell me, how do you like the place? More importantly, how do you like being your own boss? Are your employees okay? What am I saying? You haven't even put in a full week as the new proprietress of The Char-Board."

"It's a whirlwind but I think everything will fall into place. You were right about one thing, though."

"Only one?"

"Yeah, the dog. I talk to him all the time. If he wasn't here, I'd be the looney broad who talked to herself."

"Talking to oneself is normal. It's only when you answer yourself that you need to be concerned."

I handed Maddie a glass of iced Constant Comment tea and took a sip from my own. "Thanks for doing this. I know it sounds strange, but I wanted to see for myself how a place like that could get such a bad review from Edith Ellory."

"Are you sure that's all there is? Curiosity and nothing else?"

"What else would there be? Face it, we're in the infancy of our thirties and we're already in a rut. I mean, in terms of our social ventures."

"'Infancy of our thirties,' huh? I never heard it quite put that way. Fine, off to The Chanterelle we go. But first, give me the grand tour of your place, now that I can actually see it."

I walked Maddie through the rooms with Speedbump on our heels.

"Someday I'll figure out a style of my own," I said. "Meanwhile, vintage Edith will have to suffice."

"Vintage Edith works for me. Hey, we'd better get a move on if we want to have lunch. I'm not about to take out a payday loan for dinner."

I'd only seen photos of The Chanterelle and none of them did justice to the magnificent French Chateau that appeared on Parkview Avenue. It was a standalone structure that took my breath the minute we pulled up to its drive.

"It's valet parking," I said to Maddie.

She shrugged. "What else is new. Hand the man your key and start coughing up those bucks."

Minutes later, we were escorted past the opulent courtyard by a gentleman in a tux. He motioned us to a large enclave, complete with fountains and greenery, where a hostess welcomed us and asked for our reservation. Thankfully, I thought ahead and made one.

The courtyards opened up to a large dining area with decorative chandeliers and lovely sago palms softening the corners of the room. White tablecloths with silver plates and fluted glasses caught my eye as the hostess asked if our corner table would suit us. I nodded and Maddie did the same. The hostess held out the chairs for us and handed us the menus before letting us know our server would be right over. The weight of the menu took me by surprise. It was more of a vintage tome than a listing of the fare. Maybe the gold tassel that hung gracefully from the binding had something to do with my impression.

"I hate to remove the linen napkin from the stemware," I said. "Someone folded it to resemble a rose."

Seconds later, a gentleman in his late twenties or early thirties introduced himself and told us he would be taking our orders. Tall, average build, short dark hair, small diamond earring, and no visible tattoos. Next thing I knew, a petite young woman with short blond hair filled our water glasses before slipping away.

"I'll give you some time to peruse the menu," our waiter said. "In the meantime, can I get you anything to drink?"

I took a breath. "That will depend on my food selection. The water's fine for now."

Maddie immediately chimed in. "Same here."

The man nodded and started to turn. That's when I remembered why we were here in the first place. "So many patrons for a Sunday," I began. "Is that usual?"

The waiter glanced around the room as if it was the first time he noticed the diners. "It's usually busier at the dinner hour on Sundays but we command a healthy lunch crowd all week long."

"I'm glad to hear that. I read Edith Ellory's review of your restaurant a while back and wondered if it had any influence."

The man bristled. "Oh, it had influence, all right. It took Imogen months to reestablish our stellar reputation."

"Imogen?" I played dumb.

"Yes, the owner. Imogen Brodeur."

No mirrors on every wall but certainly enough of them in here.

"Self-aggrandizing twit." The words were loud and oh, so very clear. I looked to my left and tried not to gasp. Edith had seated herself across from Maddie and adjacent to me. This time in a shimmery pearl dress with princess sleeves. Not the balloon kind Cinderella or Snow White would have worn, but thinner and quite tasteful. I wanted to spit.

"Go away," I hissed.

"Pardon?" the waiter said.

"Sorry, just clearing my throat. Awful sound. My apologies."

Maddie looked at me, wide-eyed, and didn't say a word. I continued to look directly at the waiter. "I imagine Ms. Brodeur took it personally. I know I would have."

The man leaned toward me and spoke in hushed tones. "The Chanterelle is Imogen's child, so to speak. It's her passion, her raison d'être, if you will. That review was an outrage. No wonder the woman locked herself in her study and sobbed for days."

"Outrage my patootie. She was too embarrassed to show her sorry little buns."

I jerked my head to the left and glared at Edith. "Quit it."

"Quit her business?" The waiter's face flushed red. "Imogen would never have considered it."

I gulped. "Would she have considered revenge?"

"That's my girl. Go right for the jugular."

Again, I flashed a look to my left and shook my head.

"Are you alright?" Maddie asked.

"I, um, wondered how anyone could withstand such a blow to their reputation without, well, taking further action."

"I'm afraid," the waiter said, "there was no legal action to be taken. Restaurant reviews, no matter how deadly, are not considered libelous. It is an opinion and therefore, not considered defamatory. Now if you'll excuse me, I'll give you time to look over your menus before I return to take your orders."

"What the heck was that all about?" Maddie asked the moment the waiter disappeared from sight.

"Curiosity, that's all. I'm not sure what I'd do in a similar position."

"I seriously doubt you'd lock yourself in a room and cry."

Then Edith just *had* to make herself heard. "I seriously doubt that's what Imogen did. If she was locked in her study, it was probably to look up poisons on the internet. I'd ask for a tour of the kitchen if I were you."

"I'm not about to ask for a tour of the kitchen," I blurted out.

Maddie jumped back in her seat. "Who said anything about requesting a tour of the kitchen? Are you sure you're okay?"

"I'm fine. Perfectly fine. Thinking out loud, that's all."

Convinced my verbal admonishments directed toward Edith weren't working, I tried a new tactic. I tried to dismiss her with the wave of my hand. Unfortunately, I knocked over the water glass and it crashed to the ground.

I fumed. "Now see what you've done."

"Me?" Maddie asked.

"No, not you. I meant me. See what *I've* done. I went to brush off some lint from my shrug. Guess I was overly zealous."

"Boy are you a good liar," Edith remarked. "And ask for that kitchen tour. I mean it, honey. See what's under the counters."

"I'm not about to—"

At that moment, the little blonde who poured the water raced over and with a heavy towel, proceeded to clean up the shards of glass and sop up the

LAID OUT TO REST

water.

I leaned over. "I'm terribly sorry."

"This is nothing. You should have seen the glasses Madam Brodeur threw when she read that review from Edith Ellory."

Then she cupped her mouth and froze.

"Shh," I whispered. "Your secret is safe with me. But maybe I can ask you a favor."

Chapter Fifteen

Edith remained unusually quiet for the remainder of our luncheon. That worried me more than if she continued to interject her opinions and demands. Maddie and I both ordered salads—blackened shrimp, grilled asparagus, and avocado for her and chicken caprese for me. A delectable bread bowl accompanied our meals, featuring a combination of French and Italian breads along with mini zucchini and carrot loaves. I was in heaven but tried not to show it for fear Edith would do something worse than continue to make snarky comments.

When we finished our meals and politely declined the desserts, I motioned the blonde serving assistant to our table. "Remember that little favor?" I asked. "Would it be too much trouble to show my friend and me the kitchen? A quick glimpse would suffice. I'd really like to see where all the magic is made."

In that instant, Edith made up for lost conversation time. "A quick glimpse? You need to find out if that duplicitous Imogen put my lights out permanently. See what she's got stocked in that kitchen of hers."

"Cut it out." It was an automatic response.

"What was that you said?" the server asked.

"I said, I'd like to check it out."

"Guests really aren't allowed in the kitchen. Health codes and all that."

I took out one of my new charcuterie business cards and handed it to her. "I wouldn't exactly be a guest. I'm in the industry, too. Well, new to the industry with a burgeoning charcuterie business. Would that work?"

She looked around and sighed. "I suppose I could let you in for a few minutes but don't be surprised if one of the chefs has a fit."

Edith stood behind her chair and adjusted her earrings. Long jeweled ones that resembled trellises. "I'd be having fits all day if I had to work for that she-witch."

This time I didn't respond.

"I'll be back to escort you once your waiter returns with the bill."

I smiled, trying hard not to have it look like a silly toothy grin. "Thanks. We really appreciate it."

"*You* appreciate it," Maddie said. "I'm fine looking at my own kitchen."

"This won't take long. I promise."

"Liar! Liar!" Edith again. "Take as long as you need."

Again, I used every bit of restraint to keep from talking to her.

Ten minutes later, having paid our bill and given our waiter a decent tip, Maddie and I were escorted by the server to the kitchen. The poor girl tiptoed in there as if she was avoiding landmines. "That's Ms. Brodeur's office, behind the frosted glass door," she said. "Hurry up, I'd hate to have her open the door and see us."

"I wouldn't hate it at all," Edith announced. "I'd hurl the nearest ice cube at her. I'm getting pretty adroit with ice cubes."

"Enough with the ice cubes."

"What ice cubes?" the server asked.

"Uh, I wondered if they used ice cubes to cool down the food in a hurry."

She shrugged. "Wouldn't know."

Maddie didn't say a word, but I could tell she was perplexed by my strange outbursts. I had to find a way to keep Edith from getting me flustered.

Inside the kitchen, a team of sous chefs and chefs moved in synch as they prepared meals, announcing their status every few seconds. Unfortunately, they weren't the only ones with a penchant for announcing things.

"Get into that pantry over there and start looking," Edith said. "Better yet, take out that phone of yours and start snapping."

"There's not enough time." My voice had now become whiny.

Maddie put a hand on my shoulder. "Maybe you can schedule a visit another time. When your establishment gains ground."

"We don't have a decade." This time Edith was so loud that the overhanging pans shook. Maybe it was the first time something like that happened to her unearthly form, but I knew in that instant, it wouldn't be the last. Edith took full advantage of her newfound ability for distraction and within seconds, every pot, pan, and hanging utensil shook as if it was an earthquake.

"How do you like that? I can rattle the pots and pans."

And my nerves.

"Don't just stand there like a ninny-face," she grumbled. "Get in that pantry and get to work."

"I don't know what I'm looking for." I mumbled the words under my breath, hoping Maddie and the server wouldn't hear them. Thankfully, with all the clanging of the pots, I was safe.

"Look for foods that could poison someone without casting suspicion."

Oh sure. Something I do every day.

"Like what?" I whispered.

"Cashews. They have urushiol. In large quantities, it can kill you. Castor beans are worse. Ever hear of ricin? It's a Russian favorite and it's found in castor beans. Then there's rhubarb. Oh sure, the stems are used to compliment strawberries in pies, but the leaves are deadly. Mix them with soda and it's a recipe for murder."

Before I could respond, what felt like a gust of wind blew me straight ahead into the wide-open pantry doors. "I'm just going to take a peek," I called out to Maddie. She and the server were a few feet away, leaning against the wall so as not to bother the kitchen workers.

"I've never seen the pots and pans rattle like that," the server said as I stepped into the large pantry. "Must be construction work going on somewhere. When they replaced a waterline not too long ago, everything shook."

Cashews. Rhubarb. Common foods found everywhere. But castor beans? I knew castor oil was an age-old remedy for constipation, but I seriously doubted I'd find any of those beans in The Chanterelle's pantry.

While Maddie made small talk with the server, I took out my phone and aimed it at the pantry shelves. I snapped anything and everything I could at record speed while trying to hide what I was doing. If it was a game show, I would have made one heck of a contestant. *Can you find the secret poison in less than twenty seconds?*

Just then, the little blond server gasped. "It's Ms. Brodeur. She must have come out of her office when she heard the noise in here. I'll lose my job if she finds out I let you in here. She's at the other end of the kitchen. Oh my gosh. If she doesn't go back to her office, I'm doomed."

"Did you hear that?" I asked. The question was meant for Edith, but Maddie responded.

"Loud and clear. Maybe we can duck down so she won't see us. With all the chefs in here, I doubt she'll be looking that closely."

"Must I do everything?" Edith bellowed. Next thing I knew, one of the pots came loose from its hinge and landed on Imogen's head. Enough to stun her. And more than enough to have every sous chef, food preparer, and chef rush to her aid.

Maddie and I charged out the kitchen door along with the petite blonde.

"I'm so sorry to have put you through all that trouble," I told her. I reached in my bag and handed her a twenty-dollar bill. "We'd better get out of here so you can get back to work." Then I handed her another five dollars. "You deserve it."

The blonde crinkled her nose. "I really shouldn't—"

"Oh yes you should," Maddie told her. "Have a nice afternoon."

I handed the valet our ticket and took another five-dollar bill from my bag. "I think the tips and payoffs cost me more than my salad," I said to Maddie when we got into my car.

"Yeah, what was that all about? I've never seen you so distracted, so off-kilter, and well, so *off* to put it bluntly."

"I don't know. It's hard to explain." I pulled the car from the curb and headed down Parkview Avenue to connect with North Fountain Hills Boulevard and eventually the 101.

"Want to know what *I* think it is?" Maddie asked.

"Sure, why not."

"I think it may have something to do with the fact that you're surrounded

86

by all of Edith Ellory's things and it's getting to you. You know she gave The Chanterelle a crummy review and for some reason, you feel you have to justify it."

She paused for a few seconds and continued. "Please don't tell me it's because you think the woman didn't die a peaceful death after all and that someone did her in. Because I can squash that theory right there. If there was any sign of foul play, the police would've been all over it. And every real estate agent would have had to disclose that to renters or buyers."

"Maybe no one knew. Maybe she looked peaceful but maybe she ingested something that stopped her heart, or something like that. No one bothered to check. From what I found out, there was no autopsy, and she went straight to the folks at whatever cremation society she had in her will."

"The Restful Souls in Phoenix," Edith snorted. "Bing, bang, over and out. You can't check for murder if you're looking at a pile of ashes."

I glanced over my shoulder and Edith was stretched out in the backseat. Needless to say, the forty-minute drive home seemed more like four hundred. Maddie needed to leave almost as soon as we got to my place. Something about a last-minute listing she had to make. I told her I'd give her a buzz in a few days and thanked her for making the trek with me to The Chanterelle.

"Next time let's pick Olive Garden or Texas Roadhouse," she laughed. "Less drama."

I watched her pull out of my driveway and turn onto the street. Then I let loose.

"You can't pull stuff like that, Edith. Boundaries! Boundaries!"

By now, Edith had draped herself on the couch. "I thought you were referring to my late-night visits, which, as you know, I've curtailed."

I groaned. "I'm referring to any and all of your visits that aren't limited to this house."

"If I'm under house arrest, I won't be able to help you with the investigation."

"So now you're *helping me* instead of demanding I find your killer."

"You've got it, honey. By the way, how did you like my reviews?"

"I didn't. That's probably what got you in the position you're in."

"You can say it—dead. Too bad I have no recollection of what happened."

"I need to make one thing clear. My business comes first. Then, I'll take a two-prong approach to your dilemma."

"A two-prong approach? Is that some fancy lingo from your former job?"

"It's an organizational technique when two viable paths of operation are needed."

"Oh brother. To be clear, we're not done with Imogen's potluck shanty. We need to take a good look at those photos of yours and see if we can find anything incriminating. Then, we go back to the restaurant, find her recipe files and see if any of her dishes called for whatever it was that might have killed me."

"Huh? Why don't you go back, have a nice look-see, and let me know what you find out."

"It doesn't work that way. My ephemeral spirit is connected to you. Like a string you can't see. Not as if I can go willy-nilly about on my own. I'm tethered to you. Like it or not."

"I don't. You mean to tell me, you can't float around elsewhere?"

"Nope. Only where you are or the areas that you occupy. Why do you think no one else can see or hear me?"

"But you rattled pots and pans and made a commotion."

"I did, didn't I? And I was quite good at it, too. My effects can be heard and felt, but I can't."

"How convenient."

"Sarcasm doesn't suit you."

Look who's talking.

"Edith, I'm not going to sneak around that restaurant and look for recipes. I guarantee The Chanterelle's computer is password protected and probably has layers of security."

"Who said anything about a computer? Restauranteurs like her keep a hard copy of their recipes. Probably locked up in her office somewhere. The chefs are given printed copies and commit them to memory. Nothing leaves the place."

"You can't be sure Imogen was responsible for your death. And if you don't mind my saying so, you're taking a Grand Canyon leap with your theory. Food storage in a restaurant kitchen does not translate to murder so your idea of a comparison check was ill-conceived."

"Then why did you take those pictures?"

"You plagued me to death. Figuratively, I mean. Going back to The Chanterelle is out of the question. It's a restaurant, not a funhouse. And to be clear, I will not let you drag me all over the place with your wackadoodle ideas."

I was loud. I was firm. And I stood my ground. I also meant what I said. Too bad I couldn't pull it off.

Chapter Sixteen

Edith left in a huff. That is to say, a swirl of purplish-blue haze filled the room for an instant and evaporated faster than that. Speedbump, who was curled up in his usual spot on the rug, didn't notice.

"Fine!" I shouted. "When you get over your hissy fit, come back and we'll look at the photos. It can't hurt. Meanwhile, I have a life." As soon as I said that, I felt guilty. As if I was rubbing it in.

It was a little past four and slightly overcast. That meant I could take the dog for a walk without keeling over from the heat. The poor beagle was relegated to the house and yard all week and could probably use the exercise. Then it hit me—I had actually become a genuine pet owner. More concerned about the welfare of my four-legged companion than my own. If it was up to me, I would have plunked myself on the couch and remained there until dusk.

"Give me five minutes to trade this fancy get-up for shorts and a top," I said to him, "and we're off. Might as well stretch our muscles while we can."

I stuffed two plastic food bags into my pocket in case Speedbump decided to gift one of the neighbors with something unmentionable. Then I grabbed a bottle of water, leashed him, and made sure the door was locked behind me.

If I thought I was about to get any exercise, I was wrong. Moving at a speed too slow to record, the dog sniffed everything between our house and the five houses we passed. Rocks, agaves, recycling bins that hadn't yet been returned to garages, and more bushes than I could count. I rationalized that it was *his* walk and not mine.

In an effort to move him along, I tugged at his leash. At that moment, a woman called out, "Hey there! Are you the new tenant in the Ellory house?"

The voice came from behind me, and I spun around to see a middle-aged chunky woman in a floral Mus-mus. I replied, "Yes. I am" and walked toward her.

"Tsk-tsk. I don't know what's worse. Moving into that old bat's house or contending with Mr. Pleasantry next door."

"Mr. Pleasantry? Is that his name?"

"I was being facetious. It's Owen Jasper. He works for one of the utility companies in the valley. He and Edith were like oil and water. On quiet evenings, you could hear them going at each other for all sorts of things. She'd yell, 'Can't you use that leaf blower at a reasonable time?' and he'd respond, 'When hell freezes over.' Then he'd bellow, 'I can't sleep with your motion sensor light waking me up all the time,' and she'd say, 'Then take a damn sleeping pill.' Honestly, it was awful. I'm glad a new renter or owner moved in."

"Renter. Katie Aubrey. I own the sandwich shop on Main Street. Soon to be The Char-Board. A takeoff on charcuterie boards. And this is Speedbump. He kind of showed up and well, I adopted him."

"Colleen Wexby. Assistant food service manager at Valley Wide Hospital. Sadly, we don't offer charcuterie boards, but we have an abundance of puddings." She chuckled as she bent down and petted Speedbump. "I saw the posters and hoped someone would claim him."

"Oh my gosh. The posters. I forgot to take them down."

"No worries. I'll get my son and his buddies to do that. They're always complaining how bored they are during the summer."

"Thank you. Really. I haven't had a minute to catch my breath with the new business and all. It was a miracle I even managed to unpack everything."

"Well, if you need help, give a holler. This is a wonderful, caring neighborhood. Well, mostly." She leaned forward and glanced at Owen's house. "To be honest, if Edith didn't die peacefully in her sleep, I would have bet money Owen put her in the grave. All that pesticide he used. It wouldn't have taken much. Not only did he put that stuff around his house for crickets and scorpions, but he was obsessed with desert rats even though his property doesn't have any fruit trees. It seemed like he tossed those granules around his house every time I passed by."

"Granules?"

"Poisons. Like strychnine. Although that one may be dated. Unlike Owen, we have a professional exterminator take care of our property and you might want to do the same, especially with a pet."

"Um, thanks. I hadn't really given it much thought until now. Tell me, did you know Edith?"

Colleen shrugged. "Not personally, no. Only a wave here and there and the occasional conversation if I ran into her during her nightly walks around the neighborhood."

"Nightly walks? Did she follow a regular schedule?"

"She was consistent if that's what you mean. As for her schedule, I wouldn't know."

"My real estate agent told me she died quietly in her sleep. You wouldn't happen to remember if you saw her walking the night before?"

"Hmm, as a matter of fact, I did. She seemed perfectly fine. That's why I was astonished when the cleaning woman screamed her lungs out the next morning. She bellowed, 'I think Edith is dead.' I was in my driveway picking up the morning paper when I heard her. I ran over there along with half the block. The cleaning woman said she looked through the window and saw Edith's body leaning over the side of the bed. Come to think of it, it was Owen who called nine-one-one. A bunch of us clustered around Edith's front door until the sheriff's deputies arrived. Then we were ushered across the street. It was the usual gossip-fest when something like this happens. Another sheriff's car arrived but instead of an ambulance, a coroner's vehicle showed up. Then the whole hubbub was over in a flash."

"Didn't you find it odd that she was okay one minute and dead the next?"

"I suppose. But people have heart attacks or strokes. Especially at her age. She wasn't exactly in her prime. I felt badly there was no funeral or memorial service, but then again, I doubt many people would have come. Owen found out from one of the responders that Edith kept her vital information and final wishes tucked inside a large plastic bottle in the refrigerator. It was labeled 'Vial of Life.' Ironic, huh? Still, it made it easier to dispose of the body." Colleen put her palm to her mouth and swallowed. "I'm sorry. That sounds so callous. What I meant was, it made the process move smoother."

Glad the only plastic bottles I have are labeled Coke or Pepsi.

"Is that a common thing? Keeping vital information in the fridge?"

"It is around here. Especially for people whose relations are out of state, or who don't have any relatives. The fire department handed out these plastic bottle-size vials during one of those community events a few years ago with directions for folks to list their medications, contact information, and final wishes."

"I'm sure you're right. About a heart attack or something. Guess we'll never know."

Colleen looked up at the sky. "As long as Edith doesn't come back to haunt us, we'll be all right. Anyway, I should be going. Glad I introduced myself. No doubt we'll run into each other, especially since your four-legged buddy seems to enjoy his walks."

"And his sniffing." I nudged Speedbump away from an overgrown lantana bush and we continued down the block. Fine one minute and dead the next didn't cut it for me. Edith *was* right about being shoved into the next world. And maybe good old Owen's pesticides had more to do with it than Imogen's pantry favorites. Then again, how does one disguise something as horrid as rat poison or worse?

I knew in that instant that I couldn't very well hip-hop from one place to the next or one theory to the next. Maybe Edith could, but she wasn't thinking rationally. She was too emotional about the whole thing. *What am I saying? Now who's being irrational? She's a spirit. Not real.*

"I should have known better, Speedbump," I said as we approached a cul-de-sac at the end of the block, "My two-prong approach may need more branches. And I need to design a murder map to plot it out. Not that it falls in my area of expertise, but so what? I've read enough cozy mysteries to figure it out. And maybe, just maybe, if I show Edith a clearly delineated process for gathering information and reaching a viable conclusion, she'd drop the idea of rooting through restaurant pantries."

So much for that. Edith was "at-the-ready" the moment I set foot back in the house. This time she wore billowy pantaloons with a blouse that resembled something Johnny Depp wore in his last *Pirates of the Caribbean* adventure. Sprawled in her usual spot on the couch, she looked up and patted the seat next to her. "What took you so long?"

Speedbump paid no mind. He took furious gulps of water from his bowl before curling up on the rug and I made a mental note to buy one of those doggie water dispensers for walking.

"I told you I had things to do. I can't drop everything in midair and look at photos."

"I can wait. Don't let it be said that Edith Ellory wasn't considerate."

Oh brother.

"I'm going to make myself a sandwich and when I'm done eating, we can look."

As I reached for the loaf of rye bread I'd recently purchased, Edith exclaimed, "Cockspurs!"

"Is that a curse or what?"

"Not a curse, but it could be. Are you aware rye bread is the most toxic of all breads?"

"No, only that it goes great with corned beef and mustard."

"Very funny. Rye bread is susceptible to ergot, a fungus. Very deadly."

"Thanks for the warning. I'll be extra careful to watch out for mold. Now if you don't mind, I'm going to make one of those sandwiches and when I'm done, we'll look at the photos."

Edith hummed the entire time I was in the kitchen and if that wasn't bad enough, she sat opposite me at the kitchen table while I ate my sandwich.

"Good, you're done," she said. "No messy clean-up. Now we can look at those pictures you took."

Resigned to the fact that I'd never be able to get anything else done, I grabbed my cell phone and clicked the photo gallery. "Um, these are really small. It would be better if I forwarded them to my email and pulled them up on my computer."

Edith flashed a hand in the air, a move that was quite common with Cinderella's fairy godmother, only Edith was neither.

It took me a few minutes, but I downloaded the photos to the computer and motioned for Edith to join me at my desk. "Okay, lots of stuff on shelves. The good news is that the foods appear to be in their original packaging or they're in plastic containers that are labeled. Drat! The print is so small."

"Can't you enlarge it?"

"Not without having it take scads of time. And then it might turn out blurry."

"Let me take a closer look." Suddenly I was enveloped in Edith's peach-colored haze, and I realized she had moved in front of me. I got up to give her some room.

"Cooking oils, baking products, pasta galore...Hmm, looks like Imogen's got a regular bean sanctuary on the third shelf down. Black beans, white beans, kidney beans, split beans, lima beans, navy beans, lentils, and —Ah hah—those are no coffee beans. See the striations?"

"I can't see anything from back here."

"Well, I can and those are castor beans. C A S T O R beans. No one cooks with castor beans, and I doubt the restaurant is in the homeopathic medicine business as a sideline. That can only mean one thing. Imogen purchased and stored them to blend in unobtrusively with the rest of the beans."

"Like I said before, you're jumping to conclusions. If those beans are indigestible, I mean, *deadly*, then why would anyone store them on a shelf where they could be confused with other beans and wind up in someone's chili or something?"

"Seasoned chefs know one bean from another. It's not a 'grab-n-go' for crying out loud."

"Still, I think you're jumping to conclusions. Look, you gave three other restaurants horrid reviews. Not just Imogen's. Why are you so fixated on hers?"

"That's none of your business."

"It is if you want me to figure out who killed you."

"Fine. That wench claimed I plagiarized one of her term papers. Balderdash!"

"Where?"

"At the Auguste Escoffier School of Culinary Arts in Austin, Texas. You don't become a food critic without some knowledge of culinary arts. It's not the state fair pie tastings."

"When?"

"Let's just say it was a few decades ago. Miserable cheat. Hmm, now that I think of it, maybe she couldn't tell a castor bean from an espresso bean. In any case, she didn't have a bachelor's degree in English like I did. The woman couldn't even write a full sentence and punctuate it correctly. Anyway, I proved it was my paper and she was put on academic probation. And if you think that nasty little matter had anything to do with my recent review of The Chanterelle, think again. My reviews are unbiased."

"*Were* unbiased."

"Stop flaunting the fact that I now inhabit another worldly realm."

"Oh brother. Listen, Edith, before we go poking and prodding around there again, let's at least look at motives those other restauranteurs may have had. It's a logical and sequential investigative step."

"Says who?"

"Every detective and amateur sleuth who's ever solved a murder."

"Then you better get cracking. I don't know how much longer my wardrobe will hold out."

With that, the peach-colored haze turned white before disappearing completely, and I was left with a most unsettling thought—Edith, sans her wardrobe.

Chapter Seventeen

The Sunday night TV lineup looked decent but unfortunately, I chose to unwind by sitting at the kitchen table plotting out a murder map. Well, not plotting in the actual sense of the word, more like asking myself questions and coming up with answers that were pure speculation. I went back to the old composition book and got to work where I left off.

I had begun with the big three—motive, means, and opportunity and took it from there. Frankly, a bad restaurant review hardly seemed motive for murder, even given the rocky relationship Edith and Imogen had. Still, every detective always seems to utter the words, "People have been known to kill for less." In other words, *motive* was subjective. Then I realized that *motive*, along with the other two classics, needed a suspect.

My original three columns now required a fourth—suspects. Other than generalized theories, I hadn't yet put any detailed thoughts to paper or I would have been tearing out pages like crazy. When, I was convinced I was really ready to dive in, I used the edge of a plastic placemat, since I didn't have a ruler handy, and drew four columns.

Under the first column I wrote Owen Jasper, Imogen Brodeur, unnamed-as-of-yet owners for the Flaming Pit, Savor in the Heights, and Randolph's Escapade. I also added Cora and Edith's nephew, Danny. Then I added the words "disgruntled neighbors" in case anything else cropped up.

It was a daunting column of would-be killers, but I quickly filled in the blanks under motive. I wrote revenge for all of the restaurant owners, vengeance under Imogen's name, and question marks under the others. When it came to means, I wrote pesticide under Owen's name and toxic foods under the restaurant owners.

Then it came to the tricky part—opportunity. If Edith was alive and well, prancing about the neighborhood for her nightly walk, then I seriously doubted a slow-action poison had been administered to her days or even weeks ago. Horrid thoughts of continued ingestion of anti-freeze flitted in and out of my mind along with the poisons I associated with espionage. Surely, someone would have noticed if Edith was slowly succumbing to a tortuous death. Especially Edith. Nope. Whoever did her in, had to have done so between the nightly walk and the morning of no return.

Unfortunately, opportunity wasn't the only conundrum. I didn't have the slightest clue in the world as to *what* could have accomplished that aim without leaving bodily evidence that even the most inept coroner would have detected. No wonder Edith's passing was labeled a natural death. Aargh.

Across the page on the left-hand side of the notebook, I wrote "To-Do-List." Under that, I added a sub-heading—visits to Flaming Pit, Savor, and Randolph's. Then in parenthesis, I added, "record mileage as a business expense for charcuterie catering."

I also added a sidenote about researching the newer pesticides. Colleen mentioned granules but as for their contents, I was clueless. Then there was Cora. I would absolutely have to hire her in order to do more prying. Too bad it was for home or that would have been a business expense, too.

"I suppose I should add this 'to-do' list to my weekly calendar," I said to Speedbump. I stood, walked to the wall calendar, thankful I had purchased one of those huge school ones that came with cutesy stickers for meetings, parties, and miscellaneous appointments. "I've got a meeting with Suzette Vonne from the ad agency on Tuesday. She texted me she'd stop by with the new flyers around three. That means I'd be available the other afternoons to chitchat with the owners of those restaurants."

It wasn't exactly how I planned on spending my first week on the job, but since the sandwich shop closed at 2:30, I'd have plenty of time to poke and prod at those places. That is, if the owners were willing to talk and if I was polished enough to segue from introducing my charcuterie boards to asking about the ramifications of Edith's reviews.

For the first time since Edith Ellory drifted into my bedroom with her outrageous demand, I was confident I had an action plan to accomplish it. Well, maybe not a fully-developed plan, but a rather nice composition notebook that would have at least earned me a B+ if I were attending a Nancy Drew school for neophyte sleuths.

When I pulled the covers back and settled in for the night, I expected to drift off in seconds. The room was still. The dog was pressed against my feet, and for a few glorious moments, I had reached nirvana. That's when it all ended.

"Psst! Psst! Get up!"

"Huh? Wh—"

It was Edith. She hovered over me like the Canterville Ghost. Except for one thing. The Canterville Ghost never wore a crimson and puce shawl.

"I remembered something," she said.

"Now? When I was about to go to sleep?"

"I can't help that. Listen. Get up. Get dressed. We're going out."

"I told you. I'm not about to break in and rummage through Imogen's restaurant."

"Not her restaurant. Her house."

"Good grief! That's worse yet. Whatever it was you remembered can wait until morning."

"When I reviewed The Chanterelle, I remembered overhearing her tell the assistant manager that she kept a diary in her nightstand for cathartic purposes. We need to get our hands on it. If she murdered me, she'd need all the catharsis she could get."

"Are you insane? Not only break into her house but at night. In her bedroom? And her nightstand no less? I don't feel like spending the next twenty years behind bars."

"You won't have to. I have it all figured out."

If I had any thoughts of going back to sleep, the palpitations I felt in my chest indicated otherwise. "What? What have you figured out?"

Edith adjusted her shawl and plopped herself on the bed. "Imogen lives on East Milton Drive in Scottsdale. You can thank me later for doing my homework. That's just a hop, skip, and a jump from Cave Creek Road to North Scottsdale Road. Her house is between Lone Mountain Ranch and Dixileta. It's not gated. That should put your mind at ease."

"It doesn't. Nothing does. It's a terrible idea."

"You've got a better one, I suppose?"

I knew she'd never give me a minute's worth of peace but still, breaking and entering?

"This is an absolutely horrible idea."

"I need to see that diary. No one will get any peace until I see that diary. You're the only person who can make that happen."

Terrific. Now I'm David Copperfield.

"How can I be sure we won't get caught?"

"Good! You've agreed. Get dressed and start up your car. I haven't sat in a passenger's seat in a while."

"You didn't answer my question."

"Honestly," she huffed, "Imogen will all but crawl out of her skin when I really put the haunt on her. She'll be so caught up in my shenanigans that she'll pay no mind to your snooping around. If need be, I'll chase her all over the house while you steal that diary."

"Theft? Now you want to add theft to the mix? Did I say twenty years? Make it twenty-five."

"If you're not fussy, you can do what you did in the pantry. Photograph the pages going back from the night I was murdered to a few weeks prior. Surely you can manage that."

"If it will get you to leave me alone and let me continue this so-called investigation the way I want to, then fine. But only this once."

"Sure, sure. Hurry up."

"I promise I'll be back in time for your breakfast," I said to Speedbump. *Unless I wind up at the Fourth Avenue Jail.* "Meanwhile you've got the whole bed to yourself."

Traffic was practically non-existent at a little before midnight as I turned left on Dixileta and wound my way through a number of side streets before

100

reaching Milton Drive. The street looked magical with a variety of landscape lighting, including peekaboo ground lights, walkway lights, and special feature lights that shone on the palms and cacti.

"That's it," Edith said. "That expansive house on the left with the white BMW in front. Figures. Imogen always was a show-off."

I parked a few houses past Imogen's. Not that it would matter if the police were called. "Now what? And lest I forget, what if the place has an alarm system?"

"An alarm system? My energy field will stifle that sucker as soon as we approach. It's getting into that witch's fortress that may be tricky."

I was tired and irritable before I even set foot in the house. "May be tricky? Now you tell me? I thought you had this figured out."

"In a theoretical sense, yes."

Terrific. "A theoretical sense." Just like Freud, Piaget, and Jung. Only they didn't break into peoples' houses to do diary hunting.

Chapter Eighteen

I refrained from going into a tirade. "Okay Edith, what did you have in mind?"

It was absolutely quiet at that hour of the night and the last thing I wanted to do was cause a commotion.

"On nights like this, people tend to keep a bedroom window open. All they have to do is use the bypass system on their alarm panel. I guarantee that's exactly what Imogen did. Come on, let's scurry to the rear of the house."

I'm not sure I would have used the word "scurry," but I kept close to the walls and skirted around the lawn until we reached the back of the house.

"Ah-hah! What did I tell you? The window's open by at least seven or eight inches. I'll waft my way inside and make sure Imogen is too preoccupied to notice you. Lift the window, climb over the sill and keep down. Stay close to the ground."

Wonderful. A training exercise if I ever decide to join the armed forces and attend boot camp.

"One more thing," Edith said. "Don't stand up. Lay low and use your hand to pull open the drawer to her nightstand. I already checked. Only one nightstand. Makes it much easier for you."

In what world?

"Edith, even if I get my hands on that diary, I can't very well start taking pictures right there and then. Even if you *do* distract her."

"Grab the book and hightail it out of there. Hide in a closet. Imogen must have a million of them in this mansion of hers. Take the photos and leave the diary in the closet. She'll think she left it there. Or she'll blame her cleaning crew. Not my problem. When you're done, go out the nearest door and get back to the car. Easy peasy."

"And what will you be doing while I play cat burglar?"

"I'll make sure Imogen's out of bed and in the kitchen."

Her plan actually sounded workable. Until we put it to use.

Minutes later, the sound of glass crashing on a tile floor jolted me. *Edith isn't kidding. She's in the kitchen and if I know her, Imogen will need to buy more stemware.* Then I heard a voice—"Alberta, did you break something?"

Alberta? Who the heck is that? Good going, Edith. There's someone else in the house.

I peered into the room and there was no sign of Imogen. Without wasting a second, I slid the window up, and hoisted myself over the ledge. A small nightlight on the wall opposite the nightstand was the only illumination I had. Probably a good thing should Alberta, whoever she was, walk in.

Please don't let there be anything yucky in that nightstand. Why didn't I bring gloves? Why? Why?

It was impossible to stop my hand from trembling as I closed my eyes and fumbled around to find anything that met the description of a diary. I felt tissues, number one in the yuck factor, a toenail clipper, a small flashlight, and a tube of heaven knows what. I had to force myself not to let my imagination go too wild.

Yep, I laid my hands on everything in Imogen's nightstand except her diary. *Good going, Edith.*

Suddenly, I heard a husky woman's voice coming from another room. "Imogen, is that you? What did you break?"

"I didn't break anything. I thought you did. There's broken glass on the kitchen floor. Had to be one of the tumblers from the dish drain. I told you not to use the outside clips on the drainer."

"I didn't. Maybe you left it near the edge of the counter."

With Imogen and Alberta engaged in a game of "who broke the glass," and Edith somewhere around to make sure it doesn't end any time soon, I attacked the large dresser next. Nothing gross but lots of lingerie and undergarments. If Imogen did keep a diary, she didn't keep it in her bedroom.

103

Then something occurred to me. When I was in my teens, I kept a diary, too. And I made sure my mother wouldn't find it by stashing it between my mattress and the bedspring. Maybe Imogen didn't want Alberta to get her hands on it.

Next thing I knew, I reached under the mattress on the nightstand side of the bed and sure enough, I found it. One of those 5 x 7 coil-bound notebooks that could be used for anything. Drat! My first thought was that it wasn't a diary after all, but Imogen's special recipes. That would figure.

Resigned to the fact that the entire escapade would be a bust, I flipped the book open and thanked my lucky stars. Then, I tucked it against my chest and tiptoed out of the room and into another master suite. I prayed it wasn't Alberta's.

Meanwhile, I could still hear the two women arguing in the kitchen.

"You must have left it on the counter."

"Me? You're the one who never pays attention to what she's doing."

I did a mental eye roll and darted into the walk-in closet. It was larger than my bedroom and had one of those fancy islands in the center. Taking a breath, I leaned over the counter, opened the diary from the left, and worked my way back taking photos as fast as I could. Not an easy feat in the dark.

Just then, I heard a door slam. Not any door, but the one to the bedroom I was in. Then I heard a voice. Presumably, Alberta's. "If you didn't like the way I swept up the glass, you could have done it yourself, mother."

Mother? That answers my question. Alberta was Imogen's daughter. Yeesh. I could never call my mother by her first name. What else did Edith neglect to tell me? I was only partway through my picture taking when Imogen shouted, "Did you borrow my special lavender pillow? I'm going to need it if I plan to get back to sleep."

"No, I didn't." Alberta's voice was sharp.

"Well, it's not in here. I bet it's in your closet. You've got everything else stuffed in there. Go look!"

No, Alberta. Don't look.

"If it will get you off my back, I'll look but I'm telling you, I don't have it."

I grabbed a handful of clothes from the hangers behind me. No idea what they were but it didn't matter. I tossed them over my head and ducked behind the counter.

Don't bother looking, Alberta. Just tell your mother it's not in here.

Too late, Alberta turned on the closet light and rounded the counter. "What the—" she started to say when I tossed the clothes in the air and let out a wail that would have sent chills down the backs of most seasoned vampire hunters.

Edith wasted no time plunging the closet into complete darkness. Alberta, not to be upstaged by my performance, let out a bloodcurdling scream, resulting in Imogen racing into the room. It was the first time I got a look at her—dark lipstick, a long, narrow face, and not a lot of flesh on her bones. Odd, but I'd heard that description before. I just couldn't remember where.

"What? What now? Did you ruin my pillow?" Then, "The lightbulb must have blown. I'll turn on the lamp." Then, "Don't tell me the breaker tripped."

"Not the blasted breaker. There's someone in here! Call nine-one-one. It was a hideous-looking man."

A hideous-looking man? Is she nuts? True, it was late at night, and I didn't have any makeup on, but seriously? On my worst day, I'm not bad looking.

"I knew we should have purchased a gun. Hold on, I'll get the wasp spray."

"I'm not staying in here alone with a killer," Alberta shouted. "I'm making a run for my car. It's in front of the house."

Great. Now I'm a killer.

As Alberta and Imogen raced down the hallway, I made a beeline for the front door and held on to that diary like a running back with a football.

"That's him," Alberta screamed. "You're closer. Throw that heavy doorstop at him!"

"You bet!"

Those were the last words I heard. In that split instant, a force of wind enveloped the hallway and Imogen yelled, "Stop pulling at me, Alberta."

"I'm not pulling."

Then the hallway lighting flickered like a strobe and next thing I knew, a gust of wind pushed me out the door, nearly knocking me to the ground.

"I told you I'd take care of it," Edith said. "Run for the car in case those two do call nine-one-one."

"I hope you're happy," I said when I flung the diary onto the passenger seat. "Now it really *is* theft."

"Hurry up. Turn on that engine and get moving. The sooner we get back to the house, the sooner we can find out what that harpy used to kill me."

"*If* it was her. That's a big *if.* And by the way, I intend to get some sleep. I can't stay up reading that thing."

"Fine. Then I'll do it. Just don't complain if you hear loud gusts of wind. It's the only way I can turn the pages."

"No problem. I'll be sure to close my bedroom door."

As I exited Dixileta onto North Scottsdale Road, a police car, complete with lights and siren, flew by me on the opposite side of the road, causing Edith to break out in gales of laughter. "Those two must have called nine-one-one after all. I wish we could be there when the police ask what was stolen and Imogen tells them it was a lavender sleep pillow."

"You don't suppose she had one of those nanny cam or Ring devices, do you?"

My face will be on Silent Witness tomorrow.

"I disrupted all of the energy waves," she said. "Now aren't you glad we're a team?"

"*A team?* I'd rather play first base for the Arizona Diamondbacks."

Chapter Nineteen

"What a total waste of time!" Edith stood in front of the glassed shower door staring directly at me as I added conditioner to my scalp.

"Boundaries!" I shouted. As if it would make a difference. "Can't you see I'm taking a shower?"

Through the condensation on the glass, I couldn't believe today's getup—dark gaucho pants with a peasant blouse. I grabbed the shower wand and rinsed my head. "Tell me when I towel off and put on some clothes. I can't be late for work. Ugh. I hate getting up when it's dark. The sun won't rise until five-thirtyish. Forty-five more minutes."

"Stop complaining about the sunrise. Don't you realize we've hit a wall? There's nothing in Imogen's diary about her murdering me. Only endless whining about her daughter who moved in a few months ago to attend some cockamamie medical coding school."

I rolled my eyes. "Give me a few minutes. Plant or hover yourself in the kitchen. In fact, maybe see if your skills allow you to start up the Keurig."

Like it not, Edith had become a fixture in my life. That is, until her unresolved death was no longer unresolved. I'd come to the realization that I was dealing with the paranormal world and would have to get used to it. Either that, or I would need to shell out beaucoup bucks for mental health counseling.

Suddenly, the condensation disappeared from the glass panel along with Edith. I reached for a large plush towel and dried off as quickly as I could. Then I raced to get dressed, realizing I'd need to spring for more pants, capris, and tops since business suits and a charcuterie sandwich shop didn't exactly mix.

"Okay Edith," I said when I walked into the kitchen and automatically filled Speedbump's bowl and changed his water. The Keurig was untouched, but I didn't want to press the issue. I plunked a medium roast McCafé pod in the machine and turned to face her. She was seated at the table with the diary in front of her while the dog gobbled his kibble.

Her tone was brittle and sharp. "There's absolutely nothing here that would incriminate that harridan. Although she did refer to me in the most ungracious way after the review came out about The Chanterelle."

"Ungracious how?" I reached for my cup and added creamer.

"She said I had the tastebuds of a sow that couldn't distinguish between a mouthful of grass and an ear of corn. Does that answer your question?"

"Um, yeah. I guess it does." I unwrapped a package of store-bought donuts and bit into one."

"They don't call sugar 'the white death' for nothing."

"I'm in a hurry and I'm functioning on practically no sleep thanks to you. So, if you don't mind, I'll eat two donuts."

The table rattled and Imogen's diary fell to the ground. "Nice going, Edith."

"I can't stomp on it. You do it."

"I'm not stomping on her diary. You should be relieved she wasn't the one who murdered you. I mean, since you knew her and all. Besides, we need to figure out a way to return it without sneaking back in her house."

"Oh, I suppose you're right. We'll put it on the proverbial back burner."

Wonderful.

I glanced at Edith and saw she was bent over with her ghostly hands over her eyes. If she wasn't all whisp and air, I would have given her a hug. "Look, just because it wasn't Imogen, doesn't mean we don't have other leads. Three more to be precise, and those are just the restaurants you, well, um, gave bad reviews. My promotional flyers will be here tomorrow, and I'll set up meetings with those restaurants on the pretext of offering a new charcuterie service. Who knows? Maybe one of them will take me up on it."

"What if it's none of them, then what?"

"We look closer to home. Like next door. Anyway, I can't waste another second." I rinsed my cup in the sink, gave Speedbump a pat on the head, told him to be a good boy, and shot out of there at breakneck speed. I needed to set a good example for my employees and the last thing I needed, other than Edith, was to have them stand in front of the sandwich shop waiting for me to show up and open it.

"No offense, but you look awful," Lilly-Ann said when she and Matt opened the door to the sandwich shop. I had gotten in the door less than ten minutes before they did but had already turned on the lights and got the coffee machine brewing.

"Yeah," Matt chimed in. "I think you forgot to wipe the makeup from under your eyes. Kind of looks racoon-ish."

"It's not make-up. It's my natural look. There's not enough foundation in the world to cover it up. I didn't get much sleep last night."

"Anything wrong?" Lilly-Ann walked to the fridge, pulled out, and began to chop the veggies for our sandwiches.

"No, just excited about the week's events, that's all." *Unless breaking, entering, and theft are part of the equation.*

"That happens to me, too. My body's exhausted but my mind is in overdrive. Don't forget, it's bread delivery day. Brioche, Toast, and Most should be here anytime soon. Matt can take care of it, right Matt?"

"Huh? Oh yeah, sure. No problem."

"Before I forget," I said, "I'm meeting tomorrow with a woman from the ad agency who's managing the promotional campaign. She'll be here around three, right after we close. And the sign company will be installing our new Char-Board sign on Thursday. After that, it's bye-bye Cave Creek Sandwiches and hello charcuterie shop."

Matt took out two dozen eggs and put them in a large pot to boil. From there, the two of them made salads, got the lunch meats organized, and were raring to go when our first customers came in.

By midmorning, I had gotten the pace of the shop and didn't feel as if I was fumbling around. I grabbed a tuna salad sandwich at ten-thirty and while I ate, I googled the directions for the other three "Lousy Edith review" restaurants. I debated whether or not I should call them for an appointment. I'd been brought up to respect people's time and not show up someplace unannounced, but that meant I could be turned away on the phone, thus blowing my chances to see if any of those owners would harbor enough venom to put Edith away for good.

I decided to split the difference—phone one of them and show up unannounced at the others. From my desk in the kitchen, I watched as Lilly-Ann and Matt handled orders, prepared foods, and cleaned up. It was safe for me to continue my early lunchtime break.

Savor in the Heights was the farthest from Cave Creek and an impromptu walk-in might spur an immediate refusal, resulting in wasted gasoline with no reward for my effort. Yep, Savor it was. I dialed the number, took a deep breath, and prayed the owner would agree to see me.

"Good morning," I said to the man who answered the phone. "This is Katie Aubrey from The Char-Board in Cave Creek, a charcuterie food establishment." *Classier sounding than 'sandwich shop.'* "I'd like to speak with your owner or manager if I may."

"Is this about the acquisition? If so, you'd need to speak with his legal team. I can provide that information."

Acquisition? Legal team? What the heck?

"No, not the acquisition. I'd like to discuss charcuterie catering."

"Hold on a moment. I'll see if Mr. Pomeroy is available."

The moment on hold was more like two or three. "This is Wend Pomeroy. How can I help you?"

"I'm Katie Aubrey, the new owner of a charcuterie business in Cave Creek and I'd like to discuss the possibility of providing our specialized charcuterie boards for your off-site catering."

Please don't say no and hang up.

"Charcuterie, you said?"

"Yes. We create exquisite masterpieces that are as visually appealing as they are tasty. We've launched a soft opening so far and plan to have our grand opening in a few weeks."

"Charcuterie."

"Yes."

"Hmm, that's getting to be quite the popular thing. Might be one of those new trends that fizzles out, but then again, why miss an opportunity?"

"Is that a yes? You'll meet with me?"

"I suppose I can spare a half-hour, but it will need to be during the afternoon. Our dinner hour is out of the question and my mornings seem to be tied up. Savor in the Heights is in the process of acquiring some property near the Biltmore in Phoenix. We plan to build and open a second restaurant."

The acquisition.

"An afternoon would be fine."

The iPhone shook in my hand as we ended the call. We agreed on Wednesday at four-thirty, giving me ample time to finish up here and drive to Fountain Hills. I made a mental note to wear one of my best business suits. If nothing else from my position at Chan-Tech, I learned that first impressions are the only impressions.

Then I had the most unsettling and upsetting thought. What if Edith decides to join me?

"Are you all right, Katie?" Lilly-Ann asked as she wiped down the table next to where I sat. "You look as if you got bad news."

"What? No. Not at all. Good news, in fact. I'll be meeting with the owner of Savor in the Heights to discuss our new charcuterie business. I know this is short notice, but are you available tomorrow night to learn how to set up the mini-platters? I want to have them on the menu starting Thursday when our new sign is up."

"I'll be ready with bells on."

Chapter Twenty

I envisioned delectable mini-platters with all the beauty of a Roman mosaic coupled with sweet and savory cheese and meat delights for my first venture with the charcuterie boards. That meant trips to Trader Joe's and AJ's Fine Foods for specialized cheeses and cured meats, not to mention dried fruits, nuts, and chocolates. Desert Delectable Foods would most likely have what I needed wholesale, but right now I couldn't afford to wait for next month's order. Besides, the cost would even out since The Char-Board was a small business and I would have to pay additional delivery fees.

When we closed our doors at three, following a thorough clean-up, I drove to Trader Joe's in Scottsdale before heading home. Thankfully, they had everything I needed so I didn't have to go the additional miles to AJ's, even though I loved the place. Maybe another time.

Speedbump sniffed the large paper bags when I got inside the house and licked his chops.

"Don't worry," I told him. "You can have some of my meatloaf dinner compliments of Trader Joe's. Meanwhile, a dog biscuit will have to suffice." I handed him a Healthy Vet Dog Biscuit and he inhaled it before darting out the doggie door.

As I put the gouda, brie, Havarti, and Jarlsberg cheeses in the fridge, I made a note to buy more plastic containers. Next, I eyeballed the cured salamis, hams, and turkey. I may have overdone it, but I figured any extra could be used for sandwiches. Assorted olives, some stuffed with garlic or pimento, followed suit along with miniature pickles and grapes.

I left the nuts, dried figs and apricots, and chocolate candies on the counter. Then, I folded the paper bags and put them next to the food for easy transport tomorrow.

"I've got a game plan," I called out to the dog before I realized he was outside. By now I was starving and thankful I'd selected a premade dinner, even if it was microwaved. Sodium or not, I was going to devour it.

With the dinner in the microwave, I slipped into shorts and a t-shirt and returned to the kitchen in time to hear two sounds—the "done" beep on the microwave and the vibration from my cell phone, signaling a text message.

I checked the text first in case it was anything earthshattering. At least Edith couldn't communicate with modern technology. *But she could sure mess it up.* The text was from my mother, and it was short and sweet—*How R U? Call. Love, Mom*

With so much going on, I completely forgot to keep her posted. Worse yet, I'd made some nebulous invitation for my dad and her to come for dinner. Not only would I have to put that on what Edith called "the back burner," but I'd need to put it on another stove altogether.

I texted back, "Swamped with work. Will call soon. Love, Katie," and hoped it would suffice for the time being. Then, I dove into my meatloaf with mashed potatoes and peas, doling out little bits to Speedbump who had all but attached himself to my leg.

It was nice to enjoy a quiet dinner without Edith's nagging, but I doubted I'd be so lucky for the remainder of the evening. Sure enough, I spied her on the couch, still in that awful gaucho outfit.

"You can thank me, later," I said. "I'm meeting Wend Pomeroy, the owner of Savor in the Heights on Wednesday under the pretense of introducing my charcuterie business. Did you know he planned to open another restaurant? This time in Phoenix by the Biltmore."

"Heavens no! What does he plan to do? Give more people indigestion?"

"Whatever you do, do NOT give me indigestion or worse by showing up when I meet with him? Understood?"

Edith fluffed her hair and didn't respond. Not a good sign.

"I'll make it a point to pop in on the other two restaurants if I can squeeze it in this week. Believe me, I want to get this over with as much as you do."

"You'll be happy to know I figured out a way to get Imogen's diary back without setting foot in her house."

"Like leave it on her doorstep?" I asked.

"Don't be ridiculous. I've devised a sneaky little plan. Although it may have Imogen and Alberta at each other's throats. But then again, that's not a far distance for those two."

"Aargh. What's your plan?"

"We'll put the diary in Alberta's car. You remember, the white BMW that was parked in front of the house. It's Alberta's. She mentioned it when she tried to get out of the place."

"Breaking into a car? That's grand theft auto! Do you have any idea how long a prison sentence that carries?"

"Posh! I can unclick those locks before you know it. All you have to do is reach in and plunk the diary on the driver's seat. Or the passenger's seat. Makes no difference."

"No, it doesn't, because I'm not about to do that."

"Do you have a better idea?"

I tried to remain calm. "Yes. It's called get-a-night's-sleep."

"You don't need that diary hanging over your head. If you leave now, we can unload the thing and be back here in less than an hour."

"An hour? It takes forty-five minutes to get there."

"Then drive faster."

I knew I'd never get a night's sleep. Edith would most likely hover over my bed insisting we return the diary. "Okay. You win. But only this time. And no side trips back into Imogen's house. You unlock the door, I toss in the diary, and off we go. Is that clear?"

"What are you waiting for?"

For the second night in a row, I made the trek to Imogen's classy neighborhood and sure enough, Alberta's BMW was parked out front. Along with Alberta. Lip-locking with some guy, according to Edith who got a good look.

"Yeesh. Now what?" I all but shrieked. "For all we know, those two could be lip-locked for hours."

"Not if I can help it. Drive past them slowly."

I did as she said and the next thing I knew, the car horn blared, resulting in a quick exit by Alberta and company. Worse yet, it kept blaring until Imogen opened the front door of the house and yelled, "What's going on?"

"I don't know," Alberta yelled back. "It won't turn off."

"Call Triple-A!" Imogen's voice was a foghorn.

"We'll do it inside. It's too loud out here."

"Not as loud as your boyfriend's motorcycle. Tell him he can't park it on the side of our garage. I want it moved."

"I can't hear you, mother. The horn's too loud."

Next thing I knew, she and her boyfriend made a mad dash for the house, and I seized that moment to pull up, get out, open the driver's side door, and heave the diary onto the seat. I was five or six houses down when I realized the horn noise had stopped.

"I hope you're happy," I said. "You woke up the entire neighborhood. I hope no one noticed us."

"You worry too much. You need to relax."

"Tell that to the palpitations in my chest."

Edith laughed.

"That's not funny."

"I'm not laughing about that. I'm laughing because Alberta has a boyfriend who's probably giving Imogen fits."

When I turned on to North Scottsdale Road, Edith mentioned how she wished she could be there when Alberta discovers her mother's diary in the car. I all but lost control of the wheel. "Not on your life! Or, um, *death,* as the case may be. From now on, this investigation is in my hands."

Truth be known, the investigation may have been in my hands, but, like it or not, everything else was in Edith's. I got home at a little past eleven and was able to get a decent night's sleep before work the next day. I was eager and anxious to meet with Suzette and get a handle on the marketing plan she created, including a simple but inviting website to attract clients.

I had planned on starting slowly, first with the sandwich shop and then with the catering, even though I had led Wend to believe the catering part was well underway. *Good grief, I'm getting as bad as Edith.*

Chapter Twenty-One

Suzette arrived at the soon-to-be renamed sandwich shop at three on the dot the next day. Tall, slender, and blonde, with an outfit that complimented her figure, Matt offered up a zillion excuses to keep on working once he laid eyes on her. I all but threw him out, insisting nothing else needed to be sorted, cleaned, or otherwise. Lilly-Ann even helped by taking him by the arm. She told me she'd be back at seven so I could show her how to prepare the mini-charcuterie boards.

"It's not live yet," Suzette said, handing me a tablet once my employees left. "It's your new website. Simplistic, functional, inviting, and within your price range."

"My gosh, the graphics of the charcuterie boards are eye-catching. Where did you find them?"

"Some are company designs others are public domain photos. Will they work until we can photograph your masterpieces?"

"Absolutely."

She went on to review the marketing plan, beginning with targeted ads and mailers for event planners. By the time she left, I was confident my new business would succeed.

With only a couple of hours until seven, I drove home, took Speedbump for a walk, and made myself an omelet. Then it was off to The Char-Board. I had the foresight to bring my Trader Joe's purchases to the place in the morning so I wouldn't be stressed at the end of the day. Oddly enough, Edith had left me alone since we arrived home late last night, following my second sojourn to Imogen's place. Not a good sign. I worried she was up to something. Probably with good reason.

Lilly-Ann was at the shop when I pulled up front. Judging from her smile, she was as eager to get going as I was.

"Hey there! Hope you weren't waiting long," I said.

"Nope, just got here. My car's on the opposite side of the street so it will be facing the right direction when I head home. Funny habit of mine."

"Makes sense. Boy am I glad I lugged the food in this morning. That's one less thing we have to deal with." I unlocked the door and wondered if maybe I shouldn't make an extra key for Lilly-Ann, just in case. The prior owner, according to everyone, was a total micromanager who had to control everything. Maybe he wasn't comfortable giving one of his employees a spare key, but I needed to trust someone for backup and Lilly-Ann seemed reliable.

"Better keep the front lights off so folks don't think we're open," I continued. "Besides, we're going to be working in the kitchen. Once we wash our hands, it'll be look and learn."

Lilly-Ann wiped her hands on a paper towel and tossed it in the trash. "I know it's a matter of cutting and arranging the foods on a platter, but is there a secret to it? A special technique?"

"Actually, the mini-boards are more difficult in the sense that they're designed for one or two people and that means the combination of elements, that is, foods, must complement each other. When it comes to the larger platters for parties and events, it's an entirely different story. Tons of people will heap up the goodies on their own serving plates and oftentimes, they select one or two things that they like or that they're familiar with."

She nodded. "I get it. Well, more or less."

"Okay, best to start by putting all of our items on the counter so we can eyeball what we'll need. Good thing this shop has a long worktable and an equally large kitchen. I'll need it as the business grows."

Lilly-Ann and I unloaded the cheeses, meats, olives, and pickles from the fridge, and I added the dried foods that I had stashed in the corner of the counter. "Not everything has to go on one mini-board. In fact, it shouldn't. Otherwise, it will be a hodge-podge. Different story for the larger boards

118

but let's start out with these."

"I take it the meats and cheeses are the necessities."

"You learn fast. Believe it or not, when I first started designing boards, I replicated the ones that I had seen at different event venues. One of the perks of my having a photographic memory. But later on, I wanted to create my own style. Usually, I begin by selecting one meat and one cheese for small platters and two meats and two cheeses for larger mini-boards. Oh, and one of the cheeses is usually brie. I refer to it as my 'anchor' cheese since it's eye-catching and has an element of style as well as taste."

"Yeah, those soft cheeses have a certain pizazz about them. What next?"

"I either roll or fold the meat or cut and chunk it. You know, for hard salamis and the like. I also cut and shape the cheeses and place them on opposite sides of the board. I add complementary fresh fruits like small batches of different colored grapes, strawberries, raspberries, or blueberries. Then, dried nuts and fruits in small quantities."

"What about pickles and olives?"

"Good question. What I described was a standard charcuterie mini-board. Eventually, we'll offer different varieties on our menu, like a Greek-themed one, an Italian-themed one, or even a French-themed one. I bought a giant chalkboard and an easel so we can write the daily varieties on it."

"Ah, that explains it. I wondered why it was in the storage area."

"Oops. I forgot to mention it. Since the menus don't have the charcuterie selections on them, I thought we'd write them on the chalkboard with descriptions and maybe even a few cutesy drawings. I also ordered a dozen small round mini-boards and they're in back, too."

"Believe it or not, Matt's quite the artist. He'll be all over it tomorrow if you ask him."

"Great. My artwork is somewhat, well…primitive."

For the next hour, I showed Lilly-Ann how to fold and press the cured meats together so that they'd look appetizing on the boards. I told her some meats, like salamis, can be folded in quarters and fanned out, or even doubled, but if it's a thicker cut of the same meat, it can be left rounded.

"People eat with their eyes," I said. "And first impressions matter. Come on, let's take a break, sit down, and have a soda or iced tea."

Lilly-Ann sighed as we left the counter area and sat near my desk. "When you first told us about the charcuterie boards, I went home and googled it. It was mind-boggling. And complicated."

"Oh, they can be complicated all right, like a puzzle where everything has to fit in the right place. But learning the skill takes time. Meanwhile, you'll get lots of practice if these mini-boards become a hit. Oh my gosh, I can't believe we've been at it for so long. Let's put plastic wrap on the completed boards and introduce them tomorrow. In fact, I'll put a sample board in the cold food display case. That should pique people's interest."

"Thanks for asking me, Katie. It's only been a few days, but honestly, it's a joy to work for you. I actually feel valued."

"You are. In fact, I was going to ask if you'd consider doing more with the charcuterie boards if the catering part of my venture takes off. What I didn't explain was that it's usually best to get to the venue ahead of time and prepare the boards in their kitchen. Most social halls have full kitchens so it's just a matter of bringing our own supplies. That way they're fresh. Of course, time constraints and different situations require pre-arranged boards. That's why I contracted with food delivery services."

"Oh my gosh. Count me in."

"Absolutely."

While Lilly-Ann tidied up and made sure our sundries were carefully wrapped and refrigerated, I dragged the easel and chalkboard into the dining area and took out the box of colored chalks that I purchased a while back. If Lilly-Ann was right about Matt, we'd have a visual display to whet our customers' appetites.

With the lights out and the door locked, we walked to our respective cars, and I watched Lilly-Ann drive down the block from my rearview mirror. Executing a three-point turn took me a second but no sooner was I on Cave Creek Road when a yellowy haze engulfed the interior of the car and I heard Edith's grating voice. "It looks nicer when you flute the salamis. Gives it that fancy feathery effect."

"What? You watched me? Is nothing sacred?"

120

CHAPTER TWENTY-ONE

"I was bored."

"Well, like I said earlier, you better not be bored tomorrow when I meet with Wend Pomeroy at Savor in the Heights. Stay away. I don't need to worry about a looming catastrophe."

"I have no intention of making a scene. Besides, don't you think two heads are better than one when it comes to ferreting out information?"

"Not if one of those heads is yours."

I might as well have saved my breath because the word *no* simply wasn't in Edith's vocabulary.

Lilly-Ann was right about Matt's artistic ability. As soon as I showed him the chalkboard the following morning and explained my plan to introduce the charcuterie mini-boards, he immediately offered to draw the menu.

"Have at it," I said. "I'll help Lilly-Ann with your usual setup duties and when we open in an hour, our customers will know that this is no longer the Cave Creek Sandwich Shop."

When the last three customers left at a little past two, we had sold ten mini-boards and reaped so many positive comments that I was practically beaming. It was a mad rush for me to get home after we closed up, feed Speedbump, change, and drive to Savor in the Heights for my meeting with Wend Pomeroy.

"Don't you dare follow me," I announced as I started to leave the house. Speedbump cocked his head and I rushed over to pet him. "Not you, the other inhabitant who doesn't play fair."

Just then an ice cube fell from the refrigerator server and the dog snatched it.

"I mean it, Edith."

The drive to Fountain Hills, just west of Scottsdale, was absolutely lovely, even if it did mean using the highways. Savor in the Heights was located on East Via Linda, and literally took my breath away. It was a French Chateau on a small hill framed by rocket junipers and white oleanders. Mauve and gray pavers formed a curved sidewalk that led from the parking lot to the frosted glass front entrance.

A few Infinites and Audis as well as one Jaguar were the only cars in the lot. The dinner hour hadn't yet started, and lunch was long over. I imagined I'd see more pricy vehicles on my way out.

My newly printed charcuterie advertising flyer shook in my hand as I approached the door. I had to keep reminding myself that this was a murder investigation, and my burgeoning business came in second.

I introduced myself to the fortysomething hostess who greeted me at the door. Like me, she wore a tailored business suit, and I knew I had made the right choice. No cutesy summer dresses for this meeting.

"Miss Aubrey, welcome. Mr. Pomeroy is expecting you. I'll walk you to his office."

So far so good. No Edith in sight. (Bite my tongue).

We walked through a lovely atrium complete with a three-tiered classic French fountain and enough greenery to keep any landscaper busy for hours on end. Off to my left was a large dining area but since we moved so quickly, all I could do was catch a glimpse of the white tablecloths and fresh flowers.

Wend Pomeroy's office was dazzling, and I wondered how much of it was for show and how much for actual work. The French Provincial style would have dominated the room had it not been for Wend himself, who commanded a formidable presence. Tall, well-built with broad shoulders and a full head of dark wavy hair with a few wisps of gray, he would have been well-suited to the cinema had he not chosen to be a restauranteur.

"Miss Aubrey, Wend Pomeroy. Please take a seat."

He pointed to one of two floral wingback chairs near an ornate fireplace and sat opposite me. "Can I offer you anything? Iced tea? Water?"

"I'm fine, thank you."

"This is not a usual meeting for me, but as I mentioned over the phone, we are in the process of building a new restaurant in the Biltmore area. In fact, we've had good news from our legal team, and our Realtor this morning. The contract with the developer was signed. Sooner than expected I might add."

I nodded and smiled. "Congratulations."

Just then, I felt a slight draft on my neck followed by a raspy whisper.

"You're not going to sit there all afternoon gabbing about his new restaurant, are you? Get moving, will you?"

"You look somewhat surprised, Miss Aubrey. Is everything all right?"

"Uh, yes. Of course. I was just thinking about your new restaurant." *And how I can get rid of an annoying ghost before she mucks things up.*

Chapter Twenty-Two

I handed Wend the advertising flyer and broke into a well-rehearsed spiel I practiced while in the shower this morning. I told him about my venture and how I could augment his business when it came to specialized catering.

"Although I haven't seen your kitchen," I said, "I'm hopeful there would be an area for me to create the charcuterie boards. If not, I can do that in my shop and have a delivery service bring them here or to the event venue."

Wend held the flyer with one hand and rubbed his chin with the other. "Normally I'd thank you and send you on your way, but as I mentioned, things are going to be in flux for quite a while as we expand. Architect meetings, contractors, hiring. Bear in mind, this is not going to be just *any* restaurant. If you're familiar with the Biltmore area, you'll know that our new restaurant must be visionary."

Again, the cold air on my neck. "Get that blowhard to quit rambling and get to the reason you're here. The *real* reason."

"I understand, Mr. Pomeroy. Visionary and reputation go hand-in-hand. I was glad to see Savor in the Heights recuperated from that stinging review Edith Ellory gave it not too long ago."

How's that for getting to the point? And once again—Go Away!

Wend's face flushed and he shook his head. "Yes, indeed. It was quite dreadful but mercifully we had two other famed food critics that month and their reviews served to dilute Edith's. I shudder to think what could have happened had we not had the good fortune to attract renowned critics whose commentary evened things out. Not to speak ill of the dead, but when our new restaurant opens in less than a year, we'll be able to sleep easy knowing Edith Ellory isn't around to sour things for us. A toxic review like hers can destroy a restaurant in no time. Worse than a bad review on opening night for a Broadway show."

"I can imagine. Then again, your restaurant wasn't the only one that was trashed by her."

"We were fortunate. Unlike the master chef at The Flaming Pit in Scottsdale. That carpaccio remark of Edith's cost the man his job. Unlike us, there were no other reviewers to ameliorate the situation. The only thing the owner could do was fire the chef and do it immediately. It was either save the restaurant or go down in flames as the name suggests."

"How awful. Do you know if that chef ever found another job?"

"Sadly, no. None of the quality establishments would hire him. Last I heard, he was working for one of those mediocre chain restaurants that specialize in grilled meats."

I winced. "Getting back to the charcuterie boards, were you interested?"

"Oh, I thought I was clear. Indeed, I am. We've got an engagement party coming up in a few weeks. The bride's father is the CEO of a major manufacturing company in the valley. I'll have you provide a charcuterie board or two. We'll see how it goes."

"That would be wonderful."

"Patricia Milestone, our events coordinator, will be in touch." He glanced at the flyer. "Looks like I have all the information I need right here."

"Yes. The phone number for our shop and our email. Thanks so much. I look forward to hearing from you."

Wend moved forward in his seat and I followed suit. When we exited his office, the hostess approached him and said, "Excuse my interruption. Your brother-in-law called to let you know the bank transfer was received. He wanted me to inform you right away."

He nodded and thanked her as he walked me to the door. Then he said, "Family business. Sometimes it's more involved than my actual business." He pushed aside a PA speaker that sat on the edge of his desk and pointed to a gold-scalloped gallery picture frame that hung on the wall directly behind his enormous chair. "Quite the ménage, I'd say. The wife, our two daughters, my wife's brother and his partner, and our late uncle Curtis."

I squinted to get a better look and paused. One of the two men looked familiar, but I couldn't quite place him. Then again, lots of well-built, middle-aged men sported close-cropped beards. Especially if they had receding hairlines and wanted to move the emphasis elsewhere.

Unsure of what to say, I simply smiled before thanking him again. He opened the door and I let out the longest sigh of relief when it closed behind me. Not because I landed a job, or found out some rather telling news, but because for once, Edith managed to keep still.

A pinkish haze engulfed the interior of my car as I got in and buckled up. "You don't have to be so dramatic," I said. "Listen, I don't think Wend Pomeroy is your killer. He wasn't all that upset about your review since it was diluted by other ones. His words."

"I know. I heard him. He's almost as pompous as Imogen. They'd make a great pair."

"I'll tell you who I do think may have a motive—the master chef from The Flaming Pit. From the looks of things, you destroyed his career. His career! That's one heck of a motive for revenge."

"Then what are you waiting for? Let's track him down and get him to confess."

"I'm not the FBI. I don't even know where he is. Or *who* he is for that matter."

"The Flaming Pit would know. Make that your next stop."

"I'll put it on my list. Meanwhile, I intend to go home, have dinner, walk the dog, and unwind."

"You sound like an old woman. Are you planning to take an Epsom salt bath, too?"

"If it will keep you quiet, I'd take a bath in the Salt River." I glanced to my right and Edith was in the passenger seat. This time in a wide-skirted pink gown covered in rhinestones. She must have noticed my expression because she adjusted the skirt and said, "Recognize this?"

"Uh, no. Should I?"

"It was Mamie Eisenhower's inaugural gown. Pink peau de soie. French for silk skin."

"That was decades before my time. And how do you know it belonged to a former first lady?"

"Honey, that gown was plastered on all of the fashion magazines in its day. I'm not sure how it wound up on my back."

"I think I liked the gauchos better. Listen, about that chef who got the axe, maybe I won't need to pay a visit to The Flaming Pit. Maybe I can find a way to track him down by making a few phone calls. Of course, I have no idea what I'd say to him once I was face-to-face. I can't very well accuse him of murder."

"Not directly. You need to insinuate it. Use innuendo. Look him in the eye and say, 'I know about Edith Ellory.' Then don't take your eyes off of him. Make him uncomfortable. People always confess when they're uncomfortable. I call it 'pained silence.'"

"I call all of this *pained*."

I told Edith I'd pursue this latest lead if she'd agree to give me a night's peace but that wasn't good enough. For the next thirty minutes, our conversation played out like contract negotiations with the Teamsters. Somewhere between the 101 and Route 74 we struck a deal. Sort of. She'd keep out of my hair for twenty-four hours if I would track down that chef and "scare him into a confession." Her words, not mine.

We agreed to resume our dialogue the following night but at a reasonable hour. Thinking back, I should have insisted on an exact time because Edith's idea of reasonable was about as iffy as the wardrobe choices that were bestowed on her. Nevertheless, it was the best I could do.

"Today's the day the new sign gets installed on the front of our sandwich shop," I said to Speedbump bright and early Thursday morning as I refilled his water dish. He had already devoured his kibble and didn't appear too interested in the water. "From now on, it's The Char-Board. Anyway, I need to get a move on. It's already half-past five. I'd hate to keep Lilly-Ann and

Matt waiting out front, especially if the sign company shows up early."

With that, I rinsed out my coffee cup, grabbed my bag, and was out the door. This time I arrived before the employees. I knew I couldn't put it off much longer and would have to give an extra key to Lilly-Ann in case of an emergency. Given Matt's part-time college schedule, Lilly-Ann was the better choice. And if the charcuterie catering began to boom, I'd need all the help I could get, and at all hours.

Without wasting a second, I started the coffee machine and began the salad prep. Minutes later, Matt breezed in followed by Lilly-Ann.

Matt walked to the back sink and washed his hands. "Today's the day, huh? I can't wait to see the new sign. The old one is about as humdrum as they get. Hey, those small pizza-sized charcuterie boards took off like nobody's business yesterday. Word around here spreads fast, so I imagine we'll sell lots more today."

I stopped shredding the lettuce and looked up. "I hope so. Keep your fingers crossed. Oh, before I forget, it looks like we'll be catering an engagement party at Savor in the Heights sometime soon. Well, not catering in the full sense of the word, only supplying a charcuterie board or two. I'm not sure if they'll want us to prepare them here or work out of their kitchen but I'm hoping it's the latter. They'll let us know."

"Wow," Lilly-Ann said. "That's fabulous news. How'd you manage that?"

By tracking down the killer of an annoying ghost who lives at my house. "Um, uh, I took a chance and contacted the restaurant. I figured if I could get some high-end establishments to offer our boards, then word will get out."

Matt grinned. "Works for me. Geez, we'd better hustle, one blink and the customers will be here."

He wasn't kidding. I figured a third hand in the kitchen, namely mine, would make things run smoother but truth be known, there were some bugs to iron out. Specifically, who did what and when. I found myself bumping into Lilly-Ann and sidestepping Matt. I thought about creating one of those chore wheels I remembered as a kid, but quickly changed my mind. Lilly-Ann and Matt weren't third graders.

"Later today," I said, "we'll figure out who should do what. Last thing I want to do is be in your way. You guys are an amazing team."

Matt fist-bumped Lilly-Ann and they both laughed. "We'd never hear that from Mr. Kuss," he said.

The early morning raced by and sometime after ten the sign company arrived. They were able to set up their scaffolding so that it didn't block the front door, but the pounding and drilling didn't exactly make for the best eating experience. To compensate, I offered free coffees to all of our patrons. Thankfully the process took less than two hours and when they finally finished, I was in awe.

The design looked even more spectacular than it did on paper. With bright bold letters in shades of deep teal and yellow, coupled with a fantastic graphic of a charcuterie board, it was bound to attract customers. I took photos with my iPhone and sent them to Maddie as well as my mother. Then, I posted them on Facebook, Instagram, and Twitter.

"I take it this meets with your approval, Miss Aubrey," the contractor said as he handed me an invoice to sign.

"Absolutely."

"Wish every project went this smoothly. We've had three trips to Randolph's Escapade in the past two weeks because of issues with their new sign."

I cocked my head. "They didn't like the design?"

"Oh, they liked the design all right. It was theirs. What they didn't like was the angle and the way it looked when the sun hit it. As if we could move the sun. The worst part was when the owner told us it was more aggravating than some restaurant review they had gotten months ago from a witch of a food critic who passed away suddenly."

My gosh. That has to be Edith.

"Yeesh."

"Oh, it gets better." The contractor looked around before he spoke. "He said he needed a prescription for lorazepam after reading what she had written. Then one of his staff caught his arm and said, '*Suddenly* but not unexpectedly, huh? He immediately added, 'only kidding,' but I wasn't too sure. What the heck? I didn't even know who they were talking about."

No, but I do, and Randolph's Escapade is now vying with the former Flaming Pit master chef for first place in line.

Chapter Twenty-Three

I reeled from that new piece of information that had literally jumped into my lap, but I couldn't do anything about it at the time. It was lunch hour and the place filled up fast. Not only that, but the requests for the mini charcuterie boards were plentiful. I didn't want to get my hopes up, but maybe Matt was right. Maybe I did have a hit on my hands. Then again, it could have been beginner's luck, or in this case, something new for a curious lunch crowd. Only time would tell.

What I didn't expect was a full-blown catering request at twelve fifty in the afternoon. I had just cleared two mini-boards from a table of three when one of the women at the table asked if I could provide a large board for her upcoming bunco group next Friday.

"I know it's only a week's notice," she said, "but this is fantastic. Isn't it girls?" The girls appeared to be fifty or sixty-somethings, all impeccably dressed, with carefully styled hairdos.

"Is this local or out of town?" My voice had suddenly become a squeak.

"Oh, we all live here in that new development, Hidden Boulders. It's only a few miles from here," the woman said. Then she looked at the others at the table. "This will top those fondue bowls of Cherie's."

"What about Eulodie's tough-as-nails meatballs? I thought I'd break a tooth last time."

"And those mystery casseroles Deborah insists on serving?"

The women giggled as if on cue.

"Let me hand you a flyer that lists our boards and the prices. Of course, we can always customize. Since it's for a residence and not an entertainment

131

venue, it would be prepared here and delivered."

"That's perfect," the woman said. "I'm Deirdre Billings. I'll finalize everything with you when we're done with lunch if that's all right with my friends. It shouldn't take that long, should it?"

"I can get a general idea and we can fill in the details on the phone. How's that? You can pay by cash or credit card but we don't accept checks."

"No problem. Plastic works for me."

I all but danced my way to the kitchen, even if it meant adding extra hours to the following week. Then it hit me. I really did need to ask Lilly-Ann for her help and trust her with an extra key. Especially if I got caught up with my so-called investigation.

As I served customers, the word lorazepam stuck in my head. I knew it was some kind of anti-anxiety medication but beyond that, I was clueless. It didn't stick out like cyanide or strychnine, but it could make someone woozy enough to pass out long enough for the killer to deliver the final blow. Whatever *that* was. Too bad Edith had no recollection whatsoever.

It was quite possible she ingested it prior to the nightly walk she took if someone, aka the owner of Randolph's Escapade, slipped it into something she'd normally ingest. Upon her return, she could have passed out, making it really easy for him to commit murder. The only problem was there were no signs of foul play. Not overtly, anyway. No ligature marks. No bruises. No stab wounds. No gunshot wounds. No nothing. Only Cora's insistence Edith slept in her recliner and not the bed.

Given the normalcy of the situation, it was no wonder she was off to the coroner and the crematorium at breakneck speed with the cause of death listed as natural. Still, I questioned why no toxicology test was conducted. Aargh. I wasn't next of kin and would be given the brush-off from the coroner's office. Only the nephew could ask those official questions and evidently, he didn't feel the need to do so.

I had to work with what I had and so far, there were two new contenders—a toss-up for sure.

Two-prong approach, my you-know-what. I might as well offer up a pitchfork. More prongs. Or spikes in this case.

Too bad Edith drew a blank when it came to the timeline. But Colleen didn't. She was the last person to see Edith alive, other than the killer. The next person was Cora, a good twelve hours later. And from an exterior window. She pretty much gave me the rundown when we met at that coffee shop, but I felt as if she held back. After all, if she refused to tell the police that Edith chose to sleep in that Lift chair of hers, what was Cora holding back from me?

All the detectives on paper always start with the timeline. So, what was I doing monkeying around with a growing list of suspects? And while I definitely needed to have a few words with that spurned chef from The Flaming Pit, and Randolph's anxiety-ridden restaurant owner, I knew I had to get Cora to open up. Too bad another invite for coffee wouldn't cut it.

I took out my cell phone the second I rinsed off some dishes and placed the call to Cora before I lost my nerve.

"Cora Milbrand. What can I do for you?"

"Uh, hi Cora. It's Katie Aubrey. The renter at Edith's house."

"If you're having a problem with any of the appliances or something, you need to call the nephew. All I did was clean the place."

"That's why I called. I thought about what you said on Tuesday, and it turns out I could use someone to do a thorough job for me after all. My new business doesn't leave me much time for housework. And to be honest, I'm not so impressed with the professional cleaning service Edith's nephew hired before I moved in."

"Probably the Broom Ladies or worse yet, the Joyful Dusters. Cleaned a lot of places that used to hire them. Like I said, 'thirty dollars an hour.'"

"That's fine."

"When did you want me to start?"

"Well, today's Thursday, and I'm sure the rest of your week is booked, so maybe one afternoon next week for a few hours? It would have to be after 2:30 when The Char-Board closes."

"The Char-Board, huh? You didn't waste any time with the charcutee or whatever you call it business."

"Charcuterie. And the sandwich shop is still a go, we just added mini-platters and started up the catering end."

"I see. Give me a second. I need to check my book."

Matt approached the sink with more dirty dishes to rinse off. I stepped away and waited for Cora to return to the phone.

"Okay. I can squeeze you in on Tuesday but only for two hours or so. Or, you can have me for three to four hours the following week."

"Let's start with Tuesday. I don't want the place to get too dusty."

"It's Arizona. It'll be just as dusty a week later, but Tuesday's fine. I'll be there at three. How's that?"

"Terrific."

"Did I mention I get paid in cash?"

"Uh, no, but that's fine. See you then."

Cora ended the call without a word, and I must have looked perplexed because Matt asked if everything was all right.

"Sure. Fine. Just setting up a time for a housecleaner. I was able to get the same lady who cleaned for the former owner."

"Yeah, we heard about her. The owner. Not the cleaning lady. The paper said the old woman died peacefully in her sleep. Hope you replaced the mattress. Not that she was contagious or anything—was she?"

"I don't think so and yes, I bought a new mattress."

"At least she wasn't murdered in the house. That would freak me out completely."

Oh, trust me. It does.

"Not that it's any of my business, but I'd have her really vacuum the furniture and check for bedbugs. Lots of them in those college apartments."

"A professional cleaning service took care of the place before I moved in. This is only routine." *And please don't give me something else to worry about. Bedbugs. Ew!*

Matt shrugged and proceeded to rinse our salad bowls. It was a banner day by all accounts and I was glad I had the foresight to stock up on the meats and cheeses needed for the mini-boards. When I got home, there was no sign of Edith, but it was early. I changed into sweat shorts and a top, fed the dog, and took him for a quick jaunt around the block. Since I'd eaten a

134

late lunch, I wasn't at all hungry. Not for food anyway.

"Might as well make this a coin toss," I said to Speedbump as I flipped a quarter in the air. "Heads! We're starting with the recently dismissed chef from The Flaming Pit. Ugh. That means a phone call."

I was never a good liar. I'd either break out in a cold sweat or flush to the point where my face looked sunburnt. No wonder I always refused those invites for strip poker back in college. At least I wouldn't have to show my face over the phone. Only concoct a believable lie.

I retrieved the composition book that housed my murder map and located the timeline. Then I phoned The Flaming Pit before I lost my nerve.

"Hi! I'm hoping you can help me out," I said to the woman who answered the call. Her voice was chipper, and she sounded young. Maybe this would work after all.

"I'm a freelance writer in the area and I dined at your restaurant a few months ago. I was hoping I could interview the master chef who prepared my meal."

"How many months ago?"

I glanced at my notebook and told her.

The upbeat tone in her voice was gone. "I'm terribly sorry but Mr. Francatelli is no longer with us. Would you care to interview his replacement?"

I sighed and kept still for a second, but my pulse quickened. *Hallelujah! I've got the guy's name.* "The combination of spices was so extraordinary that it must be Mr. Francatelli. Do you have any idea how I can get in touch with him?"

"I'm sorry but we're not allowed to give out employee information. Confidentiality and all of that. But I understand. I was sorry to see him leave as well."

"I suppose that happens in the business. I guess master chefs aren't exempt from climbing the ladder as well."

"Climbing? In his case, he was pushed off. Oops. I shouldn't have said that. It just slipped out. Anyway, I don't suppose it's a secret. He was let go after the restaurant got a bad review from a prominent food critic. I wish I did know where Lucas wound up, but I don't."

Lucas Francatelli. Even better yet.

"Thanks anyway. I appreciate it."

"Um, before you go, our current master chef is quite good. She trained in New York and is quite conversant with the nuances of grilling. Make a reservation sometime. You may want to interview her."

"I'll keep that in mind. Again, thanks."

"Hmm," I said to Speedbump, "If I keep this up, I might be able to play poker after all."

Chapter Twenty-Four

I raced to my computer and realized in a matter of minutes that Edith wasn't the only ghost I had to contend with. Lucas Francatelli held a solid second place. The guy was nowhere to be found on Facebook, Twitter, Instagram, or even MeWe. I rationalized that few men keep up a social media presence, but one would think a noted master chef would at least have one outlet. Nope. Not in this case.

Forgoing any hope of finding him on social media, I thought perhaps I could google him. And while I perused a plethora of executive and hotel chefs, Lucas Francatelli was not one of them. As a last-ditch effort, I pulled up The Flaming Pit's website. Not that I expected to glean anything more than what my prior conversation with the receptionist offered, but I figured I might add to what little I already knew.

The website offered an array of menu photos in its gallery, but it also offered something else—an image of Lucas that no one thought to delete. I clicked on the photo and widened my eyes. No wonder the receptionist didn't want to see him go. The guy was drop-dead gorgeous. Standing over a grill in a white executive chef jacket, he appeared to be in his thirties. Clean-shaven with sandy hair, tall, well-built, and a smile that could, and probably *did,* melt hearts.

Please don't let this guy be Edith's killer.

Just then, the screen froze and the temperature in the room dropped. Edith's raspy voice was inches from my right ear, and I whisked her away with my hand.

"Don't let those good looks fool you. For all we know, that man could have the temper of a moose and the determination of one, too."

"Hi Edith," I said, refusing to look away from the screen. "Unfreeze this. You made your point."

Seconds later, the computer returned to normal, and I spun around. Edith was still in her Mamie Eisenhower getup, and I wondered how long that would last. It appeared as if she was enamored by it.

"Good. You found him. Now let's get him to confess."

"I found out what he looks like, but that's it. I have no idea where he works or where he lives."

"You're one of those millennials, aren't you? Sign on to a people search, for heaven's sake. And cough up the twenty bucks if it asks you. We haven't got all day. I've been eying a Jean Harlow dress and want it on my shoulders before the night is out."

I tried for the life of me to visualize Edith in a Jean Harlow dress but couldn't. At least she didn't mention wanting pencil-lined eyebrows and lips, the signature look of the late twenties and early thirties.

"I, um, er…"

"Just do it. Find Mr. Pretty-Boy-Fancy-Pants and let's get moving."

"It's a Thursday night. He's probably working somewhere."

"We'll never know, will we? If you keep stalling."

I rolled my eyes and googled people searches. Then I pulled up Spokeo and located the last known address for one Lucas Francatelli.

"I'll be darned. It's in Carefree. Near your former housecleaner, Cora."

"Doubt she knows him. I say you give him the once over. Worst case scenario, he's not home. If that's the case, leave one of those business cards of yours at his place with a note for him to get in touch. Write *personal* on it. That should get some results."

It was still daylight and since I wasn't hungry, I caved to Edith's request. Actually, her demand. Loud and clear.

"Fine, but this is going to be quick. I want to get it over with and make myself something to eat. Besides, I'm not so sure I can pull it off. Acting skills aren't my strength."

"Improvise."

I gave Speedbump a large doggie treat and headed out for yet another escapade on behalf of Edith. The drive was quick, and my GPS located Lucas's residence in no time. It was a condo on Mule Train Road and from the looks of it, quite a pricy one. Evidently, master chefs command a decent salary.

With a spectacular view of the mountains and lush greenery, I was in awe. The condos were Santa Fe style with flat roofs indicative of Native American architecture. I wasted no time parking my car in the lot out front and charging to his unit before I lost my nerve.

No sooner did I ring the bell, when a bald, middle-aged man with a small black dog in tow shouted, "If you're looking for Mr. Francatelli, you just missed him. He's headed to the airport."

I raced down the walkway and took a breath. "Do you know when he's expected back?"

"It could be days or weeks. He wasn't specific. Listen, if I were you, I'd forget about him. You're a good-looking girl, move on."

"I'm not—I mean, I'm here on business." Then I thought twice. *"Restaurant* business."

"My apologies. Usually, there's a steady stream of women coming and going."

"I'll just slip a card under his door," I muttered, and the man nodded.

"Have a nice evening."

Back in the car, I turned to the pinkish haze that was Edith. "Well, I guess that's it. I'll put Lucas on hold and see what I can do about Randolph's Escapade."

"Like hell, you will. You could be letting my killer fly out of here like a wasp leaving the nest. Sky Harbor Airport isn't that far, and the bald guy said Lucas left a few minutes ago. Step on it. Step on it."

"Edith, we don't even know where he's going or what terminal."

"Then ask. That man's dog is doing its business by those bushes. Pull over and ask him. He seems to have his nose in everyone's business."

Too tired to argue, I did as she said.

"Um, excuse me. Sorry to bother you again, but do you have any idea where Mr. Francatelli was headed?"

"Vegas. Southwest Airlines."

"Thanks. I appreciate it."

"See?" Edith said. "That wasn't so difficult, was it? Now step on it. Step! Step! Step!"

I swore if she wasn't an apparition, I would have shoved her out the door.

It was a good thing I was familiar with Sky Harbor Airport, having flown out on business for Chan-Tech many times. And Edith was right. It took me less than forty-five minutes to find a spot in their short-term parking and take the shuttle to Terminal 4 where Southwest Airlines was housed.

Having seen a photo of Lucas, I knew exactly who to look for. I only hoped he was still checking in and hadn't yet gotten through the TSA screening. Without a ticket, there was no way I could go beyond the checkpoint.

With bag drops and "self-tag" your bag stations, only one counter had a line, and I crossed my fingers Lucas was on it. Sure enough, he stood out like a Greek Adonis between a senior couple and a family with two sulky-acting teens. It was now or never because only a handful of people were in front of him.

I cursed Edith under my breath and made a mad dive past the rope-off to get to Lucas. Beads of sweat stuck to my hair and my hands were clammy. "Lucas Francatelli?" I asked, sounding more like a chirp than a question.

He turned and faced me. Cobalt blue eyes and all. What little moisture I had in my mouth evaporated in that second as I clenched my wrists and spoke, focusing on what Edith told me to say. "Thought you could get away with it. Boom! And it's all over. Well, I know what you did and what you're up to."

I thought I kept my voice low, but I suppose not, because in that instant, the senior woman in front of him turned and shouted, "The man behind me might have planted a bomb. A bomb! Someone check his luggage."

"A bomb! That man has a bomb in his luggage!" someone else screamed.

Suddenly the travelers at the check-in dropped their bags and ran to the exit.

"What the—" but Lucas never finished his sentence. Or the expletive that was probably on his lips. Out of nowhere, a security team that rivaled the crew on *NCIS: LA* raced over and pulled him aside. Luggage, too. I assumed the attendant at the counter activated a panic button.

And at that moment I prayed for a giant sinkhole. "This is a misunderstanding," I said but it was too late. They snatched the carry-on bag from his hands and commandeered the two pieces of luggage that were at his feet. Next thing I knew, they marched him across the sprawling lobby to a small door with a frosted glass panel.

"Wait!" I shouted, walking as fast as I could.

Lucas turned and glared at me. "I don't know who on earth you are, but I better not miss my flight."

"Please refrain from speaking," one of the security guards said. "And take a seat in the room."

With that, they ushered him inside and closed the door.

"I hope you're happy, Edith."

A cool breeze tickled my neck. "I will be if we can get a confession out of him."

"Take a number and stand in line."

"Are you speaking to me?" a woman asked as she pulled an enormous carryon behind her.

"Uh, no. Sorry. Thinking out loud, that's all."

She tossed her dark bangs from her forehead and kept moving.

"Now what?" I mumbled under my breath.

"I'll let you know. Just stay close to the door. You need to be near my aura." Edith disappeared and I was positive she slipped into the room with the frosted door.

It was impossible to not be conspicuous standing in front of a security office door. At least I thought it was a security office. With no signs, it was impossible to tell. I opted to sit on the metal bench adjacent to the door and wait it out. Ten minutes went by and the familiar Edith haze all but engulfed me.

"They rooted through his luggage and brought in a bomb-sniffing dog. That room opens up to an entire interrogation area. Now they're questioning him. Too bad you can't get inside and pick up some of their techniques. Then again..."

"Don't even think it."

But it was too late. Edith's burgeoning netherworld skills had taken off with a vengeance and she had mastered cutting the power supply. The lights went out in the lobby, and I heard someone call out, "What happened? The computers are down."

"Hurry up," Edith huffed. "Get in there and see how's it done. Sneak behind the room divider. It's a large screen. Move it! Move it! These places have backup generators and I'm not conversant with natural gas."

Thank goodness for small favors.

The words, *under the cover of darkness,* came to mind as I made a beeline for the room. Miraculously I got inside without being seen. I wasn't sure if Edith had mastered the art of unlocking doors or if the security detail didn't bother to latch it. No matter. I was behind the screen and listening to every word that came out of Lucas Francatelli's mouth.

And some of them would have taken the finish off of silverware.

What I noticed immediately was that the TSA officers asked him the same questions over and over again, varying them slightly. I figured they were hoping he'd slip up, but that never happened. Finally, they told him he was free to catch his flight and they retreated into the larger room. That left the two of us alone momentarily.

I gave the screen a nudge and stepped out.

Lucas recoiled the second he realized it was me. "You! What's this all about? Mistaken identity? What?"

Edith was right. The backup generator came on, but the lighting was dim. I clasped my hands together, all but cutting off the circulation, and took a step toward him. *Good grief. Even in the semi-darkness, this guy is hot.* "Edith Ellory destroyed your career. Tell me how you did it."

The guy didn't flinch. "Did what?"

"You know what. Tell me how you made her death look natural." I kept my gaze on him because apparently, that's an interrogation technique in and of itself.

CHAPTER TWENTY-FOUR

"What kind of lunatic are you? You think I had something to do with her death?"

I continued to stare, and it must have worked because he kept talking. "I'll admit it, that shrew cost me my job, but she didn't ruin my career. Far from it. And what's your interest anyway? Was she a relative?"

"Let's just say we were close and leave it at that. According to what I heard, you were incensed enough to run her over when The Flaming Pit gave you your walking papers."

"Who the heck wouldn't be? And for your information, carpaccio is enhanced by evenly sliced vegetables. And my dish certainly wasn't drowning in them, no matter what she wrote."

"Then why are you sneaking out of town?"

"Sneaking out of town? I'm one of the chosen contestants for *The Master Chef* in Vegas. If I win, I'll be the executive chef at Caesar's Palace. Edith did me a favor. I was hemming and hawing about leaving my position to compete, but her review made it easy for me."

Just then the lights came back on, and an announcement was made for all passengers to check the revised flight schedule.

"I've got to get moving." He slung his carry-on bag over a shoulder and with each hand, grabbed the luggage pulls from his matching Samsonite pieces. I followed him out the door and didn't say a word. When he was out of sight, Edith appeared, still in that Mamie Eisenhower gown.

"I don't think he's our guy," I said.

"Evenly sliced vegetables my patootie!" And with that, she left for the night, leaving me to make my own way to the shuttle, the parking lot, and home.

Chapter Twenty-Five

I wasn't sure if Speedbump was ecstatic to see me when I came inside or to get ahold of the giant bag from McDonald's. In any case, his tail wagged furiously and I reached in the bag to grab him a burger. "You're a good boy. And I'm a lousy investigator. If this keeps up, Edith will be here for eternity."

The dog devoured his treat in one gulp, and I tore into my Big Mac with the same fanaticism. I didn't even bother to get a plate. Only a bottle of Coke to wash it down along with the fries. "From now on, I'm doing things my way, beginning with whatever else is on that computer of hers. But not tonight. I've had more than enough of this for one night."

I plunked myself on the couch and watched the final three minutes of *Bull* before the nightly news came on. The tension in my neck had evaporated and the muscles in my body were no longer strained. Then, the news teaser came on and I stiffened up as if rigor mortis had set in.

"Close call at Sky Harbor Airport earlier this evening."

I winced and held my breath. It was worse than I imagined. Someone in the small lineup of passengers, most likely one of the sulky teens, recorded the entire scenario and sent it off to KPHO channel 5. It was impossible to miss me. Talk about a full-frontal view. Had I smiled, I'm sure a few fillings would have been visible.

I could be heard saying, "This is a misunderstanding," right before Lucas got dragged off and the small throng of passengers bolted for the doors. I snatched the remote and flipped to FOX 10 and they had the story as well. Another two flips and channels 12 and 15 were on it, too.

"This is horrible," I said to Speedbump. "Worse than horrible. Mom and Dad watch the nightly news before turning in."

I debated whether or not to call them and ultimately decided not to, in the oft chance they tuned in late. "I hope you're happy, Edith," I groaned, but there was no response. At least not from her. Seconds later the phone rang, and I was positive it was my mother.

"Katie! Was that you on the news? What the heck were you doing at the airport and who's the heartthrob?"

It was Maddie but words couldn't form in my mouth to explain, and everything came out garbled.

"I don't understand you," she said. "Are you dating him? Why didn't you tell me? What did he have in the luggage? Was he dealing drugs and you found out?"

Somehow, I got my voice back. "I'm not dating him. He's the former chef from The Flaming Pit. Just a slight misunderstanding about my charcuterie catering services, that's all."

I hated like heck to lie to my best friend but what was I about to tell her? That the resident ghost in the rental house she found for me is twisting my arm to find her killer?

"But why were you at the airport?" Maddie sounded genuinely perplexed. *Good question.*

"Um, there was a misunderstanding about my catering services and when I found out, I learned that the chef was on his way to Vegas for a competition, so I thought I'd clear things up before they got out of hand. Someone in the pre-check line misunderstood what I said to him."

"Oh brother. Guess you can cross him off your list for a possible date. He looked darn-right ticked."

"Yeah. You could say that."

"Give me a buzz this weekend. We'll catch up. Hey, I'd be careful picking up the phone tonight if I were you. If I saw the news, I bet your mother did."

"Ugh. Bite your tongue." *But at least I've got the party line nailed down.*

Maddie laughed and we ended the call.

"She's right, you know," I said to the dog. "Next call goes to voicemail or the answering machine. My money's on both. 'Leave no stone uncovered' is my mother's motto."

Either my parents were preoccupied, or they turned on the news after that segment had aired because I never got a call. I crept into bed at a little past eleven and was up with the roosters for Friday morning breakfast at The Char-Board.

Unfortunately, Lilly-Ann and Matt both caught the nightly news.

"It's none of my business," Lilly-Ann said, "but that was quite a scene at the airport last night."

Matt, who had just started up the coffee machine, tried to choke back a laugh. "Did you see the woman with the cane? She flailed it everywhere and cleared a path for herself out the door."

I shuddered. "Um, no. Not really. It was a misunderstanding with an area chef. No big deal."

Lilly-Ann motioned for Matt to get to work and whispered, "It won't affect that engagement party from Savor in the Heights, will it?" She bit her lower lip and waited for me to respond.

"No, a different situation altogether. Not a problem."

"Whew. Believe it or not, I've been reading up on charcuterie designs and telling everyone I know about your new business."

"That's great. Say, how about if you design a few of the mini-boards for today? It'll give you some practice and I'm sure you'll do great."

"Say no more. I'm on it!"

I started for the kitchen when my phone buzzed. *Drat! A text from my brother.*

Evan wasn't bad enough? Why R U chasing men at the airport?

I texted back. *Business misunderstanding. Not love life. Not a word to Mom.*

Seconds later, another text. *"Lucky she missed it."*

Thankfully the only drama we had that morning wasn't even ours. There was a minor fender-bender across the street and the entire cavalry came out. It didn't appear as if anyone was hurt, only aggravated given their body language when Lilly-Ann, Matt, and I peered out the door along with a handful of our customers.

"They either drive like maniacs on this road," one of them said, "or they window shop from their cars and don't pay attention."

Her friend bobbed her head. "Face it, Cave Creek is becoming a tourist destination. Next thing you know we'll be the next Scottsdale."

"I wouldn't go that far," another woman added.

The lunch crowd was larger than usual, and it kept up until two, making me wonder if I shouldn't expand the hours we stayed open. One thing at a time I told myself. It was barely approaching three weeks and I already had two catering jobs, both of which could become real business launchers. If that turned out to be the case, expanded hours at The Char-Board would be the last thing I needed.

Surprisingly, I hadn't heard from Edith and wondered if she wasn't otherwise occupied concocting another one of her nefarious little plans. Ugh. Nothing like waiting for a shoe to drop. Or in this case, a miserable apparition.

One shining light - I enjoyed a quiet evening taking Speedbump for a stroll and nuking a frozen dinner. The next day, Saturday, came and went, and still no sign of Edith. I did, however, get a phone call from Wend Pomeroy with the exact date of the engagement party. And no, it wasn't weeks away. It seemed he confused the date with something else. The engagement party was on a Saturday, only two weeks from tonight and he wanted something spectacular—a charcuterie board or two that would defy the imagination. Talk about pressure.

But it wasn't until the following day when I turned on the Sunday morning feature news for Arizona that I realized just how important Wend's reputation was. As I sipped my second cup of coffee and leaned back on the couch, I heard one of the anchors say, "Hold on to your seats, viewers, because an epicurean masterpiece is about to unfold in the Biltmore area."

The second I heard the word "Biltmore," I turned up the volume and listened intently to the morning host. "I'm sure many of our viewers are familiar with Fountain Hills' spectacular Savor in the Heights, but now, their owner, Wend Pomeroy, has embarked on a project that will bring the same elegance, taste, and vision to his soon-to-be-built restaurant in the Biltmore area. And frankly, the word *restaurant* won't come close to describing the vision Mr. Pomeroy has for this daunting project."

Next thing I knew, I was staring at artist sketches of a building that looked more fitting for Dubai than the Phoenix landscape. If that wasn't enough, Wend appeared in the studio to talk about the culinary masterpieces that would soon find their way onto people's palates. Yep, my charcuterie boards had better blow them away or it would be curtains for my burgeoning business.

I spent the rest of the morning creating my own sketches. From the traditional to the exotic, I would offer the hosts of that engagement party options like never before. It was a make-or-break opportunity for me, even if it had come as a result of a ruse to eke out information regarding Edith's demise.

Maddie always said "opportunity is where you make it, not take it," and I knew what she meant. Then why did I feel guilty focusing on my new enterprise rather than working out a coherent plan to find out exactly who was responsible for Edith's death? True, I wanted to rid myself of her annoying presence and her unceasing demands, but I had to admit, there was something about Edith that livened up the moment, even if it gave me indigestion. Funny, but in the past twenty-four hours, I noticed her absence with a certain amount of alarm. What if she wasn't coming back?

In retrospect, I should have known better. Driven personalities like Edith are ruthless when it comes to getting the job done. And apparently, I wasn't the only one who had to come to grips with her persistence and tenacity. However, I was the only one who had to deal with her in this realm.

Chapter Twenty-Six

I spent the rest of the day toggling between charcuterie boards and my murder map. And while I had narrowed down two potentially promising designs for the engagement party, and a handful of nifty options for Deirdre Billings's bunco group next Friday, I was nowhere near finalizing my approach for Randolph's Escapade.

Short of taking out a personal loan, there was no way I could afford to eat there. Not until my own business loans were on solid ground. As far as broaching the subject of charcuterie catering with Randolph's, I had already taken on more than I expected and didn't want to risk fouling things up altogether.

I put a big question mark next to Randolph's Escapade with every intention of figuring out how to question the owner without resorting to downright deceit. Of course, if Edith had her way, deceit would be the least of my worries.

I made myself a grilled cheese sandwich for dinner and washed it down with iced tea before settling on the couch for some much-needed channel surfing. That's when I smelled a horrific smokey order coming from the kitchen.

"Oh my gosh." I jumped from my chair. "Something's burning."

Convinced I might have accidentally left the burner on, I turned to face the kitchen and gasped. Thick black fumes were everywhere yet the smoke alarm didn't come on. I immediately opened the nearest window and began to fan the smoke. It dissipated slightly and morphed into an ugly brownish color. Speedbump looked up from his place on the rug and went back to sleep. Nothing was burnt on the stove and there was no sign of fire. The odor took on a sulfuric smell and I wondered if perhaps something went wrong with the HVAC system.

By now, I had opened three windows and was on my way to the front door when Edith's form appeared a few feet from me. *That explains the smoke and fumes.* Her hair was disheveled but that wasn't the half of it.

"Edith!" I shouted. "What happened? I thought you were after a Jean Harlow gown. You look like you stole something from Ethel Mertz's closet."

"The green stripes are hideous, aren't they? And the dress is frumpy with a capital F."

"I don't understand. Is that why there's black smoke everywhere?"

"It exemplifies my mood. Apparently, I ruffled a few feathers in the afterworld. Honestly, some spirits can be utterly vindictive."

"Uh, how long will you be wearing that dress?"

"Until they get over it. And *that* could be an eternity. No one's in a rush in the outer realm. That's why you need to hurry things along. I refuse to relive the drab and unimaginative nineteen fifties any longer than I have to."

"Um, I seem to have hit a snag with my approach to Randolph's Escapade."

"What do you mean, 'a snag'?"

I winced and bit my lower lip simultaneously. "I'm clueless."

"Thankfully, I'm not. This Wednesday, the Women for Greener Air will be holding their monthly luncheon at the restaurant. Don't you ever follow these things on social media? They're pushing for a law to mandate air-purifying plants in all Fountain Hills public buildings."

I opened my mouth and managed a shrill gasp.

"All you need to do," Edith went on, "is mill around while they gather for hors d'oeuvres in the outer lobby. Seamlessly blend in and chitchat. It's customary at those things. I should know. I've been forced to choke down some rancid-tasting appetizers while waiting for one symposium or another."

"Mill around?" I was incredulous. "What will that accomplish?"

"Honestly, Katie. Think! It's your chance to break away and coax the truth from Sterling Moss."

"Sterling Moss? That's the owner's name?"

"That's the current owner. Randolph Rinderknecht sold the restaurant in the late nineties. Forget social media, honey. You really need to learn how to use Google."

"What? I'm the poster child for Google. How do you think I located Lucas? And forget Google, if you haven't realized, I'm working on Wednesday. The Char-Board doesn't close until two-thirty."

"You're the boss. The boss! You can come and go whenever you want. Haven't you figured that out by now? And if you want that catering business to take off, that will mean you need to meet with future clients. Put that retired school employee in charge for the afternoon. Give her a title if it will make you feel any better. People love titles. Assistant charcuterie chef. How does that sound?"

"Scary."

"Learn to delegate. If you haven't noticed, it's an art I've perfected."

Oh. Is that what you call it?

"I'll iron out the details. Wednesday. Be ready by noon. The luncheon starts at one-thirty."

And like that, the black smoke evaporated, leaving only a foul-smelling mustard haze in the air.

"Can you believe it?" I asked the dog. "She wants me to hobnob with some wealthy ladies' group that doesn't have anything better to do than worry about purifying indoor air with plants. Okay, maybe I'm overreacting. The ladies' group is my ticket to Sterling Moss and if he's anything at all like Wend Pomeroy, I may seriously gag."

I went back to the couch and reached for the remote when the heavy hand of guilt washed over me. "Fine Edith! I'll google the guy."

At first, I thought I had typed something incorrectly because the image that popped up for Sterling Moss looked like Sir Peter Ustinov when he played Hercule Poirot. *Terrific. Another officious bugger to deal with.* I read the articles associated with Sterling Moss and my stomach tightened. Like Edith, he was a graduate of a prominent culinary school in New York and managed his family's foundation. Whatever that involved. Then I read further. The man had a penchant for beagles and worked with area agencies to foster and adopt the homeless hounds.

"I've got an 'in,'" I shouted to Speedbump. "Or should I say, *we* have an 'in.'"

Without wasting a second, I took photos of the dog the second he looked up. "I'll simply tell Mr. Moss I read about his beagle rescue and show him your photo. Then, I'll tell him I read the review Edith had written and hoped it didn't negatively impact his restaurant." *If I can even find a way to speak with him.*

Suddenly a number of ice cubes hit the kitchen floor. "Don't sweat it, honey. I'll make sure you speak with him."

Oh no! Do not tell me she can read my mind.

The next day, I took Edith's advice and asked Lilly-Ann if she could manage the sandwich shop on Wednesday afternoon. It was after the breakfast crowd left and we were in the kitchen washing dishes. Matt was out front wiping tables.

I mentioned something nebulous to her about a business meeting and marketing. I swear, the woman's smile couldn't have gotten any larger and she couldn't stop saying yes. I also mentioned needing to leave early on Tuesday since I arranged for a housecleaner.

"Any time, Katie," she said. "I love working here and frankly I'm chomping at the bit to learn more skills. As a teaching assistant, my focus was math support, so this is an entirely new thing for me. It's the hands-on I like. And the fast pace. It doesn't give me a lot of time to dwell on the fact my daughter and her family moved to Houston for her husband's job. They wanted me to relocate there but my home is in Arizona. Oh my gosh, I shouldn't be going on like this."

"It's okay. I'm lucky my family's in Chandler even though they can be really intrusive at times."

Lilly-Ann laughed. "That's what makes them family."

It was that moment I chose to give the spare key to her. "This business is going to succeed and expand. *Either that or I'll be back at Chan-Tech with my tail between my legs, heaven forbid.* That means, I'm going to need someone I can trust in my absence. I'm already getting pulled away with the marketing end of things." *And a murder to solve.* "Hold on a sec." I walked to the desk and took out the spare key from my bag. "Here, take this. And I'll pay time and a half if you wind up getting stuck here or opening early."

I expected Lilly-Ann to shriek for joy, but instead, she welled up and had to grab a paper towel to blow her nose. "I don't know what to say except that I won't disappoint you."

"I know. And that means I'll be able to sleep better at night knowing someone's got my back."

The next day and a half blew by, and I found myself hustling out of The Char-Board in order to let Cora into the house. I was positive the woman was a wealth of information when it came to Edith and some of that knowledge might give me a decent clue as to why Edith insisted she was murdered.

I had absolutely nothing to go on. Zip! Nada! Nothing! Not a shred of tangible evidence on Edith's body and no indication of forced entry. Even the coroner didn't waste any time. It was only Cora's insistence that Edith slept in her recliner chair and not the bed that made me question her death.

Like the amateur sleuths in all those cozy mysteries I read, I plodded along with the little I had—the names of restaurants whose reviews might have resulted in major business losses and a darned good motive for murder.

Sure enough, Cora arrived at my front door at three. Not a moment sooner. The second I opened the door she announced, "I begin with the bathrooms, and I bring my own supplies unless you're one of those people who insist on organic cleaners. Then you're on your own. I use my own vacuum, too, and I clean the bottom of the machine before it goes into another house."

Next to where she stood was a fairly new Shark vacuum and one of those multi-purpose cleaning supply caddies that I'd seen in hotels. She also had a mop bucket and one of those Cedar mops.

"Edith had me use my own cleaning products but like I said, if you want your own, I won't argue with you."

"That's fine. Come on it. You know where everything is so let me know if you need anything."

I figured I'd let her get started and then see if I could wheedle any more information out of her. With a quick nod, Cora put her cleaning supplies in the kitchen and took what she needed into the master bathroom.

"I always like starting from the back and working my way forward," she announced.

Not wanting to get in her way, at least for a little while, I told her I'd be out back with the dog. It was a perfect time for me to get caught up with my personal email and messages. Speedbump sniffed around the yard, and I fiddled with my iPhone. Between an offer from Verizon and a tandoori chicken recipe from a professional cooking site, I spied a message from Maddie. The subject simply said, "Yeesh," and when I read her note, I understood.

"Did you know Evan's in a relationship? I should have unfriended him on Facebook the minute he gave you the brush off, but I didn't give it much thought since he rarely posted. I unfriended him today when I saw a poolside photo of him fawning over a tall redhead with super long curly hair. Must be his preference in women, huh? I went to his profile page figuring he took advantage of a selfie opportunity, but lo and behold—the jerk's in a relationship. Her name is Via. What kind of name is that? Doesn't it mean road or something in Spanish? Anyway, call me when you get a chance. You're lucky to be rid of him."

I wasn't exactly bummed that Evan moved on, but so soon? And in a relationship? That lowlife must have been two-timing me while we were dating. Yeesh is right. Still, it did sting a bit.

I glanced at the other emails, and nothing required a response. "Come on, Speedbump," I called out, "let's see what Cora's up to."

When I got back in the house, the bathrooms were done, and she was in the kitchen. "If you want me to take out the dishes and clean the insides of the cabinets, I'll have to do it at another time."

"The shelves were pretty clean when I moved in, but I wiped them down with vinegar and Dawn to be on the safe side. Edith's nephew left a full set of dishes because it was too much trouble to sell them. He told me that the estate sale companies don't even like dealing with dishes. Anyway, I have a set of Corelle but if I ever have a big party, I'll be prepared. Um, speaking of parties, did Edith ever entertain?"

Cora dropped the sponge she was holding into the sink and looked up. "Edith? Entertain? Not likely."

"I ran into one of her neighbors the other day. A nice woman by the name of Colleen Wexby who works at the hospital. Colleen told me Edith took a nightly walk and that she had seen her the night before you, well, um, found her dead. She said Edith seemed perfectly fine."

"No kidding. If it walks like a duck and quacks like a duck, it's a duck. And that quacker was most likely murdered."

Chapter Twenty-Seven

"I'm afraid the coroner didn't concur, but I'm with you, Cora. I have a nagging feeling Edith's death was anything but natural. Colleen told me Edith and her next-door neighbor, Owen, went at it like a pair of fighting hens."

"The Neanderthal from hell? I caught that show on more than one occasion. She told him if as much as one little itty-bitty gram of pesticide got in her yard, she'd turn him into a eunuch. Could be he wanted to make sure that didn't happen."

"Think she could have let him in the house that night?"

"Not unless she was holding a Smith and Wesson. Nope, not a chance. I'm going to start vacuuming now. Then I'll mop. Those cleaning services do a surface job when it comes to picking up a vacuum. They'll do the floors all right but forget about the furniture. Not me. I use the attachments and get under all the cushions and sidearms. You'd be surprised what I pick up. Usually dried up foods like raisins and chips. Sometimes wadded up tissues that clog the machine."

"Um, great. I'll be at my desk if you need me."

The hum of the vacuum wasn't exactly conducive working at the computer, so I grabbed my iPhone and shouted to Cora that I'd be on the back patio. Then, I phoned Maddie to ruminate over the email she sent me.

Her voice was louder than usual when she took the call. "I know it's cliché but you're better off without him."

"How did you know it was me?" I asked.

"Caller ID, dummy. Hey, I shouldn't have sent that in an email, but I was pressed for time."

"It was good that you did. It gave me time to let it sink in."

"Evan is a stinker, you know. And I'm not just saying that to make you feel better. Maybe you can smooth things out with that hunky chef from the airport."

"Not in this lifetime. Besides, I'm on a hiatus from men."

"Is that what they call a slump?"

"Very funny."

"Listen, when is that grand opening for your new sandwich shop and charcuterie business? I don't want to miss it."

Oh my gosh. Neither do I.

"I haven't set a date yet. So far, this has been a soft opening with tentacles."

"Tentacles?"

"Uh-huh. I added mini-charcuterie boards to the menu, and not only did they take off, but I'm catering a bunco party and an engagement party. Well, the engagement party was sort of self-initiated, but still..."

"Katie, that's wonderful. It hasn't even been a month. Let me know what you need for your grand shindig. I wouldn't wait too long if I were you. We'll have to catch up later. I've got two back-to-back appointments. Condo properties in Tempe. A hot market."

"Hot and pricey. Good luck. And don't fret over breaking the news about Evan. I would have found out one way or another."

Evan was the least of my concerns. I couldn't believe I'd forgotten about the grand opening for The Char-Board. I told Suzette from the ad agency that I'd let her know the specifics and she said "no rush." That was over a week ago. I fumbled to pull up her number on my list of contacts and held my breath.

"Suzette? It's Katie Aubrey."

"Katie! I was about to call you this afternoon. You must have read my mind. Have you decided on a date for your grand opening? Also, I need to know when we can send a photographer to take some shots of your custom platters. Don't worry if it's only one or two charcuterie boards. Like I mentioned earlier, we can infuse public domain photos and artist designs into the catering menu flyer you requested. I know you're using a handmade one for now."

"That's a relief. I've been so busy with the start-up that I haven't settled on a date. Worse yet, all sorts of little things took up more time than they should have." *Like an amateur murder investigation without evidence.*

"No worries. I can work around your schedule."

"Good. Because this Friday night I'll be catering a bunco party in Cave Creek. Maybe you can send a photographer to my shop in the late afternoon to snap some photos."

"Not a problem. We're going to be right down the road at that new custom-made furniture shop to photograph some of their designs. We'll pop over between four and five. Does that work?"

"Perfectly."

"By the way, what's your plan for the grand opening?"

"I envisioned a charcuterie day with all sorts of platters for customers to sample and promo menus with photos and prices. Maybe a few giveaways for mini char-boards and one grand prize winner for a standard board, redeemable within the next six months."

"Sounds good. Giveaways always pull people in. With that in mind, I'll get a promo going for you. Let me know the date ASAP."

"I will. Thanks, Suzette. You're a lifesaver."

Speedbump ambled over to where I sat and put his head on my knee. I gave his ears a good rub and rolled my eyes. "I can't believe I totally forgot about the grand opening for my own business. What kind of budding entrepreneur does that make me?"

The dog leaned in closer for more rubs and I continued to pet him. "Well, I guess we'd better see how Cora's faring, although I doubt she needs my help with anything." I got as far as the door and could still hear the hum of the vacuum. "No sense going back inside," I told the dog, "I might as well make this a banner afternoon and call my mother. Geez, I promised I'd have her and Dad over for dinner once I got the sandwich shop going and got settled in. Good thing I wasn't specific."

My mother's usually chipper voice was even more ecstatic when she heard mine. "Oh sweetheart, it's good to hear from you. Every time I told your father I was going to give you a call, he said, 'Give the poor girl a break. She's probably up to her elbows with work. Text her if you must.'"

I laughed. "Dad was right. It's been exhausting. The good news is that my employees are fabulous and—Can you believe it? – I got two catering requests already. One is for a bunco game and the other for an engagement party at Savor in the Heights."

"Savor in the Heights? How on earth did you manage that?"

"Sheer determination." *And not for the charcuterie boards.*

"I'm sorry if I didn't have confidence in you. It's just that, well, I've always been one of those low-risk people. I'm glad you didn't inherit those genes."

"I inherited all the right stuff. Hope you don't mind, but that dinner I promised you and Dad will need to wait a bit. I'm still—"

"It can wait as long as you need. We understand how stressful moving is, not to mention starting a new business. Maybe we'll meet for dinner in a week or so. As long as it's not Savor in the Heights. Who can afford that?"

"The same people who'll be able to afford their new restaurant in the Biltmore area."

"Either the owner must have an untapped source of wealth, or a long, long list of backers. I caught the tail-end of a news segment."

"Me, too. If my charcuterie board is a hit, I might be in the black by year's end."

"I know you're independent, but if you need any support, financial or otherwise, pick up the phone. Okay?"

"Okay, Mom."

When I ended the call, I was relieved I didn't have to add one more thing to my already overflowing plate. Not until I wiped it clean. Or at least cleared out some space.

By the time I said goodbye to my mom, Cora had finished vacuuming. The only sound coming from the house was a high-pitched whistle to the tune of "Take Me Out to the Ball Game."

"How's it going?" I called out.

Cora replied from the other end of the house. "You've got a full canister of dust and dirt. I told you those companies don't do deep vacuuming. By the way, I felt something under the front closet door when I vacuumed so I opened it and found an eyeglass lens wedged underneath by the hinges. No wonder it didn't open all the way. The door was fine last time I was in the house. It's where Edith kept her special lamb's wool duster. Has to be your lens since she only used readers and her lenses were small and narrow."

"Not mine. I have contacts. And my sunglasses are those huge wrap-around kind."

"See for yourself. I put it on the counter next to the toaster."

I walked into the kitchen with the dog trailing behind me and stared at the lens. It was more square-shaped than rectangular and had to have popped loose from its frame. I couldn't see any tiny holes, indicative of a wire-rimmed design, like John Lennon glasses, so I went with my first hunch—the lens hadn't been properly secured in its frame. I should know, having lost a few sunglass lenses that way.

Thinking I might glean more from its prescription, I went to grab it and suddenly stopped short. "Cora!" I shouted. "Can you come in here for a minute?"

"I'm six feet away. Not six hundred. I finished mopping the back of the house and I'm working my way to the front."

"Uh-huh. Listen, about the lens you found, you didn't get your fingerprints on it, did you? That lens may turn out to be the first piece of tangible evidence regarding her death."

"Harrumph. When I find things on the floor, I pick them up. I don't go around thinking they might be evidence in a murder. By the way, when's that nephew of hers going to repaint this house? Usually, that's what they do when new tenants move in. Or when the paint starts to peel. Whatever comes first. In this case, it's a toss-up."

"What do you mean?"

"Look at the sides of the closet where I found that lens. I wouldn't have noticed right away if I wasn't up close and personal. The paint is chipping on both sides midway up the door frame."

I walked to the closet door, opened it, and took a good, hard look. Sure enough, the white paint had peeled off on the edges midway up the door, leaving a hideous dark beige color in its place. Not that it really mattered, since I kept the closet door closed, but still…it was time for a refresher.

"Edith's nephew told me he'd get the house repainted in a few months."

"I'd tell him to narrow down the timeframe for you."

My gosh. She sounds like Edith. What is it with these women?

I eyeballed the doorframe again and tapped my teeth. A bad habit I had since middle school. Especially when I was stymied. "Cora, what if Edith opened the door and the person on the other side caught her off guard and killed her? Quite possibly they might have struggled by the closet door and the lens in the killer's glasses came loose. That would explain the paint chips midway up the door."

Cora looked at the closet and shook her head. "Seems to me the struggle would have started at the front door." To prove her point, she flung the front door open and looked. "Hmm, paint's fine here."

"That's because the killer got inside. Then Edith might have opened the closet door to get something to fend them off. You know, like a golf club, or a can of bug spray."

"Edith didn't golf."

I did a mental eye roll. "I'm just saying."

"Okay, okay. I suppose that makes sense. She could have fought them off by the closet door but how did they kill her if no evidence was on her body?"

"Chloroform over her mouth?"

"You'd need a gallon of it. They couldn't even kill the cat with it in *I Remember Mama*, but you're too young to have read it. Or seen the movie."

"I saw it. Black and white on Turner Classic TV. As I recall, they knocked out the cat but didn't kill it. Maybe that's what happened. Whoever it was, knocked out Edith but she wasn't as lucky as the cat. They had to have rendered her unconscious in order to do the deed or there would have been signs of a struggle."

"No sign when the body was found, but that doesn't mean the killer didn't pick up after himself. Or herself."

"No sense worrying about fingerprints on this lens," I said as I picked it up and held it in front of my eyes. "On second thought, the marshal's office would pooh-pooh my theory. By the way, it's a progressive lens. A bifocal. My father has these. Now all I need to do is find out where it came from."

"Let me know how that works out for you. Face it, you're not going to bring her back. You'd be spitting in the wind." She turned to resume her mopping and then turned back to face me. "Then again, no one deserves to die without justice."

"Are you saying you're interested in finding out where the lens came from?"

"I'd be interested in finding out what *you* find out. I'm not the one who has to sleep in this house, you are." She moved the mop around for a few more seconds and paused. "If the books I dusted on your shelf are any clue, you're a mystery reader."

"Huh?"

"What I'm saying is that you should figure out who crossed paths with Edith recently. Too bad that giant wall calendar of hers probably wound up in a landfill."

"Would she have put that information on her computer?"

Cora pursed her lips and made a sharp smacking sound. "Maybe. But a lot of good that's going to do you. Most likely the computer's sitting next to the calendar under mounds of compressed garbage."

Nope. It's sitting in the back of my closet. With a blanket draped over it.

She resumed her mopping but kept talking. "There's bound to be a busybody on this street. Every neighborhood's got one. Figure out who it is and ask them what they know about Edith's sudden death."

I may be one step ahead of you already.

"I'll, uh, keep that in mind."

Cora finished her cleaning and I had to admit, the house absolutely gleamed. I made an arrangement with her to clean twice a month and for the first time since we met, she smiled. Well, maybe not a big, wide smile but more like an upturned curve on the side of her lips. Still, it beat the usual scowl.

Chapter Twenty-Eight

I couldn't drag the computer out of the closet fast enough the moment Cora got in her car and drove off. Not that I needed her to prod me along. Edith was doing a bang-up job on her own. What I needed was to find her schedule and narrow down the timeline of her death. In one of the mystery series I read, the author referred to it as the post-mortem-interval, but those words sounded way too clinical for me.

"You won't find anything on the computer if you're looking for a calendar." It was Edith's raspy voice, but she was nowhere in sight. A faint orangey haze appeared in the kitchen as I looked around. "I kept a big calendar on the wall like most normal people. What was I supposed to do? Log on to the darn computer every time I needed to check on an appointment?"

"I was hoping to find a timeline or any indication of who you were in contact with prior to your death."

"You mean, *my murder.*"

"Fine. Your murder. You know, you're not making this any easier with that lapse of time thing going on. Are you sure you can't remember anything?"

"Of course I'm sure. I'm dead, not senile."

The orangey haze dissipated, and Edith stood a few feet from me clothed in a polka-dotted orange and white shirtwaist dress. Still stuck in the late fifties or early sixties.

"Don't you dare mention this outfit," she said. "I should have things cleared up by tomorrow so that I'll look, shall we say, a bit more fashionable when we arrive at Randolph's Escapade."

Another mental eye roll on my part. "No one can see you. Only me. I'm the fortunate one."

"It's a matter of pride. And by the by, Cora had it right about the neighborhood busybody."

"You were here all along?"

"Someone had to make sure she didn't cut corners. You were too preoccupied making phone calls. Cora was also right about that eyeglass lens. Google Imogen. There must be scads of images for that she-witch. See if any of them show her in glasses that have that kind of lens."

"We've been through this before. I seriously doubt she's your killer. And she didn't wear glasses when we saw her."

"I'm not crossing her off my list. Oh, and be sure to put on one of your best business suits for that luncheon. Even if they are a bit stuffy."

"Yeah, about that luncheon...what plan did you have for me to chat with Sterling Moss? Edith? Edith?"

Too late. Along with the remnants of the orange haze, Edith vanished, leaving me staring at the computer screen. Speedbump sauntered over to the table and rubbed his head against my knee. "I know, I know. You're probably hungry. But thankfully not as demanding as our resident ghost. Give me two or three minutes to google Imogen so I can tell Edith I was right."

The dog continued to rub my knee, so I did my computer search onehanded. I must have eyeballed at least two dozen shots of Imogen, and none of them showed her wearing glasses. Funny, but her image never varied even though the photos encompassed the past decade. Photos that depicted a pencil-thin brunette with short, frizzy hair, bright red or coral lipstick, and large, round stud earrings.

"She looks exactly the same as she did that night Edith and I got into her house," I mumbled. Then something clicked. "Oh my gosh. That's the same description Lilly-Ann and Matt gave me about the customer who told them Edith's house most likely had bad energy. Yikes. That woman was Imogen. It *had* to be."

The more I thought about it, the creepier the situation got. Why on earth would Imogen Brodeur traipse all the way over to Cave Creek in order to leave a message for me. And how did she know I was the new tenant in Edith's old house? Maybe Edith *did* know her better than I thought and maybe I was a bit too eager to dismiss Imogen as a possible murderess. Still, none of her photos showed her with glasses.

"Okay, dog," I said. "Enough with computer searches. I've got to leave a detailed list of must-dos for Lilly-Ann tomorrow so I can play 'catch a killer' with Edith at a swanky restaurant."

Like a new parent writing detailed instructions for the babysitter, I did the same for Lilly-Ann and Matt even though I knew it was overkill. At least it absolved me from some of the guilt I felt leaving The Char-Board in their hands as I attended to other matters.

Since Cora wouldn't be returning for another two weeks, I left the computer on the table just in case I had another epiphany. Then I took Speedbump for a walk before returning home to prepare a pasta salad with tuna for dinner.

One would think I'd be used to stepping into awkward situations given my brazenness with Wend Pomeroy and Lucas Francatelli, not to mention my sheer idiocy when I snuck into Imogen's place. Still, I was jittery and unsettled at the thought of mingling with The Women for Greener Air.

For one thing, I hadn't a clue as to what I could say, other than the usual banalities about the environment and global warming. And while I was tech-savvy and knew my way around the business world, something told me I'd need a whole new skill-set for that luncheon. I could only pray Edith would hasten things along so I could duck out and have a face-to-face chat with Sterling Moss.

Needless to say, I had a horrible night's sleep culminating with a dream that had me tossed out of Randolph's Escapade while my ex-boyfriend made out with the hostess. When morning came, I needed two cups of coffee to pry my eyes open and form intelligible words.

I knew I'd never appear perky but with sufficient undereye makeup and an extra dab of blush, I managed not to look like death-warmed-over when I opened the doors to The Char-Board the next day.

Lilly-Ann pulled me aside almost immediately and told me not to worry, everything would be fine in my absence. Three hours later I gave Speedbump a treat, changed into one of my classier suits, and took off for Randolph's Escapade.

At least this is the last restaurant Edith scorched. I don't know how many more charades I can pull off.

With slow and methodical breaths, I drove straight to Paradise Valley telling myself I could blend in with the air-purifying women *and* eke out information from Sterling Moss. All I had to do was refrain from making any accusations. Simple enough. Except for the wild card who, hopefully, had ditched the orange polka-dotted dress.

Randolph's Escapade sat high in the Camelback Mountains off of East McDonald Drive in Paradise Valley and not too far from Wend Pomeroy's soon-to-be-built extravaganza in the Biltmore Estates.

If nothing else, I was certainly getting acquainted with the upper echelon of dining establishments. It was difficult to keep my eyes off of the spectacular mountain views as I navigated the flowing driveway that led to Randolph's. Edith must have smoothed things out with the forces-that-be because she no longer looked like a cast member for *Annie.*

"It's not the Jean Harlow gown I wanted," she said, "but it'll do. Recognize it?"

I glanced to my right and shook my head. "No, should I?"

"Myrna Loy wore this in the opening scene of *The Thin Man.* You really should become better acquainted with classic movies. Then again, maybe it's best you're not familiar with that scene."

"Uh-huh." I had no idea what she was talking about, but in retrospect, I should have pressed further. Truth be known, I was too worried about whatever she had in store once we got inside. For a ghost who couldn't stop yakking, Edith was oddly quiet about her intentions. Then again, maybe I wasn't listening.

As I approached the modern structure with its glass panels and breathtaking masonry, a lump formed in my throat. "This place takes my breath away." When a valet greeted me, I could almost hear Maddie say, "Ka-ching.

Ka-ching."

Taking a deep breath, I strode to the entrance where an usher opened the door and directed me to the hostess.

"Find out who designed her dress," Edith whispered in my eye. "It's a must-have."

"Shh!" I don't know why I shushed her since I was the only one who could hear her, but it was more of a reflex action.

"Beg your pardon?" the petite young hostess asked.

"Sorry. Clearing my throat. I'm here for the Women for Greener Air Luncheon."

"It's in the bougainvillea room off to your left. Just past the koi pond. You can't miss it."

"Thanks."

I wasn't a member. I didn't have an invitation, and I was positive I would be booted out of there within seconds. *If* that long. However, I should have known Edith would have other plans. I felt a pull on the shoulder of my blazer and enough force to turn me around.

"The clean-air women or whatever you call them are only a ruse. Come on, we're headed to Sterling Moss's office. It's past the bougainvillea room on the right. Behind those enormous wooden doors." Before I could argue, the force that spun me around shoved me down the corridor without giving me a second to think.

Terrific. I am going to slam right into those wooden doors and get a concussion. Nice work, Edith.

I took a breath, closed my eyes, and next thing I knew, I stumbled into Sterling's office and landed on the floor. With my arms outstretched and my bag sailing under his enormous mahogany desk, I wanted to throw myself off the nearest cliff. It would have been an easier and less humiliating experience.

"Good heavens!" Sterling announced, looking more like Hercule Poirot than the actors who were paid to portray him. He stood and thundered toward me, his large girth knocking into a side table causing a potted plant and a framed photo to crash on the tile floor.

I will never be able to show my face in this state again.

"I, um, er—" but I never got to form a complete sentence. Or any sentence for that matter. Sterling's shoe caught on the leg of his desk and within seconds, he was face down in what would have been a spectacular bellyflop had he been in a swimming pool.

The framed photo landed inches from me and I picked it up as I stood. "I'm so sorry," I finally managed to spit out. "Can I help you up?"

"No need. I'm fine. Good thing I had cataract surgery last year or I might have broken a pair of glasses. I take it you survived the fall as well." He brushed off his dark slacks and straightened his tie. Up close, he appeared to be in his early fifties and was much heavier than the Belgian detective I'd seen on screen. And unlike the fictional detective, Sterling's dark mustache didn't curl up so noticeably. I handed him the framed photo, positive my cheeks were beet red.

"Thank you." He glanced at the photo and turned it so that it faced me. "Montgomery, my beagle. He passed away a year ago at age fifteen."

"Aw, I'm sorry. He looks so sweet. I've got a beagle, too. Speedbump. Hold on a second." I dove under the desk, retrieved my bag, and tapped my cell phone to reveal one of the zillion photos I took of the dog.

"Purebred?"

I shook my head. "I wouldn't know. He showed up at my doorstep when I moved to Cave Creek a few weeks ago. No one claimed him so I adopted him." Without wasting a second, I proceeded to scroll through Speedbump's album making sure the pictures were eye level with Sterling.

"Nothing like a beagle and from the looks of things, yours is quite contented."

"Quite spoiled at this point. He's even taken over my bed."

Sterling smiled and offered me a chair. "Would you like something to drink? Water? Iced tea? Lemonade? Fountain drinks? I don't know about you, but that fall took the breath out of me. I'm not getting any younger."

"Water or iced tea would be wonderful. Thanks."

He picked up the phone on his desk and asked for a pitcher of iced tea with two glasses. Then he tilted his head. "Cave Creek, you said? Quirky little town. I was there not too long ago on a business matter. I went to see a restaurant reviewer who gave Randolph's Escapade a scorching review. The only one who made out like a bandit was my gastroenterologist who raked it in from my resulting indigestion and anxiety. Oh goodness. I can't believe I'm going on like this. It must be from the fall, only I didn't hit my head."

"Go for the jugular. Go for the jugular," Edith ranted from across the room. She draped herself on his desk leaning her hazy head against an elbow. "Ask him if he murdered me."

Chapter Twenty-Nine

I turned my head away from Edith and widened my eyes. "I'm renting a house that used to belong to Edith Ellory. Her nephew owns it now. That's not the reviewer you went to see, was it?"

Sterling nodded. "That's the old crone all right and I don't use that term lightly. One stroke of her pen, or should I say, 'tap on her keyboard' and next thing I knew, we were riddled with cancellations. So I did the only thing I could."

Edith literally flew off the desk and landed right behind Sterling. "I knew it. I knew it. He killed me. Get the confession in writing. No, better yet. Ask him again and record it on your phone when he's not looking."

"What was that?" I bit my lower lip and hoped he didn't notice how tightly clenched my fingers were.

"I went to her house, asked if she'd consider doing another review in the next week or so but the miserable battle-axe slammed the door in my face."

"And then what?"

"What more could I do? I drove back to Paradise Valley to lick my wounds. I suppose I could have forced my way inside her house and refused to leave until she listened to me but I'm not that sort of person. What was done, was done."

At that moment, a server came in with two pitchers of different iced teas and a small tray of assorted butter cookies.

"Don't be so impressed by the tea and cookies," Edith huffed, still standing behind Sterling. "It's cheaper than a lawsuit if you claim the floor was slippery."

"Peppermint or regular?" he asked.

"Oh, peppermint for sure."

Sterling handed me a glass and pointed to the butter cookies. "That fall must have knocked my senses out as well. Forgive me. As you've most likely surmised, I'm Sterling Moss, the owner of Randolph's Escapade. Not to be confused with Stirling Moss, the racecar driver. Only his name is spelled with an I and not an E."

"Katie Aubrey, former manager at Chan-Tech and now the owner of a burgeoning charcuterie business in Cave Creek, The Char-Board."

"Is that what brought you here? Introducing your charcuterie enterprise?"

"Actually, I was interested in what the Women for Greener Air were all about but apparently I landed at the wrong doorstep."

Sterling laughed. "They're all about being bored and needing something to do. My sister is on the board. I should know." Then he put a finger over his lips and laughed. "Don't say a word."

There was something so inviting, so refreshing, and so comfortable about Sterling that I couldn't imagine him having anything to do with Edith's death. Plus, he mentioned cataract surgery so that eyeglass lens couldn't possibly be his.

I smiled. "You may have saved me from a long-winded luncheon." I handed him my card and invited him to visit my little sandwich shop the next time he stopped by Cave Creek. Then, as I was about to leave, he said, "Shrew or not, Edith Ellory appeared to be in perfect physical health. I found it odd she was found dead of natural causes a few days after my attempted conversation with her."

I swallowed the sip of tea I'd taken and widened my eyes. "Are you thinking foul play?"

"I'm no detective but something's off. Murder isn't always transparent."

I thanked him for his hospitality and bolted out of there before Edith had a chance to wreak havoc with whatever ludicrous idea popped into that ghostly head of hers at the last minute. It was only when I was seated behind the wheel of my car that I began to relax.

"That was a total waste," Edith muttered. "Unless he did poison me."

"What are you saying? How?"

"I always make sunshine tea and I put the glass jug in front of the house on the porch. Maybe Sterling laced it with something. Too bad I don't remember bringing it inside or anything else right before I was shipped off to well...you know."

"What was the last thing you remember?"

"Talking to my nephew about my will."

"Your call or his?"

"Mine. And it's a good thing I decided to put my affairs in order, or the darn house would have gone into probate for Maricopa County. My nephew would have been on social security by the time that was settled."

"What about the little things? Like what you ate? What you watched on TV? You know, everyday stuff."

"Honey, I couldn't remember that on a good day. Once you reach a certain age, life becomes impressionistic, not realistic."

"Well, if the timeline for your death clears up, let me know, will you? So far we have a plethora of suspects and one eyeglass lens. Even Sherlock Holmes would be pulling his hair out."

"You're not giving up, are you?"

"No, but I've got to focus on those charcuterie boards. Deirdre's get-together is one thing, but that engagement party can be a deal-maker."

"I still say Imogen is not off the hook."

"Enough with Imogen. Let it go."

Seconds later Edith evaporated. Just like that. I drove home mulling over the situation and muttering to myself. While Imogen and Edith certainly had their issues, there was no way I could prove Imogen poisoned my ghost. Even if her restaurant kitchen had castor beans on the shelf.

As for Lucas Francatelli, he was on his way to possible culinary stardom in Vegas, something he would not have considered had he remained at The Flaming Pit. Then there was Wend Pomeroy, family man and entrepreneur. He brushed off Edith's review like dandruff on a shirt, insisting it was mollified by the other reviews Savor in the Heights received.

Today's unannounced interview with Sterling Moss gave me no indication

172

the man would ever consider something as heinous as murder in order to salvage the reputation of his restaurant. Besides, Randolph's Escapade seemed to be doing just fine.

That left Edith's neighborhood, but I seriously doubted someone would do her in because she put a note on their recycling bin or asked about their private bedroom habits. Intrusive, yes, but not rising to the occasion of murder. Unless of course, the situation between her and pesticide aficionado Owen Jasper next door was more toxic than Colleen Wexby thought.

But pesticides? Not something easily disguised in food or drink. Still, it was worth a look-see. Not as if I had many options left. And while I was at it, I could take a very close look at his glasses. *If indeed,* the guy wore them. I was curious, that's for sure, but I wasn't crazy. Last thing I wanted to do was knock on his door. No, I had to find a way to unobtrusively bump into him. Preferably in daylight. In front of lots of people. Good luck with that.

It was late afternoon, and I was famished. The lovely butter cookie I ate at Randolph's Escapade didn't get me too far. As soon as I got out of my business attire and into grubby sweats, I moseyed into the kitchen, took out a bagel from the freezer, nuked it, toasted it, and made myself a cream cheese and jelly sandwich, something I hadn't eaten since I was a kid.

Speedbump nuzzled my knee, and I gave him a taste of the cream cheese. The silly beagle couldn't stop licking his tongue, so I gave him another bite before taking out his food dish and feeding him the usual fare.

"I've got to figure out a way to bump into Owen next door," I told the dog, "but in the meantime, let's see if he's got anything going on social media." With my iPhone in hand, I pulled up Facebook, Twitter, and Instagram, not really expecting the man to show up on any of the sites, but surprise of all surprises—he had a Facebook profile.

The intro said he worked for the local electric company in the east valley of Phoenix and graduated from Glendale Community College. Other than that, not much information. His photos weren't much help, either. Even his profile shot was a side angle of him against the background of the Grand Canyon.

The last thing I wanted to do was send him a friend request, so I tossed up my search as a total bust and stopped looking at the phone. "Come on, Speedbump," I said, "might as well make the most of this afternoon and take a walk. In another month, it will be impossible."

The dog perked up his ears at the word *walk* and went straight to the front door. Minutes later, we were halfway down the block when I noticed a few large green recycling bins on the curb.

I've got to write this schedule down. Recycling day is tomorrow—Thursday.

"Remind me to put out the recyclables, Speedbump, or I'll forget by the time I get home."

We enjoyed an uneventful walk and waved to a few passing cars, but that was the extent of my interaction with the neighbors. As I approached my house, I glanced at Owen's and realized he hadn't yet put out his recycling. If I was lucky, he'd do it fairly soon and not wait until after dark or prior to dawn when the waste management company made its rounds.

And while I would have much preferred channel surfing or designing the charcuterie boards I needed for Friday, I chose instead to pull out my M.C. Beaton novel and read it from the front porch while I waited for Owen to make an appearance with his large green recycling bin.

It was a gamble but one I was willing to take. I figured the second I saw him, I could shout something like, "Oh my gosh, I forgot the recycling." Then, I'd walk over for a little chitchat. A little chitchat with my iPhone in my pocket and at the ready in case I needed to tap nine-one-one. Yep, I may have been determined, but I wasn't stupid.

A full hour went by and while I enjoyed a glorious early summer sunset, I was resigned to the fact that Owen either didn't recycle or was one of those last-minute folks who dragged the bin to the curb when they heard the waste management truck making its way down the street.

Speedbump, who made himself comfortable on the porch, stretched and pawed at the front door. Even he knew when it was time to go inside. I stood and started for the door when a beige van pulled into Owen's driveway. I couldn't see who got out but seconds later I heard Owen and a man talking. In the evening stillness, their voices carried, and it was impossible not to recognize Owen's distinct voice. "I told you I'm slowing down for a while.

CHAPTER TWENTY-NINE

We need to be under the radar right now. Not taking more chances."

"That never bothered you before."

"That's because I thought no one was looking. Things got a little dicey a while back and I had to take care of that matter. Like I said, I don't need to raise any eyebrows right now."

"Just so you know, the copper cable market isn't going to stay this hot for long."

"I hear you. I'll be in touch. Give me another couple of weeks."

"It's your bank account."

I couldn't see the driver get back in his van, but I heard the door slam followed by the engine starting up. Seconds later, Owen dragged his recycling bin toward the curb.

I let the dog in the house and made a beeline as fast as I could to the side of my house where my green bin stood against the wall. Taking a breath, I had one thought quickly followed by another—Don't blow it. Owen Jasper may have a darn good motive for murder.

Chapter Thirty

With my hand firmly grasped on the handle of the recycling bin, I thundered down the driveway in time to see Owen casually walking back to his house. No glasses. Drat!

"I can't believe I almost forgot about the recycling," I called out. "I really need to put it on my calendar."

"What? Oh yeah, the recycling." He turned away and kept walking and for a moment I was at a loss of what to say that would make him stop. Then, it hit me—his pesticide use. Anyone that fixated on eliminating insects and vermin would most likely have a few hints.

"Wait! Before you go inside, I have a quick question. What kind of granules are you using to prevent scorpions and bugs from getting into your house? I don't have an exterminator and probably should do something before one of those horrid things gets inside."

Owen walked toward me and looked at Edith's house. "The only scorpion you would have needed to worry about is long gone. Hmm, I probably shouldn't have been that blunt. Anyway, you can't really poison scorpions. Best you can do is eliminate their food source and they'll find another location. What you need is good old-fashioned cricket and insect killer—diatomaceous earth. The stuff's not toxic but it gets the job done. I use it all over the place.

"So it's not a pesticide?"

"Nope. It's even a food source. You can buy it at any hardware store or at the grain and feed places in the valley."

I made a mental note to let Colleen Wexby know that she and the other neighbors needn't worry about Owen poisoning the ground with pesticides. However, I *needed* to know what sneaky deal he was in with the driver of that van. The nightly news stations always reported on thefts of copper cable and if Edith found out he was dealing in stolen cables, she might have threatened to turn him in. Too bad that part of her memory went kaput, but her knowledge of high-profile wardrobes seemed to be well intact.

"I understand Edith used to take evening walks around here."

Owen shrugged. "Wouldn't know. Kept as far away from her as possible."

"Colleen Wexby from down the block said she saw Edith walking the evening before her body was found."

Again, Owen shrugged. "Found all right. From the screams coming out of her cleaning lady's mouth, you would have thought she'd come upon a grisly crime scene, not someone taking their final zzz's in the bed."

"Yeah, that was odd."

"What do you mean?"

"Edith slept in her lift chair, not the bed, due to a bad knee."

"What are you getting at?" Owen scratched the back of his neck and then the underside of his elbow. Nervous maybe?

"Not that anything could be proved, but I suspect she was murdered, and someone moved the body. Staged it, to be more specific."

"Moved, staged, whatever. It doesn't matter. She's not coming back and that's that. My TV show's about to start. Don't want to miss it. See ya."

Owen made a fast retreat, and I was left open-mouthed standing by the side of his driveway. Unless I could find some definitive proof that he was in possession of stolen property, and convince the authorities that Edith somehow found out and he killed her, there was nothing I could do. I turned and headed back to the house when a gust of wind came out of nowhere and slapped me in the face.

"You're not going to let him get away scot-free, are you?" A dizzying whirl of wind, leaves, and paper trash engulfed me. "Don't stand there. Snoop around his place. He's probably engrossed in some high-action drama with idiotic dialogue."

I looked around to make sure no one was nearby. "What am I supposed to do? Break into his house while he's watching a show?"

The mint-burst disappeared, and Edith stood in front of me in a leopard lounging outfit. "Not the house. He wouldn't stash copper tubing in the house. Too bulky. And houses in this part of Arizona don't have basements. That leaves his garage. You need to ferret through his garage."

"I most certainly will not. I'll get arrested. Besides, how would I get inside?"

"Ah-hah. You're thinking about it, aren't you? Or you wouldn't have asked about getting inside."

"I, um, er.."

Another mini-burst and I was once again the hapless victim of Edith's antics.

"I'll get the garage door to go wonky. Then I'll shut off the power to Owen's TV. Dollars to donuts he'll be on the phone with the cable company. You go inside that garage of his, turn on the spunky little flashlight on that phone of yours, and do some digging around. If you find anything, take a picture."

"Can't you look around like you did at the airport?"

"We need proof. It's not as if I'm carrying around a Kodak camera."

"But, but…"

I never choked out another word because, in that instant, Edith had managed to create a localized windstorm that blew me straight into Owen's now-opened garage.

"Be quick about it," she commanded. "I'm not that familiar with how long I can sustain the power fluctuations."

Wonderful. Exactly what I need to hear.

I took the iPhone from my pocket, tapped the flashlight feature, and looked around. Owen's Dodge Ram truck took up most of the space in the garage but that didn't prevent him from stashing all sorts of cartons, crates, and boxes on the shelves that lined two of the walls. I was certain that if his washer and dryer weren't set against the third wall, it would have been floor to ceiling with more boxes.

Having never had a use for copper cable, I had no idea what I was looking for. At first, I pictured long cables like the kind on utility poles but nothing of the sort was visible. With the flashlight feature still on, I googled "copper cable images" and fixed my eyes on photos of cable wire on assorted-sized spools. Hallelujah! At least I knew what to look for.

No sense checking out the boxes that required a ladder. On a good day, I avoid heights like the plague. Besides, if Owen was moving stolen goods, he'd want them in an accessible place, not one that required additional work.

Starting on the wall to the right of the garage door, I opened box after box only to find assorted hand tools, used paint spray cans, and broken solar lights. The first two boxes on the right didn't reveal the grand prize either. Only broken table lamps and miscellaneous cords. Apparently, Owen was one of those people who thought he'd get around to fixing those things but never did. As for me, into the trash they go.

I continued to look but without enthusiasm. That is, until I opened a large box filled with copper spools. Then another. And another. Without wasting a second, I took photos of my findings before picking up one of the spools to check out the label on the plastic—CT -2100—03. Then I looked at the one next to it—CT 750 -03. All sizes and lengths of spools. Still, it didn't exactly scream out STOLEN. Not until I flipped it over and looked at another tag. This one with a barcode and the name of the utility company.

For an instant, I froze. Unsure what to do next. That's when the lights came on in the garage and the door started to close. I raced to the utility door where the door opener switch was located and pushed it. No time to see if I had put the spools back where they belonged in the box on the shelf. No matter. I wasn't about to check.

The second the garage door rose, I raced out of there, heart thumping and cold prickly sweat running down my face. I was positive Owen followed me but when I pushed the door closed and bolted the lock, I looked out the window only to see an empty street. That didn't mean he hadn't seen me, though.

Great. There's a thought that will keep me up all night.

When I walked past the kitchen into the living room, Edith was still in that atrocious leopard lounger sprawled out on the couch. She gave her curls a tussle and looked directly at me. "I was right, wasn't I? Sorry if I couldn't sustain the energy field. I'm new to this."

"I could have been the next person he murdered," I sputtered.

"Not likely. I managed to unload a ton of ice cubes on his kitchen floor. He would have slipped and fallen on them. Hmm, for all we know, maybe he did. Anyway, show me what you found."

I flashed the photos of the copper spools in front of her ghostly face and she actually gave her chest one of those self-satisfying pats.

"Okay, Edith, we've got proof he stole property from the utility company but now what? Do I show it to the Cave Creek Town Marshal? The Black Mountain Police Department? The Maricopa County Sheriff's Office? And how do I explain how I happened to come across them without incriminating myself?"

Edith grimaced and made an annoying humming sound. "Good point. You don't do any of it. You blackmail him."

"What?? I think the pressure of your unexpected death has rendered your thinking a bit off. I most certainly am not going to blackmail him. That's worse than breaking and entering. Although, I only entered. I didn't break in."

"Not blackmail in the sense of a threat. Blackmail as in a jumping-off point."

"I'm not sure I follow but it doesn't matter. No one is going to admit that they killed you."

"I suppose you're right. We'll have to resort to more drastic measures."

"Like what?"

"Like I'll need some time to think of them."

"Take all the time you need because I will be tied up with charcuterie boards for that bunco party and the engagement extravaganza at Savor in the Heights. Maybe you can explore new and different fashion opportunities in the meantime."

"Don't be snippy. As you know, the couture is not always up to me."

I started to reply but like that, Edith was gone, leaving a swirling mess of confetti in her wake.

"Thanks a heap!" I shouted. "Now I have to drag out the vacuum."

Chapter Thirty-One

I wanted to believe we had really found Edith's killer, but something told me I was wrong. Not so much a logical conclusion but more of a gut feeling. Still, Owen had a decent motive. Heck, he had the *only* viable motive at this juncture in time.

Rats! I'm so conflicted about Owen.

True, those restaurant owners faced enormous business losses thanks to her but was it enough to engage in homicide? I wasn't so sure. The one thing I was certain of, was the fact I needed to get cracking on those charcuterie designs if I expected my new enterprise to take hold.

Deirdre Billings told me she wanted something eye-catching and delectable. Beyond that, it would be up to me. I emailed her three different possibilities, and she selected the first platter—ripe cherries and blueberries, brie, Havarti, cubed pepper jack, Genoa salami, spiced ham, mortadella, almonds, and assorted crackers. It was the perfect combination of taste, color, and texture. My hands all but itched to get started and I imagined Lilly-Ann felt the same way.

The design would have to be stunning since Suzette was sending over a photographer that afternoon to take a few promo shots. If people really do eat with their eyes, I wanted them to all but inhale those pictures.

Fortunately, Desert Delectable Foods was able to accommodate me and would only charge me a minimal delivery fee. Given how pressured and strapped for time I was, it was well worth it. They promised to have all the products at The Char-Board by ten a.m. at the latest on Friday. That would give Lilly Ann and me plenty of time to create the masterpiece I envisioned.

Then, there was the engagement party the following Saturday. Patricia Milestone, the event coordinator, informed me the bride-to-be was Olivia DeLonde, and that her father was hosting the engagement affair. I never thought to ask the fiancé's name. Not that it mattered. Olivia was marrying him, not me.

The mere thought of their engagement party made me shaky. It was a make-or-break opportunity, and I couldn't blow it. A stellar review from Savor in the Heights would go a long way for my reputation as a charcuterie caterer.

With a tightening calendar, I decided to hold our grand opening on the Friday following the engagement party. I chose Friday because Fridays seem to bring in lots of Cave Creek foot traffic. Also, there was ample time for Suzette to make sure the advertising was in place. So as not to waste a minute, I phoned her and gave her the date.

"Perfect timing, Katie," she said. "I can get ads in for the local papers and flood social media with your announcement. Don't forget, our photographer will be at your shop this Friday to snap a few shots of that platter for the bunco party."

"I won't. I've got it in bold print on my calendar. And on a Post-it on my fridge."

She laughed. "My notes indicate you want a photographer for your grand opening. Is that still the case?"

"Absolutely."

"Great. We'll flesh out those details later. Meanwhile, I'll get started with what we have."

I thanked her and sank onto the couch, too tired to rig up something to eat but too hungry to let it pass. "Popcorn's a vegetable," I said to the dog. "And if I sprinkle parmesan cheese on it, I can say I had a milk product as well."

Speedbump, who had now taken over the rug near the coffee table, lifted his head as if to acknowledge my comment. I got up, nuked a package of microwavable popcorn, and counted the minutes until it was ready. Then I added processed grated cheese to it and took the entire bowl to the couch along with a bottle of iced tea.

For the next fifteen or twenty minutes, I was in food heaven. Until I heard that annoying raspy voice of Edith's. It sounded even more grating than usual. "That processed food is going to kill your insides, you know."

"As long as my outsides look good, I'll take the risk. I suppose you're back because you figured out some nefarious little plan to get Owen to confess to murder."

"Not yet. I'm still working on it."

"Um, I hate to sound defeated, but what if we can't prove anything? Does that mean you'll be here indefinitely?" *Heaven help me.*

Suddenly a plume of black smoke engulfed the room followed by Edith's announcement, "Not if I can help it."

Seconds later, everything returned to normal, and I finished the remaining kernels in my bowl.

I'd become more comfortable with the routine at The Char-Board with each passing day and the following morning was no exception. Lilly-Ann, Matt, and I breezed through Thursday as if the three of us had been working for months, not days. I gave Lilly-Ann a sketch of the charcuterie board we were going to make for the bunco party and asked for her input, something that literally made her beam.

She suggested adding edible flowers in addition to the sprigs of dill and spinach leaves that I had chosen. It was a fantastic idea and one I hadn't considered since finding edible flowers wasn't always easy.

"I've used decorative flower sprigs before," I told her, "but not edible flowers."

"Maybe Petals and Plants a few doors down would have them. I can give them a call."

Thrilled that Lilly-Ann was taking the initiative, I gave her the okay and told her that if the flower shop sold them, she could select a handful that we'd use to embellish the board. "But only if they're pesticide-free," I added.

The next morning, Lilly-Ann ducked out of The Char-Board and returned with a small bag of bachelor buttons, nasturtiums, and zinnias. She informed me that they had calendulas, too, but she felt the daisy-shaped flowers were too large and better suited for fall-themed platters. The woman caught on quickly and I couldn't have been more pleased.

"I'm supposed to deliver the board to Deirdre at six-thirty tonight," I told her. "That should give us plenty of time to work on it once we close for the day. It's a short drive to her development and the platter will fit nicely in the back of my car. The good news is that she'll drop off the empty board tomorrow. Incidentally, those boards are costly, so I include a non-refundable charge if they're not returned or if other arrangements aren't made. Next Saturday, however, will be a whole different story."

"The engagement party. Right. Nothing's changed where I'm concerned. I'm available the entire day and well into the evening."

"I don't think we'll have to worry about 'well into the evening,' but we will need to craft two large boards on-site at Savor in the Heights. I can drive you or you can meet me there if you prefer. Someone from his staff will return the boards to me on Monday. Wend, the owner, told me I'd have full access to one of his kitchens. His event planner will be contacting me so I can check it out first."

"*One* of his kitchens?"

"Uh-huh. When the restaurant was built, two kitchens were installed in order to handle large parties while the regular diners ate. You should have seen that place. It was enormous. I can only imagine what his new venture will look like in the Biltmore area."

"Yeah, I caught part of that on a TV special but it's way out of my league. *Way* out."

I chuckled. "It might as well be on another planet as far as eating out is concerned. Listen, as we get closer to next Saturday, we can fine-tune our operation."

"Sounds good to me."

While I was confident and assured everything would run smoothly with my two catering assignments, I was a blithering wreck when it came to my so-called murder investigation and absolutely terrified at what kind of devious plan Edith would concoct. Thankfully, she didn't. In fact, I wound up being Edith-free well into the start of the week. I didn't question it.

As for later that evening, Deirdre was blown over by the charcuterie board I delivered to her house at twenty-past six. Lilly-Ann surprised me with her innate sense of design when it came to positioning the items so that the textures and colors would augment each other. And not only was Deirdre overjoyed, but I wound up taking two more orders for subsequent months. It seemed Eulodie was willing to give up her leathery meatballs and insisted Deborah toss aside one of her casseroles for "something more recognizable." Finally! I made a dent at Hidden Boulders and kept my fingers crossed more orders would come in.

With the success of Deirdre's bunco party behind me, I felt confident I could deliver a spectacular charcuterie board experience for that engagement party. I ordered all sorts of cured meats and assorted cheeses from our distributor and went overboard with the fruits, nuts, and specialty items. Lilly-Ann insisted we find out if the soon-to-be wedding party had already selected a color theme so we could use it with the edible flowers if at all possible.

A quick call to Patricia and I relaxed. No color scheme was selected for the engagement party. "At least that's one less thing to worry about," I told Lilly-Ann the following Monday when I arrived at The Char-Board.

She stood near the sink chopping onions and celery for our salads. "I'm all but twitching when I think about this coming Saturday. It's the high point of my social life. Oh, who am I kidding? It *is* my social life. And, it's the closest I'll come to elegant dining. If we weren't going to be in the kitchen preparing food, I'd almost spring for a fancy dress."

"Me, too. I think a plain white or light-colored top and slacks will be fine. The new aprons I ordered with our logo should be here by Wednesday at the latest. We should look pretty snazzy in them."

"Snazzy *and* professional."

I wanted to share Lilly-Ann's elation but the "Owen situation", for lack of a better description, hung over me like the Sword of Damocles. I pondered calling Silent Witness, but it wasn't the theft that gnawed at me as much as his role in silencing Edith for good. I'd come to the tenuous conclusion that Owen Jasper was her killer, but deep down I was afraid it was more conjecture than conclusion. Still, my mind played it out as if it were a TV drama.

Lamentably, Edith had no recollection of the timeline leading up to her death. Only a few snippets here and there and they weren't much good. My imagination, however, was on overdrive and I had no problem filling in the blanks with a well-crafted scenario. I envisioned Edith catching Owen in the act of unloading the stolen goods and confronting him. I also pictured Owen denying it and telling her to mind her own business. Then, I visualized Owen knocking on her door and forcing his way inside, followed by a struggle that resulted in her loosening the lens from his glasses. Maybe he held a hand over her mouth, and she suffocated. That might have looked like a natural death.

The only sticking point was that eyeglass lens, and while I hadn't actually seen Owen wearing glasses, that didn't necessarily mean anything. Maybe his vanity won out and he only wore them for TV viewing, driving, and close-up reading.

"Katie, are you alright?" Lilly-Ann asked. "It looks like you're deep in space."

"Huh? No. I was thinking about Saturday, that's all."

"Sure you're okay with driving me over there?"

"Absolutely. It's only a mile or so from my house to yours. No problem."

I hurried out of the kitchen and into the dining area to check on our customers. Matt stood at a four-person table and took orders while I tried to shake the Owen scenario out of my head for the time being.

I seriously considered confronting Owen, but after the Lucas fiasco, that was the last thing I intended to do. Instead, I actually found myself wondering if Edith was able to come up with a better plan.

Chapter Thirty-Two

No plans from Edith. No nothing. I figured she was either up to some hanky-panky in the netherworld or they restricted her movements. She must have gotten under someone's skin in the afterlife, but knowing Edith, she'd find a way around it. Much like she did with restoring her wardrobe. More or less.

Then Wednesday arrived and I was positive Edith had returned. Strobing red, white and blue flashers illuminated my bedroom at dawn. I sat up and stretched, pinching my shoulder blades while Speedbump continued snoring at my feet. "It's not July 4th," I said. "You can quit the sideshow."

Not a word. I looked around the room and realized the lights were coming from outside the house. With a quick toss of the blanket, I walked to the window and looked. Sure enough, one sheriff's car and one sheriff's van were in Owen's driveway, lights a blazing.

Oh no. Please don't tell me he's the next victim on this block.

I threw on a sweatshirt and shorts, let Speedbump out the doggie door, and ran my fingers through my hair before I stepped outside and onto the porch. A few people stood on the sidewalk, some with coffee mugs in their hands, others with dogs on leashes. As I got closer, I saw Colleen Wexby.

"Um, what's going on?" I asked as I walked toward her. "I don't see an ambulance or the paramedics. Is Owen, um, well...dead? Did they remove his body already?"

"No, he's not dead," someone shouted. "We should be so lucky. Take a good look. The sheriff's deputies are removing cartons from his garage. *Lots* of cartons. Don't think it's anything hazardous or the Hazmat team would be here."

Colleen motioned me aside. "Owen works for one of the utility companies. He leaves for work around four. My guess is something happened at work and whatever it was, it sent the deputies to his house."

"Can they just do that? Go inside and remove stuff?"

Colleen shrugged. "They can if they've got a search warrant."

The two of us stood silently for a moment watching what appeared to be an endless line of deputies removing cartons. I began to think maybe Owen stashed more stolen copper cable in a guest room or something.

"Well, no sense standing around here." It was another voice. This time a woman's. "I've got to get to work. Whatever it is, they'll have it on the news."

"I always knew Owen was a bit off," Colleen whispered. "But if you ask me, I think he was dealing in stolen goods. Couldn't be drugs. Not in all of those large cartons. I don't even think the cartels house that many in one place. Go figure. Someone lives on your block for years and you have no idea what they're really up to."

"I suppose."

"If it is stolen goods, chances are they came from the utility company where he worked. I bet one of his co-workers tipped off the authorities. No one around here would have an idea. I mean, it's not as if the guy ever let anyone into his house."

"What about Edith? Would she have known? Being his next-door neighbor and all?"

Colleen crinkled her nose. "I don't know but it wouldn't surprise me. Edith struck me as one of those people who knew exactly what was going on. Anyway, she couldn't have been the one to blow him in considering she died not too long ago. Nah, my money's on someone from that utility company."

"Think they arrested Owen?"

"If they didn't, they will now. Take a look at that carton. It's got the name of the utility company on the side. Boy, talk about chutzpah. Either that, or Owen was too darn sure of himself. Oh my gosh. I've been standing out here way too long. I need to be at work in an hour. Nice chatting with you."

"Uh, yeah. Same here."

The endless parade of cartons being removed from the house and placed into the van continued but the crowd dispersed, leaving only two women. I gave them a quick wave and retreated back to the house. Speedbump was already inside staring at his empty food dish.

"Hang on. Your kibble's on the way."

I poured a healthy handful into his bowl and started up the Keurig. Then I looked around and announced, "If you're in here, now would be a good time to make an appearance, Edith."

Nothing. Absolutely nothing. The only sound was Speedbump crunching those dry morsels of food. Like the voice in the crowd, I, too, figured whatever Owen did would be on my news app, not to mention the noonday news. Those TV stations have their scanners everywhere and wouldn't dare take a chance at being out-scooped.

"Whoa," I said the second I glanced at the oven clock. "Forget the coffee. I've got to get a move-on. I'll drink coffee at work." With a quick tap of a finger, I shut the Keurig and raced to get washed and dressed. True, Lilly-Ann would have been more than happy to open The Char-Board, but I didn't want her or Matt to think I was going to be one of those lackadaisical bosses.

"We had some excitement on my block," I said when Lilly-Ann and Matt arrived to work. I had already started up the coffee machine when they walked in.

Matt's ears perked up. "What was it? A shooting? Fire? Hostage situation?"

I shook my head. "Nothing that dramatic. Only two sheriff's vehicles and a few deputies removing cartons of goods from my next-door neighbor's house. The guy I told you about. The pesticide spreader. Only it wasn't pesticide. It was diatomaceous earth."

"In the cartons?" Lilly-Ann asked.

"More like stolen goods would be my guess." *And firsthand knowledge.* "I'll check my news app around noon. Meanwhile, that apron delivery should be here this morning and I can't wait to see how they turned out. Right on time, too, for Saturday's first major charcuterie catering event. I'm counting the bunco party as the dress rehearsal for our debut at Savor in the Heights."

"Break a leg," Matt laughed as he charged toward the kitchen. "If you want me, you know where to find me—boiling and peeling eggs for salads."

Lilly-Ann didn't waste any time either as she followed suit. Meanwhile, I made sure all of our tables had napkins and condiments before placing a call to Desert Delectable Foods to confirm the delivery arrangements I made previously. I'd decided it would make more sense if they delivered the raw goods, aka cheeses, meats, and the like, directly to Savor, rather than to my location. One less thing to worry about. And I was worried enough. My charcuterie boards had to make a stellar impression in order to jumpstart my reputation.

An hour and a half into our breakfast rush and the aprons arrived. I ordered everyday white aprons as well as black ones for special occasions like Olivia's engagement party. The last time I was this excited about a delivery, I was eight and stayed up late to catch a glimpse of Santa Claus. Now it was the FedEx truck and I all but chewed my nails off in anticipation. The design sketches Suzette gave the company were one thing. It was the end result that mattered.

As Lilly-Ann and Matt put the term "food service" to good use racing back and forth from the dining area to the kitchen, I plunked the box on the only available space I could find at the end of the worktable and cut through the tape on the box. I held my breath as I removed the first white apron from the packing material and held it up in the air. At that exact moment, Lilly-Ann brushed past me with an armload of dirty dishes.

She spun her head around and looked at the apron. "Wow! That's even more striking than I thought they'd be. I love how they were able to replicate the logo."

Matt, who was right behind with his own armload of dishes, crinkled his nose. "Yeah, got to admit, they're not dorky or too feminine."

"I prefer the old-fashioned ones that look like cute little pinafores. The ones with those ruffled sleeves."

I all but dropped my apron when I heard Edith's voice. "No one asked you."

"Huh?" Matt took a step back.

"Oh, um, not you. I mean, that's not what I meant to say. I meant to say,

190

CHAPTER THIRTY-TWO

"No one asked you if you'd like any help with those dishes."

"Um, uh, I'm okay. I'm just putting them in the sink to wash off."

I caught my breath and kept my fingers crossed Edith decided not to add any additional commentary. To be on the safe side, I put the apron back in the box and made a beeline for the trash. "Lots of eggshells in there," I said. "I'll tie up the bag and take it to the alley out back for pickup before they get too odorous."

Matt all but raced me to the trash bin. "I can do that for you."

"It's fine. Really it is. I could use a breath of air."

He shrugged as I removed the plastic bag from the bin and darted out the door. Once outside and out of earshot, I put my hands on my hips and looked around. "Boundaries, Edith! Geez! Do you want my workers to think I've gone bonkers? And now, of all times. You've had days to chitchat with me."

A filmy, murky gray haze engulfed the alleyway, and I was glad no one else was around. Not that I thought they could see it, but they could see me talking to myself.

"Let's simply say I've been tied up. And don't you dare mention this outfit. It's a loaner."

"From who? Liberace? Never mind, talk to me later. When I'm home."

"I might not get the chance. Everything's in flux at the moment. But don't worry, honey, it'll get sorted out by tomorrow when we pay Owen a visit at the Fourth Avenue Jail. I'm positive that's where he's headed. And if I'm right, I'll haunt the truth out of him. Theft wasn't enough. He had to resort to murder. Too bad I can't remember any of it. And all this time, I was banking on it being Imogen. And by the way, I'm not done with her, either."

"Whoa! Slow down!" I outstretched my arms, palms up, and prayed no one was in the vicinity. "What did you mean by 'when we pay him a visit?' Not *we*. I'm not going if Owen winds up there."

"You have to. I can only manifest myself in your presence and its immediate surroundings."

"Well, manifest yourself elsewhere because the Fourth Avenue Jail is out of the question. Have you ever seen that place? I've only seen the outside of the building and it's worse than anything George R.R. Martin could have dreamed up for *Game of Thrones.* Nope, I am definitely not going to the Fourth Avenue Jail."

"What's that about the Fourth Avenue Jail?"

I turned and found myself face-to-face with the middle-aged lady who owns the pottery shop next door. Mercedes something-or-other. Heavy-set, tight salt-and-pepper curls. Maddie had given me the names and info regarding the other shop owners within a quarter-mile radius of The Char-Board. "For reference," she said. I made a mental note to introduce myself prior to my grand opening but with Edith breathing down my neck and the opportunity to get my charcuterie catering going, I never got the chance. Now, I found myself in an alleyway with one of them.

"Terrible habit, having this Bluetooth in my ear," I said. "I just heard my neighbor was arrested and taken to that jail."

"Must be the copper cable thefts. It's been all over the news this morning. Right down the road here in Cave Creek. And that was only the tip of the iceberg."

"The tip?"

"Didn't you hear? They also found extensive amounts of electrical grounding wire and all sorts of other wires and cables. Not to mention catalytic converters. Used to be one had to worry about their jewelry being stolen. Go figure."

I nodded, too numb to say anything else.

The woman shook her head and sighed. "It goes to show you, you never really know who your neighbors are. Oh goodness. That must have sounded awful. How rude of me. I'm Mercedes Alvarez. I own the pottery shop next door—The Galloping Goose."

"Katie Aubrey. New owner of the former sandwich shop. It's now The Char-Board. We've got the same sandwiches as before, but we've added mini-charcuterie boards."

"I love those. I'll make it a point to stop in for lunch one of these days when I get a free minute."

"I'd like that. And your first mini-board will be on the house."

"That's so sweet of you. If you need anything, give a holler. It's just me and my daughter-in-law running the show. We contract with a number of artists in the Greater Phoenix area so everything we sell is handmade right here in Arizona."

"That's great. I'd love to chat but—"

"I know. I've got to get back inside, too. Nice meeting you. And remember, if anything comes up, just yell."

Understatement of the year.

When Mercedes was a good seven or eight yards away, a filmy gray haze appeared. "Still obstinate about the Fourth Avenue Jail?"

"Yes! With a capital Y. But if you leave me alone, I'll talk with you about it tonight. At a reasonable hour. Reasonable!"

The haze deepened into shades of ocean blue and teal before evaporating. I walked back inside The Char-Board as if all I did was take out the trash.

Chapter Thirty-Three

T he customers came in waves with a few lulls in-between. It was rush-rush one second and soaking in the silence the next. Still, at the end of the day, we'd done a decent amount of business.

"I'm going to meet with Patricia Milestone at four-thirty today," I told Lilly-Ann as we walked out the door together. Matt had left moments before so as not to be late for a pre-arranged conference with his college advisor. "Patricia's the events coordinator at Savor in the Heights but I get the feeling she handles more than that."

"Yes, I think I remember you mentioning her."

"She's going to show me the workspace they've set aside for us to prepare the charcuterie boards. They've also reserved shelves in one of their refrigerators for our supplies from Desert Delectable Foods. That delivery is scheduled for Friday morning."

"Sounds like you've got everything under control."

"The only things I need to transport are our large charcuterie boards and the knives we'll be using."

"Don't they have knives and other cutlery they'll let you use?"

"I'm sure they do but I like using the ones I'm accustomed to. I always used to think renowned chefs were fussy and weird when it came to knives since they only use their own, but once I started making charcuterie boards, I understood."

"I hope I can get to that point. I really do."

I smiled and double-checked the lock in the door behind me. "You will."

With a full food bowl and freshly changed water, Speedbump was all set until I got home for our evening walk. I needed to familiarize myself with the setup at Savor so that my timing would be on-the-nose for the event, and I could guide Lilly-Ann without losing precious work minutes.

In spite of the near-rush hour road traffic, it was a pleasant enough drive to Fountain Hills. With striking mountains in the distance and desert landscaping, I could almost ignore the rude drivers, the distracted drivers, and the slow-moving-I'll-get-there-when-I-get-there drivers.

Although I had spoken with her on more than one occasion, I hadn't met Patricia in person but envisioned a cross between *Blue Bloods'* Erin Reagan and *Harry Potter's* Professor Minerva McGonagall. Turned out, I wasn't far off.

Tall, slender, and striking with sleek dark hair in a French bun, Patricia Milestone greeted me at the hostess station when I arrived. I made note of her steel blue business suit and high heel pumps, resting assured that I made the right choice by selecting an iceberg blue outfit for the visit.

Wasting no time, she escorted me to the kitchen I'd be using and showed me the area they had reserved for the charcuterie boards. She also offered me water, iced tea, or lemonade. All of which I declined for fear of spilling something. For the life of me, I didn't understand why I felt so intimidated but maybe it was because this job would determine The Char-Board's future catering success and I didn't want to blow it.

Patricia pointed to a wall with three large stainless-steel refrigerators. "We received a call from Desert Delectable Foods and Shawn, one of our sous chefs, will make himself available to see to it everything is properly stored in the refrigerator to your immediate left. Mr. Pomeroy was insistent you'd have everything at your disposal to ensure a quality outcome. So that you're aware, we've hosted numerous receptions, many of them high-profile, but this is the first time we've hosted for the DeLondes. Between you and me, I'm not sure if we're catering to the family or to Athenon-Intel Industries."

Athenon-Intel? That's a Fortune 500 company. I need to pay more attention to what goes in my ears.

I gulped and nodded. Not necessarily in that order. "Thank you. I appreciate it." I kept my hands close to my body so she wouldn't see them shaking. Technically, I had the charcuterie boards all configured. It was merely a matter of working the food into the magic of the design. And not slicing my fingers off in the process.

For the next few minutes, Patricia showed me where I'd find everything from paring knives to nutcrackers. She explained that once the boards were completed, their staff would move them to the serving area in the large banquet room. Again, all I could do was nod. If I kept that up, I could double as one of those bobblehead dolls.

"Do you have any questions?" she asked.

"Not at this time."

"If you do, don't hesitate to call."

We left the kitchen and walked down the long corridor where Wend Pomeroy's office was located. As we got closer to the office, I could hear two loud male voices and recognized the first as Wend's. "Hold your horses. You'll get your money."

"I expected that final bank transfer two days ago. What's the holdup?"

"I had other accounts to settle. You know how these things go."

"Look, I risked everything to save your ass."

"Don't play martyr. You knew what you were doing. When the new restaurant is off the ground and the greenbacks come rolling in, you'll thank me."

"I'd thank you now if you'd hurry along with that transfer."

Patricia turned to the closed office door and sighed. "Sorry about that. Mr. Pomeroy's been under tremendous stress with his new enterprise. So much on the line, so to speak. He's apparently in conference with one of the investors."

"I saw the TV special about the new restaurant. An endeavor like that would need investors. Or a very generous bank."

"Banks aren't *that* generous. Investors can be, if the payback is worth it."

We walked another step or two when the man in Wend's office spoke again. "I expect to see that money in my account by Friday or you'll be seeing me again real soon. And it won't be for a family function."

196

"In this case," Patricia continued, "the investor is a family member. The brother-in-law. Not the best scenario in my book, but I'm not the one in charge. Come on, I'll walk you to the main entrance."

I got the sense she didn't want to delve any further into her perspective regarding how Wend Pomeroy ran his business, so I segued into a more pressing topic—the engagement party.

"It sounds like Saturday's celebration is going to be quite the deal."

"Complete with ribbons, bows, balloons, and a highly sought-after band. Not to mention a four-course dinner for sixty or so guests. It will rival anything Buckingham Palace can create."

"So the charcuterie boards are the welcoming teasers?" I laughed.

"They'll be the first impression for the guests, and you know what that means."

Tiny beads of moisture ran down the back of my neck.

Yep. Don't mess it up.

When I got into my car, I remembered the conversation I had with Wend when I first met him. Someone interrupted us with a call about a bank transfer to his brother-in-law. Wend dismissed the matter as "family business" and we moved on to talk about my catering proposal. Not that any of this had anything to do with me, but I wondered why he was so cagey about the matter. The snippet of conversation I overheard a few minutes ago was even more perplexing.

Usually, investors *give* the money. They don't receive it. Not until the enterprise gets going and the returns are in. Even if it is a family business. Still, not my problem. I had enough of my own.

Chapter Thirty-Four

True to her word, Edith waited until the ten o'clock news came on before making her entrance. Speedbump was snoring away on the floor while I sprawled out on the couch. A sudden gust of wind shook both of us from our reveries. Seconds later, Edith stood in front of me, a black boa wrapped around her neck like a noose.

With an exaggerated gesture, she put her hands on her hips and leaned forward. "I heard the news. That scoundrel *is* locked up in the Fourth Avenue Jail just as I thought. It would be more dramatic if I haunted him at night but like I explained before, you need to be with me. I suppose sometime tomorrow will have to do."

"No, it won't. I'm not going there. Alcatraz is more inviting. Maybe even San Quentin. Listen Edith, you know I've got a make-or-break catering affair this Saturday and its outcome may very well determine the success – or heaven forbid, the failure – of the charcuterie end of my business. I need to concentrate on my designs, walk Lilly-Ann through the process, and make sure Desert Delectable Foods doesn't screw up the order."

"And I need to trap that killer into a confession. Do you think I enjoy drifting around in the afterlife? It's run by middle management and some of them can be downright obnoxious."

Where's a mirror when I need one?

"How about this? After the engagement party this Saturday night, I will totally devote myself to catching your murderer. Even if it does mean visiting hours at the jail." *I have finally lost my mind.* "All I ask is for a bit of time and space between now and Saturday night. Come Sunday, I'll be at your service.

Fair enough?"

Edith made a few huffing sounds and readjusted her boa at least half a dozen times. "I suppose it will have to do. Harumph. I keep trying to remember the events right before I left this world but all I get is fuzz. Probably just as well."

"Owen did have a motive. I mean if he thought you knew about his stolen goods. That's more than a jealous restauranteur or a business getting a bad review. I wager you'll be able to eke a full confession out of him by the start of the week." *Or I'll pull the hair out of my head.*

"I'm holding you to it." The whiteish haze exploded into shades of deep gray and charcoal and when it fizzled out, Edith was gone.

In the two days that followed, there was no more news about Owen's arrest other than what I already knew from my brief conversation with Mercedes Alvarez. Nothing had changed except the extent of the news commentaries. They branched out into all sorts of spinoffs including uses for copper cable, the international copper cable market, and market fluctuation regarding the purchase of ground wiring.

Then everything changed when I got home from work on Friday. No sooner did I pull into my driveway when a taxi pulled away from the curb in front of Owen's house and Owen charged up his driveway to the garage. I couldn't for the life of me imagine all charges were dropped against him by the county, so I figured he was able to post bail. After all, as far as his arrest went, it was for theft, not murder.

Unfortunately, there was no way I could ignore him. One quick turn of my head and we were pretty much eye-to-eye, even from a distance. I waved from the driver's side window and without waiting for a response, pushed the garage remote and drove straight ahead. Once inside, I made sure to push it again and close the garage door.

Horrible thoughts raced through my mind. Each one worse than the other. *What if he thinks I was the one who ratted him out? If he killed Edith, nothing is stopping him from doing the same to me. What if he knocks on my door?*

Speedbump must have sensed my anxiety when I opened the utility door to the kitchen because he walked right up to me and leaned his head against my knee. Not his usual nudge for food.

"Everything's fine, boy," I said but there was certainly a quiver in my voice. "As soon as I'm done checking to be sure all the windows are locked, I'll feed you."

The dog followed me around the house and stood patiently as I tried each window. It was a habit of mine to keep them locked, but I did make exceptions. Especially in the evenings when the temperature dipped down and I wanted to let a breeze through the house. So much for that.

"From now until November the AC stays on." I patted the dog on the head and poured kibble into his bowl. Then I retreated to the bedroom and got into sweat shorts and an old faded Cardinals top. At least there was a silver lining: With Owen out on bail, there was no need to visit the Fourth Avenue Jail to have Edith haunt a confession out of him. Nope. She could do that right in his own backyard. *And I could buy a jumbo can of wasp spray if it all went south.*

At least I didn't have to worry about it until Sunday. If nothing else, Edith had shown she could keep her word. In twenty-four hours, I'd be working on my charcuterie masterpieces in Savor in the Heights' kitchen. Lilly-Ann at my side. I took a deep breath and told myself to relax. Then I grabbed my cell phone and dialed Maddie.

"How would you like to spend the night here?" I asked. "It would be great fun. We haven't had a sleepover since we were in high school."

"What's going on? What happened?"

"Okay. Fine. In case you haven't caught the local news, the sheriff's office raided my next-door neighbor's house a few days ago. You remember him. The guy who needed a shave. We knocked on his door when we were trying to find Speedbump's owner."

"Drugs? Explosives?"

"Stolen goods. Anyway, I get the feeling he thinks I may have had something to do with his arrest."

"Why? Why would he think that?"

"Um, uh, more like a look he gave me when I pulled into the driveway. It was one of those *I'll get you* looks."

"He was probably aggravated that he got caught and that everyone knows what he was up to. Look, if the guy was that much of a threat, they wouldn't have released him from jail. Not without upping the bail money so he couldn't secure it."

It was one of those moments when I desperately wanted to tell all to Maddie, but I couldn't. Even without mentioning Edith, how could I possibly explain what I was doing rooting around the guy's garage that night?

"I suppose you're right."

"Hey, what do you say we get together for brunch on Sunday? You can tell me how your first major catering affair went. Savor in the Heights, right? The engagement party."

"That's the one. Sunday sounds good. Text me where and when you want to meet."

"Got it. And stop worrying about your neighbor. He's probably way too busy getting his story straight for his lawyer. But lock your windows anyway."

"Already done. Maybe I can convince Speedbump he's really a Rottweiler in disguise."

"Ha! Good luck with that."

I spent the rest of the evening jumping at every little sound I heard until I finally came to the conclusion Owen wasn't about to do me in. At least not right away. Somehow, I managed to get a few decent hours of sleep before a full day at The Char-Board.

To save time, Lilly-Ann agreed to drive to my house, and we'd leave for Fountain Hills before four. Factoring in the drive, we'd have a good three and a half hours before the charcuterie boards made their way to the banquet room. Plenty of time.

To be on the safe side, I had called Patricia around one to make sure Desert Delectable Foods had delivered everything I ordered. Two thumbs up. I was all set. If nothing else, working at The Char-Board and chitchatting with customers was the perfect distraction I needed during the day, so I'd stop worrying about the evening.

All I had to do was convert the two designs I'd created into visual masterpieces on the large wooden boards. And unless a major power failure gripped the valley, what could possibly go wrong?

Chapter Thirty-Five

I had chosen two distinct country themes for the charcuterie creations—Italian and French. I was sure to let Patricia know so that she could pair the boards with appropriate wines. Among the items I had selected for the Italian board were prosciutto, capicola, soppressata, an Italian staple, mortadella, and Genoa salami for the meats, manchego, and soft ricotta for the cheeses, and an array of olives, artichoke hearts, pepperoncini, and almonds. Thinly sliced Italian bread went without saying.

The French board was a tad more complex, featuring a chicken liver pâté I whipped up earlier in the day, mild dry-cured sausage, mild ham, Gruyere and brie cheeses, fig jam, sweet pickles, red and black grapes, and small pickled cucumbers known as cornichons. Naturally, I offered crusty baguette bread and an assortment of artisan crackers.

Lilly-Ann made sure we had the right amount of edible flowers to compliment both boards in keeping with their themes. Thank goodness Petals and Plants had everything we needed.

Now, at twenty minutes to five, I pulled past the large parking area in the front of Savor and drove to the employee parking area in the back.

"Someone from their kitchen crew will bring our boards inside," I said. "I think we can manage with the flowers."

Lilly-Ann's face was glued to the window. "Did you get a good look at the cars in front? BMWs, Jaguars, and Mercedes."

"That's just the regular dining crowd. Wait until the guests for that engagement party show up. I wouldn't be surprised if some of them had Bentley's or Rolls Royces. We'll get a good sneak-peek at the crowd when the servers bring out our platters. After all, we need to make sure nothing gets jousted between the kitchen and the banquet room."

Like most restaurants and event venues, the rear parking lot led directly into the kitchen. Within minutes, I asked one of the workers to let Patricia know we had arrived and that the boards needed to be carried inside.

"No problem. We've got some strong sous chefs who probably want to catch a breath of fresh air," a young female server who couldn't have been older than twenty announced. Judging from the numerous ear piercings sans earrings, I was fairly certain Savor in the Heights had a certain dress requirement for its workers.

She walked across the room, said something to a tall man with reddish hair, and returned to where Lilly-Ann and I stood. "Your delivery is in the fridge to the left. Please let us know if you need anything. Miss Milestone said she showed you where everything was. Oh, and feel free to help yourselves to the bottled water or iced tea in the middle fridge. It gets really warm in here even though it's air-conditioned."

I thanked her and then proceeded to open the fridge and sort out the assorted meats, cheeses, and condiments. There was ample room for the completed charcuterie boards to remain refrigerated if need be, but I was sure our timing would work since the meats and cheeses had to reach room temperature prior to serving.

"I'm putting the flowers in the fridge," Lilly-Ann said, "since I don't want them to wilt. They're wrapped in some sort of moisture tissue paper with tons of newspaper around that. If we get bored, we can always read the month-old news."

I laughed. "Bored is the last thing I'd worry about."

The great news was that Patricia had given us plenty of workspace and for the next hour we sliced, diced, and chopped our meats and cheeses. Not as easy as it sounded since the different items required specified widths. Midway through a large chunk of Manchego, I needed a restroom break and left the kitchen for the one I had seen in the corridor during my last visit.

No sooner did I approach the ladies' room door when I heard a door slam, followed by a voice I recognized—Wend Pomeroy's. His vocal cords had all the fury of a tempest and the intensity of a gravel mixer. "You'll get your damn money when I'm good and ready. I've got a five-star affair going on tonight and I've got other things to do."

The next voice was equally loud but not as throaty. "You're not brushing me off that fast. I had to finagle all sorts of things to make sure you got what you needed, now it's my turn."

"We can talk about this another time."

"The hell we will. I'm not going anywhere."

With my hand poised over the restroom door, it was a case of either satisfying mother nature or my own curiosity. No surprise there. Mother nature won. When I exited the restroom, the arguing had ceased. Given what I heard, I was fairly certain that Wend's combatant was the brother-in-law. The investor who demanded his return.

Patricia had the right philosophy about not doing business with family members but "not the best scenario" was an understatement as far as I was concerned. The conversation was heated and one step away from volatile as I interpreted it. I imagined no one else heard them since I was the only one in the corridor at the time and it was none of my business.

When I returned to the kitchen, Lilly-Ann and I completed the prep work and perused the sketches I'd drawn indicating the placement of the foods on the board. Since this was our first major event, and Lilly-Ann was new to the process, I wanted us to work together. Hopefully, she'd gain mastery so that in the future we could create separate boards with our own artistic flavor.

As we neared completion of the Italian board, Lilly-Ann looked over her shoulder.

"Is everything all right?" I asked.

"Uh-huh. I just had the strangest sensation we were being watched, that's all."

"There's lots of sous chefs in and out of here." *But most likely, it's Edith. She simply can't stay out of things. Aargh!* "Might as well unwrap the edible flowers. I can't wait to see what you picked out."

"Same as before, only more. Zinnias, bachelor buttons, calendula, and nasturtiums."

Lilly-Ann removed the newspaper pages that held the flowers and spread them out on a separate table. "Wow, here's an article I missed about a new playground proposal. Oh, and one featuring our county employees for some sort of a recognition day a month ago according to the date."

I glanced at the giant quarter-page spread featuring the emergency response team for Cave Creek, including its coroner and the county officers. A second later, my jaw dropped. "I've seen a photo of the coroner before. Drat. That's the problem with a photographic memory. I recognize stuff but I have no idea when or where I last saw it. Hmm, seems pretty recent though."

Lilly-Ann shrugged. "It's local news. That guy's probably been in the papers before."

"But I've only lived here for a month or so. That's going to plague me all night. Phooey."

When the board was completed, two servers placed it on a large rolling cart and I followed them out to the banquet room. "I'll be right back. I want to check the setup and make sure everything's hunky-dory. Meanwhile, you can start on the French one."

The banquet room was breathtaking with a centerpiece ice sculpture of two swans, their necks entwined, surrounded by fluted champagne glasses that promised an evening of continued toasts to the lucky couple. A special alcove had been reserved for the charcuteries and its offset lighting gave the spot an air of fantasy. Lovely white linen tablecloths and calla lilies in crystal vases completed the venue. Not to be upstaged, a fabulous black, gray, and gold banner was draped across the ballooned archway entrance and read, "They're engaged! Congratulations Olivia and Evan."

Evan! I could have spit just seeing that name. True, it wasn't the Evan jerk who dropped me with a text message in the middle of an upper management meeting, but seeing that name filled me with an unsettling combination of anger, nausea, and revulsion. Evan! Ugh! If ever there was a social climber, that was the rat I almost got hitched to.

I hope your Evan is better than mine was, Olivia. (Whoever you are).

After making sure the Italian board looked perfect, I moseyed back to the kitchen to work on the French one. That process went quicker since Lilly-Ann and I knew what to expect.

"Want to follow me out to the banquet room with this one?" I asked her as the servers moved the French board onto the rolling cart.

"Absolutely."

The two of us stood and admired our work as if we had completed construction on the Eiffel Tower. I was so engrossed that I didn't hear the oohs and aahs coming from behind me. Female giggly voices.

"This is *so* over the top, Via. I am *so* going to hold my engagement party here. *If* I ever get engaged."

"Yeah, Via. You are one lucky girl for sure."

Via! Olivia! Oh my God! This can't be happening. How many Olivia "Vias" who are engaged to an Evan are there?

I turned my head to spot the tall woman who looked like a supermodel. Her slightly ash-red hair was swept to one side, revealing perfect diamond studded earrings. All moisture left my mouth as I choked out the words, "I need to make a call. I, um, told my mother I'd call. I forgot. I'll call from outside."

Lilly-Ann nodded. "Sure thing. I'll be in the kitchen."

I don't remember bolting out of there and onto the patio, but I must have been quick. Next thing I knew, my finger tapped the speed dial for Maddie, and the words cascaded out of my mouth. "Worst nightmare of my life. I can't go back inside the restaurant."

"Katie? What's going on? Did one of your boards drop? Food all over? Did something spoil? Did someone upchuck from eating those cured meats? What?"

"Evan."

"What do you mean 'Evan'? Don't tell me he's one of the guests."

"Worse. He's the fiancé. Via is *Olivia*."

"Holy cannoli."

"Holy cannoli's right. Next to her, Karlie Kloss and Cara Delevingne look like toads."

"Yeesh. What did Evan say when he saw you?"

"He didn't. I mean, he didn't see me."

"Are you finished? Maybe you can just make a quick exit before he does. Or hide in the kitchen. It's not likely he'll go in there."

"I need to find the nearest sinkhole and throw myself in it."

"No. Evan does. He's the ratfink jerk. Look, go back inside, finish up and get out. It's almost eight and knowing you, everything is prepared and ready to be served. Am I right?"

"Uh-huh."

"Then get out before it becomes really awkward."

Lamentably, that didn't happen.

Chapter Thirty-Six

I slunk back inside the banquet room and froze. Evan stood a few feet away, his back to me, conversing with a few of the guests. There was no mistaking him even from the rear. Great physique, sandy hair styled just right, and perfect posture. *Perfect posture. Now I see the red flag.* I was about to walk through the room to get to the kitchen. My hands shook as I turned and flew out the patio door.

Fine. Even if I have to walk around the entire perimeter of this restaurant, I will.

From my new vantage point, I could see the rear parking lot. A quick jaunt to the kitchen entrance. Then I remembered another door Patricia had shown me, one that led directly to the long corridor where Wend's office and the restrooms were located.

"I doubt the kitchen door will be locked," she said at the time, "but if that's the case, use the corridor entrance. It's always open."

Not only was it open, but it was much closer, and I raced inside, all but colliding with a wispy-haired man who had just exited the restroom. Something about him looked oddly familiar but I couldn't pinpoint it. I was too fixated on the Evan disaster in the banquet room.

Maddie was right. Lilly-Ann and I had completed the charcuterie boards and we were free to leave the premises. I'd call Patricia on Monday to make sure the boards were returned and let her know I'd be emailing her an invoice. The only thing Lilly-Ann and I needed to do was make sure we cleaned up our area. Nothing is worse than hiring a caterer who leaves a mess for the event holder to deal with.

The wispy-haired man muttered something before thundering past me toward Wend's office. A quick slam of that door and it was as if a zillion puzzle pieces began to connect. The Evan sighting left a fog in my brain, but that delayed reaction didn't last long. Hallelujah. My photographic memory hadn't failed me. The wispy-haired man's photo was plastered on one of the newspaper sheets Petals and Plants had used to wrap our edible flowers and, on a county promotional flyer left on my car windshield a while back. Not only that, but it hung on the wall in Wend's family photo.

The coroner. That's who it was—the coroner. No wonder he didn't waste any time with an autopsy. He and Wend were in cahoots. But why? Wend told me Edith's review of Savor was marginalized when other reviews came in. Still...I had an inkling of what really happened.

Hells bells. I need to let Edith know what I think—Owen Jasper isn't her killer. Darn it. Where is she when I want her? She's usually right on top of me.

In all the cozy mysteries I'd ever read, the sleuth had a clearly articulated plan to catch the culprit. Unfortunately, the only thing I caught was Evan on his way to the restroom.

I felt his hand tap my shoulder before he spoke. "Katie, is that you?"

Funny that I didn't recall turning around to face him, but I must have because the next words out of his mouth were, "I don't believe it. You're working here as a server? Geez. I heard you left Chan-Tech, but I didn't expect you to climb down the ladder so fast."

"Climb down the ladder? You arrogant piece of dung!" My cheeks burned and my heart raced. "I happened to have started my own business—a catering enterprise and I hope you choke on the delicacies we've served up on the charcuterie boards. Too bad you're not footing the bill, but I suppose that stands to reason. You're not marrying Olivia DeLonde. You're marrying her father's money. Better invest what you can before she realizes what a good-for-nothing swine you are and sends you packing."

"Jealousy doesn't become you."

"Jealousy? Why you rotten stinker!"

Suddenly a whirlwind of black smoke wrapped itself around Evan, giving off a fetid odor that made me gag.

"Is this the man who murdered me?" Edith's voice was more of a growl than actual words. "Who is he? I heard you say something about the coroner. Is this him? The coroner? Why would the coroner kill me?"

"The coroner didn't kill you," I exclaimed.

"What did you just say? Something about the coroner? Are you threatening me?" Now it was Evan's voice that was guttural and sharp. "Forget it. Something must be burning in the kitchen. Do you smell that? Damn! They better not mess up my engagement party."

Before I could respond, Evan charged down the corridor and back to the banquet room.

The black smoke morphed into a dark purple color and Edith's form began to materialize. This time in a flowing caftan that looked like something straight out of the bible.

"Was that my killer? Don't stand there, chase him and get a confession out of him."

"He's not your killer, Edith. He's my horrible ex. Soon to be Olivia DeLonde's husband."

"Oh bother. I'm not interested in Olivia whoever-she-is. I want to catch my murderer."

"So do I. Give me a minute or two, will you? And if you want to do something useful, see if you can pop those archway balloon displays for Evan's engagement. Make them pop like there's no tomorrow."

"I can't be too far away from your energy field, but I'll give it a try. Meanwhile, find my killer!"

The purplish haze turned smokey white before it dissipated completely. By now, my mind was on overdrive as I charged toward Wend Pomeroy's office.

Do not let me mess this up.

The earlier argument I heard from behind the office door resumed, only this time with more intensity. Enough to drown out the music playing from the engagement party a few yards away. I slowed my pace and stood against the wall, cell phone pressed to my ear so as to convince anyone who passed by that I was in the midst of a conversation.

"Don't threaten me, Carter." It was Wend's voice. "You'd only be threatening yourself."

"The stunt I pulled could have cost me my position. *And* my retirement."

"Relax, will you? Once the new restaurant is up and running, you'll get your share. Enough so that you won't have to worry about your measly retirement money from the county."

"You think it was easy covering up that insulin overdose you gave her? I take it you stockpiled the insulin whenever you visited my wife's great aunt in her retirement village. No wonder you were always visiting her."

"A quick and painless death."

"The insulin didn't kill her, by the way. The fall she took did."

"Glad something worked. I couldn't risk having her give the new restaurant a bad review like she did with this one. It would have destroyed everything. Everything! Do you have any idea how many investors I would have left hanging?"

Holy cow! The motive! It's not what Edith did. It's what she might have done.

Too bad this wasn't a Hallmark movie, or I would have burst inside the room and confronted the men like a true amateur sleuth heroine. Instead, I stood against the wall, mouth wide open, wondering what on earth my next move would be.

As the fates would have it, I didn't have to stand there much longer. Shrieks, screams, and the sound of plates crashing came from down the hall. The banquet room! *What the heck did Edith do?*

I seriously doubted there'd be much reaction to balloons popping, even if they did comprise the focal point of the room. Most people would have attributed it to too much helium pressure and let it go. No, I was positive the sounds I heard had nothing to do with balloons popping.

Then, an all-too-familiar voice. "This isn't an exact science."

"Edith? What have you done?" I made sure to keep my phone near my ear so it wouldn't appear as if I was looney. "Never mind. I'll see for myself. Good thing I'm not wearing heels."

The twinkling fairy lights that circled the banquet room blinked as if they were strobe lights on steroids and a sticky, gooey substance coated the floor. But that wasn't the worst of it. The guests who had fallen on the floor struggled to get up in the semi-darkness.

"This better not be anything toxic," I muttered, making sure to step gingerly as I looked around. "It's not toxic, is it, Edith?"

"Since when is wine toxic?"

"Wine? You managed to coat the floor with wine?" I was flabbergasted.

"The balloons didn't pop. The wine bottles did. Riesling, Zinfandel, Chardonnay, Merlot, Cabernet Sauvignon, and Moscato. They didn't bring the champagne out yet."

"This serves Evan right, but still, it's a bit much."

"I told you I needed to be closer to your physical essence in order to invoke my newfound skills."

"Your newfound skills stink, if you must know. Oh, and by the way, I know who killed you and why."

The strobing fairy lights went dark, and the room dropped at least twenty degrees.

"There's an electrical problem," someone shouted. "No one move."

Then another voice, "The backup generator's not working either. Someone get Mr. Pomeroy. Now!"

As if the room wasn't in enough turmoil, Edith managed to conjure up a low-level fog made visible by the exit lights over the doors. The last time I'd seen anything like that was during my high school's production of *Brigadoon*.

"Why is it foggy in here?" Another voice in the crowd. Female, this time.

"Change in air temperature," someone else shouted.

More voices followed in a frenzied cacophony.

"Can someone get the generator going?"

"Where the heck is Mr. Pomeroy?"

"My dress is ruined. Wine stains don't come out."

Then, the most bizarre thing happened. A crackling voice came out of nowhere and it took me a second to realize it was from the restaurant's speaker system.

"I'm not going down as an accomplice to Edith Ellory's murder."

Chapter Thirty-Seven

With the combination of low-level fog and dim lighting, I felt it was safe enough for me to reach out to Edith. For all anyone knew, she could have been one of the guests. Still, I kept my voice low and made sure no one was near me.

"Edith? Can you hear me? That voice we heard was the coroner. Carter. He's Wend Pomeroy's brother-in-law. He was the one who gave you the fast track to the Restful Souls in Phoenix. He covered for Wend by writing off your death as natural causes. You were right. You were murdered. Injected with insulin to be specific. Followed by a fall. He killed you so that you wouldn't write a scalding restaurant review for his new enterprise in the Biltmore area. He was protecting his investment."

"Not for long." And poof! Edith vanished.

With that, the lights came back on, revealing a catastrophic mess on the banquet room floor. I looked over to the alcove where my charcuterie boards stood, and thankfully, nothing was disturbed. Meanwhile, a hysterical Olivia sat off to the side of the room, head between her knees, sobbing uncontrollably.

Between sniffles, I heard her say, "This better not be a bad omen for my future life with Evan."

Oh. It is. Trust me. It is. Run now while you have the chance.

As much as I wanted to tell Olivia what a snake-in-the-grass Evan was, I figured she'd find out for herself. But I didn't figure she'd find out so quickly. With his shirt partially unbuttoned on the top and the shirttail hanging from his dark trousers, he emerged from the back of the room, pausing to adjust his attire and run a hand through his hair. As he approached Olivia, a stocky young woman with curly chin-length hair beat him to it. She shook one of Olivia's hands away from her face and said, "Ask your bridesmaid, Sherri-Lynn, what she was doing sucking face with your fiancé. I saw them by the exit doors when the lights went out."

"Olivia!" Evan shouted, brushing past the woman. "I can explain."

I really wanted to enjoy a front-row seat at the soap opera being played out in front of me, but I had a murderer to catch and an unpredictable ghost to contend with. Not to mention Lilly-Ann, who I left in the kitchen to tidy up.

Regrettably, I left the Evan-Olivia saga to play out while I took off for Wend's office. I was positive Edith had already made an entrance, but I knew her skills were limited the further she was from me.

Terrific. I'm chasing after an apparition who's chasing after her killer. Every woman's dream of how to spend a Saturday night.

The expression "think on your feet" never carried as much meaning as it did in the thirty or so seconds it took me to pull open Wend's office door.

"It's over!" I shouted, making good use of a hackneyed phrase uttered by every detective known to TV. The only trouble was, Wend wasn't in his office and neither was Carter. A chair was overturned near the large French Provincial desk and the long cord that connected the restaurant's PA system to a wall outlet had been ripped from the receiver. So much for Carter's impromptu announcement. Not that anyone at Olivia and Evan's ill-fated celebration would have known who Edith Ellory was, or even cared. But it mattered to Edith. Big time. She'd hold her killer accountable even if it meant absolute mayhem at Savor in the Heights. Then again, Evan's kissy-face actions with Sherri-Lynn still commanded first place in that regard.

I crossed my fingers that Edith and I were too far apart for her to wreak havoc, but what did I know? With my eyes fixated on the overturned chair, I tried to second guess where the men could have gone. Certainly not the banquet room.

Drat! They're probably duking it out in the men's room.

Thoughts of poor Lilly-Ann, wondering where I was, flashed through my head and I figured I'd better get back to the kitchen and make some lame excuse to linger a bit longer. I had to confront Wend before I lost my nerve. More importantly, I had to do it before Edith got to him first. As far as Carter was concerned, most likely he'd tumble like a pile of wooden blocks once Wend confessed. *If* I could get him to own up.

The instant I stepped inside the kitchen Lilly-Ann rushed over.

"Is that the owner over there?" she asked me. "I think the poor man is suffering a psychotic break. See for yourself. He's over in that corner by the freezers screaming for everyone to stay back."

Not everyone. Edith. She's managed to haunt him. So much for energy proximity and all that hoo-ha.

Sure enough, Wend Pomeroy plastered himself against a large Kelvinator freezer and held his arms straight out. "Leave me be. Stop blowing that cold air on me."

"See what I mean?" Lilly-Ann said. "The air's probably coming from the commercial freezer, but he thinks someone is causing it."

Wend's voice got louder, and he flailed his arms. "Stop it, I say. I won't stand for it."

"Call nine-one-one," a young sous chef cut in. "The guy's having some sort of a breakdown."

Wend stomped across the room to the sink and grabbed the long hose used for rinsing dishes. "I'll put a stop to your devilry, you no good food critic!"

"No one's criticized the food, Mr. Pomeroy," one of the dishwashers blurted out.

"It's a nervous breakdown," the sous chef continued. "My aunt Martha had one years ago and it wasn't pretty."

"Leave me be, you harridan! You're supposed to be dead. Dead, I tell you."
Oh my gosh. He can see her.

With that, Wend turned on the water and proceeded to spray the kitchen as if it was a waterpark. Seconds later, Patricia Milestone rushed in but before she could say a word, the full force of the water hit her straight in the face.

"Now will someone call nine-one-one?" the sous chef shouted. "I don't have a cell phone on me."

Patricia grabbed a dishtowel and wiped her face. "Don't anyone make any sudden moves. I'm dialing them now."

As she proceeded to place the call, my cell phone went off and I jumped. I'd forgotten it was in my pants pocket. A quick glance and the name "Maddie" came up.

"Is everything all right?" I asked her.

"You're asking me? I'm the one who's worried about you. Are you still at Savor in the Heights? Facebook and Instagram are exploding with photos of the place. I haven't checked Twitter. That engagement party's a free-for-all. There are five different shots of Olivia hurling plates at Evan. You must be in the kitchen, unless you got lucky and you're on the road."

"Not lucky. You were right the first time. I'm in the kitchen. Wend Pomeroy, the owner, is having a meltdown."

"Who can blame him? Did someone call nine-one-one? Those party guests could go ballistic and trash the place. Call me when you get home. Geez, I hope this doesn't ruin your future charcuterie catering gigs."

"Actually, I—"

Whatever I was about to say got cut off in the mayhem. Wend chose that particular instant to grab a broom from the corner of the room and use it like one of those crazed villagers wielding pitchforks in horror movies. I ducked under one of the tables to avoid getting whacked with the broom and shut my phone. Maddie would understand.

"You'll have to forgive Mr. Pomeroy," Patricia announced. "He's been under monumental pressure with his new restaurant endeavor."

The only pressure he's under is coming from a feisty seventy-seven-year-old apparition who doesn't know when to call it quits.

A horrified kitchen staff watched in absolute silence as Wend continued to brandish the broom. A murky gray haze separated him from the rest of us, but I was pretty certain I was the only one who could see it.

"Stop with the shrieking noises!" he shouted. "I'll lose an eardrum."

"Like I said," the sous chef mumbled, "nervous breakdown."

In the distance, I heard the faint sound of sirens, but unfortunately, Patricia's call to nine-one-one wasn't that specific. Instead of sending EMTs to the kitchen, the dispatcher responded by sending sheriff deputies in full force to the banquet room. I only know this because Lilly-Ann, who happened to be standing by the door to the corridor, shouted, "They've got an army of sheriff deputies running to the banquet room."

If my charcuterie boards survive this unscathed, I might have a chance at my newfound career.

The murky gray haze took on a darker color and that meant trouble. As if the Savor hadn't had enough of it already. I was positive Edith was using every bit of her ghostly energy to force Wend into a confession, but I hadn't counted on the Olivia-Evan fiasco to upstage her.

By now, Wend had trapped himself between the sink and the edge of the freezer. He held steadfast to the broom as if it was a bayonet and shouted, "Get away from me. Get away from me."

"Maybe I should get one of those deputies to assist us in here," Patricia said. "I don't know how the dispatcher could have gotten it wrong." She walked to where Lilly-Ann stood and looked down the corridor before glancing back at Wend. "Poor Mr. Pomeroy. He's been under enormous strain. Surely, they don't need all of those deputies in the banquet room. I'm on my way."

Unfortunately, Patricia never made it out the door. A crazed Olivia bumped into her, nearly knocking the woman over. "Is he hiding in here?" Olivia shouted. Then she turned her head every which way. "Too afraid to show your face? Well, I'll show you something!" She reached for a ceramic colander but luckily the sous chef snatched it away before she could hurl it at someone.

"I hate him! I hate him! I hate him!" she shrieked.

Take a number and get in line.

"Evan's not in here," I said.

Olivia looked at me, the disappointment evident on her face. "I'm having him arrested for adultery."

"Um, I think you have to be married for that first."

"Then I'll have him arrested for intent to commit adultery."

218

CHAPTER THIRTY-SEVEN

"I don't think that's a thing either," the sous chef added.

Just then, the very louse appeared and leaned his head into the kitchen. "I'm pressing charges for assault, Olivia. That plate you threw decapitated the swan heads and missed me by an inch. An inch! That's felony assault."

With that, Olivia sprung at him like a tigress after her prey but that wasn't the worst thing to happen. The overhead gallery pot rack, complete with frying pans, soup pans, and an assortment of large miscellaneous cookware, came loose from the ceiling and crashed to the ground, but not before whacking Wend in the head. It was the Imogen incident revisited but much worse.

Good going, Edith.

Chapter Thirty-Eight

"Is he conscious?" someone called out. A crowd of sous chefs, kitchen helpers, and waitstaff clustered around their boss, who was now lying flat on his back on the kitchen floor. Behind me, I could hear Olivia and Evan struggling by the door and when I turned my head, she had managed to snatch up the broom Wend had been holding and whomped it right between her fiancé's legs. *Ouch!*

In a split second, Wend wasn't the only one on the ground.

Lilly-Ann made her way toward me and whispered, "All this time I thought cafeteria food fights were bad. Yikes."

I opened my mouth, but no words came out. Just then, Patricia returned, flanked by two burly sheriff deputies.

"That's him!" she pointed. "My boss. The older man on the floor. Mr. Pomeroy. Wend Pomeroy. He may have had a stroke or something."

"What about me?" Evan called out. "I have worse problems."

"The EMTs are on their way," one of the deputies said. "Hang on."

What happened next is still a bit fuzzy in my head. Mainly because Evan kept whining while Olivia spewed expletives and it was impossible to ignore them. When I finally turned my attention to Wend, it was too late. Edith was inches from his nose, her arms crossed, and nostrils flared. Too bad I was the only one privy to that spectacle.

"Go away. Go away," he mumbled. "I'll admit to it if you leave me alone."

Patricia surveyed the crowd and shrugged. "Admit to what? What's he talking about?"

"He's delirious," the sous chef said.

Finally, I found my voice. "Um, maybe we should hear what he has to say." I walked over to Wend, bent down, and spoke softly so that only he and Edith could hear me. "It'll go away if you admit to the truth. It's the only way."

He propped himself up by the elbows but remained on the floor. "Edith Ellory didn't die of natural causes. I was responsible for her death."

A frigid burst of air took me by surprise and gave Wend a start. He shook for a moment and then added, "What I mean, is, I killed her. And now her spirit is haunting me."

"He's out of his gourd," one of the waitstaff exclaimed.

"No," Wend replied. "I'm as sane as anyone in this room." Then he looked over at Olivia and Evan, who were still at each other's throats. "Well, almost anyone."

Patricia walked toward us, and I stepped back, allowing her to converse directly with her boss. "What are you saying, Mr. Pomeroy?"

Wend stared directly ahead, refusing to make eye contact with anyone. Meanwhile, the two deputies took out iPads and scribbled notes.

"I'm *saying*, that I murdered Edith Ellory in her home. She left me no choice. It was *that* or my new restaurant would have gone up in flames. *Figuratively.* A scathing review from her and there would have been no way I could repay my investors. Do any of you have the slightest idea what an investment of that magnitude costs?"

"I, I, don't understand," Patricia stammered.

Wend looked at the two deputies and got up from the floor. He leaned against the Kelvinator and ran a hand through his hair. "The night before her body was found, I went to her house in Cave Creek under the pretense of asking her to review our restaurant again. She refused to let me inside, but I shoved my way in and before she could stop me, I jabbed her with a syringe of insulin I brought with me. Enough to make her wobbly but not kill her. She yanked my glasses from my face, and they fell underneath me. Then she collided with the doorjamb to her entry closet and fell, hitting her head on the hard tile floor. I didn't have much time. I retrieved my glasses and realized a lens was missing but I couldn't stop to deal with that. I had to make it look as if Edith died naturally."

"So you staged her death by putting her in her bed?" I asked.

"I wasn't about to leave her by the front door."

"Then what?" By now I was on a roll and relishing every second of it.

"Then I wiped down the doorknob and doorframe with a hanky and did the same with anything I came into contact with in the bedroom. Anything that would have shown fingerprints. I locked the front door with the bottom door lock since it wasn't a deadbolt and got the hell out of there. Next, I called my brother-in-law who happens to be the coroner in Cave Creek, and offered him the investment of a lifetime."

"That's why there was no complete autopsy. No toxicology report. Only a write-up indicating she was seventy-seven years old and died a natural death."

Wend nodded. "Yeah, yeah. Heart attack or something of the like."

"We'll need a complete statement at the sheriff's office," one of the deputies said.

And wham! A hundred-and-eighty-degree turn! Wend Pomeroy suddenly realized what he had done. Not the murder. The confession. He looked around and rubbed his head. "Whoa. This hurts. I must have taken a hit to my head. I don't know what I'm saying. Utter gibberish."

No sooner did the word gibberish come out of his mouth when two EMTs entered the room and asked who required assistance.

"I do!" Evan announced. "My manhood could be at stake."

"That's fortunate for the rest of the world," Olivia responded.

"The man over there," the sous chef pointed. "I think he had a mental collapse or something."

I turned my attention to the deputies who were still fixated on their iPads. "What he had was an admission of guilt and I can prove it. I rent Edith Ellory's house and my cleaning lady found the missing eyeglass lens. I guarantee it will match up to the one his optometrist has on file. In fact, I'm positive it will fit his frames with no problem. Oh, and did I mention fingerprints? Because my cleaning lady was very careful when she picked it up."

The deputy who mentioned the sheriff's office turned to his partner.

"Better round up the coroner and get his statement. Something tells me we've got a long night ahead of us."

"What about me?" Evan exclaimed. "I need medical attention."

As if we didn't have enough excitement in the kitchen, the stocky woman with the curly chin-length hair, who ratted on Sherri-Lynn, walked in and rushed to Olivia's side. "Olivia, we've been looking all over for you. Your party kind of broke up while you and Evan disappeared. Some of the guests are asking if they can get doggie bags to take home the tasty hors d'oeuvres."

"Whatever." Olivia followed the woman out of the kitchen without as much as giving Evan a second glance. A few seconds later, Wend was read his Miranda rights and led out of the room by the deputies leaving Lilly-Ann, Patricia, the kitchen staff, and me looking as if we'd survived a tornado.

"I had no idea," Patricia said to no one in particular. "He seemed like such a nice man."

"I hope this restaurant doesn't close," the sous chef said. "I need the job."

In that second, it hit me. I was never going to get paid for my charcuterie boards since I literally had the restaurant owner arrested. In fact, I wasn't even certain the boards themselves would be returned to me.

Still, it was a glorious moment. I would be rid of Edith Ellory once in for all. She could move on in the afterlife and do whatever it is people do once they get there. I gave the kitchen one last look as Lilly-Ann and I vacated the premises. The thick grayish haze turned slightly pinkish, and I left with the satisfaction that I had done well. Even if it meant I'd be paying off business loans well into my nineties.

"What a night!" Lilly-Ann exclaimed when we got into my car. "I hope all of these events aren't going to be so dramatic. And what a coincidence about your cleaning lady finding an eyeglass lens that turned out to belong to a man who killed the former house owner. I bet you were surprised to hear Wend's confession."

Not as surprised as you think.

"Probably not as surprised as Olivia about her fiancé's cheating."

"Yeah, that was a shocker, too. Boy, we'll have a lot to tell Matt on Monday."

"Sure you'll be okay driving home?" I asked her when I pulled into my driveway. "You can leave your car in front of my place, and I can get you in the morning."

"I'll be fine. I'm so wired, I'll be up for hours."

"Me, too, I'm afraid."

I watched as she drove off and then looked to my right at Owen's house, thankful he didn't turn out to be the culprit after all. The guy had enough going against him. And I didn't relish the thought of getting a pistol permit.

"We did it, Edith!" I called out the minute I unlocked the front door. "Happy afterlife."

No response from Edith but Speedbump was all over me with doggie bumps and slimy kisses. A great way to end the night.

Chapter Thirty-Nine

I t was too late to make it into Sunday's *Arizona Republic* newspaper, but every news station in the Greater Phoenix area covered the DeLonde engagement party fiasco and the subsequent arrest of the venue's owner for murder. Not only that, but it made national headlines on CNN, FOX, and MSNBC. "Engagement Melee Results in Murder Confession" and "Charcuterie Boards Survive Murder and Mayhem."

From nine twenty-six until a little past ten, I fielded calls from my mother, my brother, and Maddie. I assured them I was fine and far removed from last night's action. Boy, was I getting good at lying.

Then, as I made myself comfortable on the couch with an iced coffee and a muffin, I got another phone call. This time from Cora.

"You could have warned me the sheriff's office would be at my door. On a Sunday morning no less. Two deputies just left. They wanted a statement regarding the eyeglass lens I found at your house. Well, Edith's house in a manner of speaking. I told them I thought she'd been murdered but who could argue with the coroner's findings. Ha! I knew it. He was on the take."

"Did they mention the marshal's office wanting a statement, too?"

"No, but it wouldn't surprise me. All of these local and county authorities tripping over each other. Turns out that the eyeglass lens is the evidence they needed to make that arrest stick. Now, aren't you glad you hired me to do your house cleaning? Who knows what I might find next?"

"Yeesh. Nothing, I hope. Sorry I didn't give you a heads-up. I'm still wrapping myself around last night's events. You see, I made these charcuterie boards for an engagement party at Savor in the Heights and—"

"Yeah, yeah. Save your breath. I caught it on channel 10 right after the weather report. One of the guests sent the station a video from his phone of the fiancée throwing plates across the room. Better the engagement party than the wedding I suppose."

"Uh-huh. Well, have a good day, Cora. See you next time when you clean."

"I may have to raise my rates if I find anything else that points to murder."

Wonderful.

The remainder of the morning was uneventful. I threw in two loads of laundry because it was either that or a trek to Target to buy more underwear and towels. At a little past three, I took Speedbump for a walk and ran into Colleen Wexby who asked "Was that you I saw on channel 12 this morning? They showed a clip of an engagement party going wild and I could have sworn that was you in the corridor."

"Uh, yeah. It was me all right. I did some of the catering. The charcuterie boards. Anyway, the bride-to-be caught her fiancé cheating and the place exploded. The owner had some sort of breakdown, most likely from the shock of it all, and confessed to killing Edith Ellory in her house the night before Cora discovered the body."

"No kidding. No way." Colleen put her hands to her mouth and took in a deep breath. "Like I said, I only caught a little bit of it before I left for church. So Edith was murdered? She didn't die naturally?"

"Apparently not."

"How awful. You should get a reduction in rent or something. Isn't there a full disclosure law about renting or buying places where a murder has been committed?"

"I'm not sure. It doesn't really matter at this point. The house is fine."

Colleen put her hand on my arm and sighed. "If you need anything, let me know. And here I thought it was bad enough you had to live next door to Owen. I don't imagine he'll be sticking around long. Not with those heists."

Cora's right on the money with the neighborhood busybody.

Lilly-Ann was a regular chatterbox the next day as she told Matt, and anyone else who would listen, about the catastrophic experience I endured at the

226

hands of a murderer at Savor in the Heights.

"The only thing I'm going to endure," I told her, "is a raft of bills since Wend Pomeroy is not likely to pay up."

"Didn't you see the note I left you on your desk?" She crinkled her nose and waited for a response.

"I must have overlooked it. What note?"

"Patricia Milestone called while you were in the dining area serving breakfasts. She said to tell you to email the invoice for the charcuterie boards to Mr. DeLonde and gave you the address. He had agreed to pay separately for them and that you can expect payment by the end of the week. Said you should let her know if you don't get it."

"Oh my gosh! That's fabulous! Absolutely fabulous." I gave her a giant hug, almost taking the breath from her. And that wasn't the best part. As we were about to close for the day, the phone rang, and I picked it up. Sterling Moss was at the other end, and I had to ask him to repeat what he said because I couldn't believe it.

"Granted, the footage was brief, but one look at those charcuterie boards of yours and I knew we'd need to offer them for our affairs at Randolph's Escapade. Are you still interested?"

"I, um, uh, yes, sure, of course. That's wonderful."

He explained that his restaurant manager would send me a tentative calendar of events and then provide details with ample time for me to design and deliver the boards. Had it not been for the Olivia-Evan fracas, he never would have seen them. Talk about silver linings…

I was in seventh heaven for the remainder of the day with one exception—no word from Edith. Not even a small sign like an ice cube landing on the floor. I had at least expected a thank-you for all the trouble I went through. From sneaking around Imogen's house, accosting Lucas at the airport, making my not-so-grand entrance at Randolph's Escapade, and ferreting through Owen's garage, I had given the term "amateur sleuth" a whole new meaning.

"Guess we can move on," I told Speedbump when I got home, but the place felt empty and even with my coaxing, I knew Edith was gone. Not that

I wanted her back. I mean, who in their right mind needed that kind of stress? What I wanted was closure. Closure that could only come from that annoying, demanding ghost.

Still, I had the satisfaction of knowing I kept my word and the relief that I could now concentrate on what really brought me to Cave Creek: The Char-Board.

Epilogue

I t had been a full week since Edith's killer confessed and I was still jumpy, even though she vanished in a plume of pinkish haze, grumbling "Dammit. I wanted it to be Imogen."

The Char-Board was bustling, and I could finally give my attention to my burgeoning business instead of amateur murder investigations. As I prepared mini-charcuterie boards in the kitchen, I was thankful Lilly-Ann and Matt had the sandwich making under control. Saturday mornings were usually hectic and today was no exception.

I reached for the thinly sliced Genoa salami and was about to fold it onto one of the plates when I felt a cold breeze on the nape of my neck and heard a croaky, throaty voice. "Flute the edges. Flute the edges. It looks better if you flute the edges."

I dropped the plate that held the salami and shrieked. Matt was at the kitchen door in seconds. "Is everything okay?"

"Uh-huh. I thought I saw a mouse, but it was only a wadded-up dishrag by the side of the fridge. Sorry about that."

He laughed. "No problem. Did anything break?"

I looked at the floor. "Nope. The plate's still in one piece." *But my nerves aren't.*

"Good deal," he said as he walked back to the dining area.

Edith stood, inches from the sink, in a hideous floor-length Hobble skirt, straight out of the early 1900s. The only thing worse was her white Edwardian blouse. If the neckline was any higher, it would have covered her mouth.

"What? No grand entrance? No haze, smoke, or odor?" I asked.

"Don't try to cheer me up."

"Why are you back? I thought you moved on. You said you'd move on once you found out who killed you. We found out. He was arrested. Why are you still here?" I couldn't seem to stop the words from spewing out of my mouth.

"Why, indeed!" Edith plopped herself on a stool and leaned a translucent elbow onto the counter. "Apparently, I've been sent back to work on my humility. Humility! And look what they chose for me to wear. At this rate, I'll never get my hands on that Jean Harlow gown. Can you imagine a worse insult?"

At this point, I can imagine anything.

I took a slow, deep breath and forced myself to stay calm. "So, uh, what are your plans?"

"You mean, 'What are our plans?' Why, I intend to assist you with your catering business. After all, *I'm* the one with the degree in culinary arts."

"Humility, Edith. You're supposed to work on your humility."

From the crack in the doorway, I could see Lilly-Ann and Matt clearing off tables. Any second and they'd be in the kitchen.

"Does this mean you'll be, well, you know…hanging around here all the time?" My stomach tightened and a sudden twitch tickled my eyelid.

"Honey, I said I would assist you, not work full-time."

I walked toward her and crossed my arms. "We're going to need some boundaries. Boundaries!"

"I knew you missed me."

Like fire ants at a picnic. "As long as we don't have to solve any more murders, I suppose I can deal with it."

Edith disappeared the same second a handful of ice cubes flew from the refrigerator, and I knew I was in trouble.

Ingredients for Basic (but dazzling) Charcuterie Tray

- Wedge of Brie cheese
- Small circular Camembert Cheese
- Chunked cheeses such as cheddar or Havarti
- Small dish of fig jam
- Small dish of hummus
- Small dish of mixed nuts
- Sliced Italian salami
- Rolled Prosciutto
- Row of folded ham (Black Forest, Honey, or any cured ham)
- Sliced baguette bread
- Grapes (green or red)
- Sprigs of parsley or edible flowers to suit your taste – Optional

Design

Begin with the larger items first. Place the Brie and Camembert cheeses in the center of the tray and surround them with the folded ham, the Prosciutto, and the sliced Italian salami. Place the bread on the outside edge of the tray. Position the hummus, grapes, mixed nuts, and fig jam in-between the larger items.

Be sure to use little round dishes for the hummus, nuts, etc. Otherwise, small items may fall off!

Don't forget to have serving utensils!

Have fun! Play around with the placement so it looks aesthetically pleasing. If it is too overwhelming, cut out some items or lessen the quantity.

Serves 5 – 8 people, but can be adjusted to fit your number of guests

About the Series

The Charcuterie Shop Mysteries are humorous cozies that feature an enterprising charcuterie chef, a laidback beagle, and a feisty food critic who just found out she's a ghost. Together they forge a wacky relationship as they tackle one whodunit after another so the ghost can get enough "brownie points" to leave the earthly world for good.

Acknowledgements

We always take a deep breath when we start a new series, but knowing that we've got an amazing crew of beta readers and tech savvy professionals, makes the process less daunting.

Thank you Tammy Barker, Becky Clark, and Susan Schwartz for your keen insights, thoughtful reflections, and downright good advice when it came to putting our ducks in a row for this one. We genuinely appreciate all of your time and support.

Again, we thank our tech crew, Larry Finkelstein and Gale Leach, for coming to our rescue any time our computer programs went wonky. We seriously could not have managed without you.

Of course, none of this would have been possible without our amazing agent, Dawn Dowdle, at Blue Ridge Literary Agency. Her guidance and knowledge have been invaluable.

Special thanks goes out to our editor at Level Best Books, Shawn Reilly Simmons, and the entire team at Level Best for giving us this opportunity to shine with our first paranormal cozy series.

About the Author

Ann I. Goldfarb and James E. Clapp, writing as J.C. Eaton

Ann I. Goldfarb

New York native Ann I. Goldfarb spent most of her life in education, first as a classroom teacher and later as a middle school principal and professional staff developer. Writing as J. C. Eaton, along with her husband, James Clapp, they have authored the Sophie Kimball Mysteries (Kensington), The Wine Trail Mysteries (Kensington Lyrical Underground and Beyond the Page Publishing), and the Marcie Rayner Mysteries (Camel). In addition, Ann has nine published YA time travel mysteries under her own name. Visit us at:

www.jceatonmysteries.com
www.jceatonauthor.com
www.facebook.com/JCEatonauthor/
www.timetravelmysteries.com
https://twitter.com/JCEatonauthor

James E. Clapp

When James E. Clapp retired as the tasting room manager for a large upstate New York winery, he never imagined he'd be co-authoring cozy mysteries with his wife, Ann I. Goldfarb. Non-fiction in the form of informational brochures and workshop materials treating the winery industry was his forte along with an extensive background and experience in construction that started with his service in the U.S. Navy and included vocational school classroom teaching. Visit the website at www.jceatonmysteries.com and the blog at www.jceatonauthor.com

AUTHOR WEBSITE:
   https://www.jceatonmysteries.com

Also by J. C. Eaton

Kensington Publishing:
   Booked 4 Murder
   Ditched 4 Murder
   Staged 4 Murder
   Botched 4 Murder
   Molded 4 Murder
   Dressed Up 4 Murder
   Broadcast 4 Murder
   Railroaded 4 Murder

Kensington Lyrical Underground:
   A Riesling to Die
   Chardonnayed to Rest
   Pinot Red or Dead?
   Sauvigone for Good

Beyond the Page Publishing:
   Divide and Concord
   Death, Dismay and Rosé
   From Port to Rigor Morte
   Mischief, Murder and Merlot (release in 2022)
   Saddled Up 4 Murder

Camel/Epicenter Press:
   Murder in the Crooked Eye Brewery
   Murder at the Mystery Castle
   Murder at Classy Kitchens

CPSIA information can be obtained
at www.ICGtesting.com
Printed in the USA
LVHW101909230722
724251LV00005B/61

9 781685 121525